BASKETS
AND BEIGNETS

A Miss Fortune Mystery

NEW YORK TIMES BESTSELLING AUTHOR
JANA DELEON

MISS FORTUNE SERIES INFORMATION

If you've never read a Miss Fortune mystery, you can start with LOUISIANA LONGSHOT, the first book in the series. If you prefer to start with this book, here are a few things you need to know.

Fortune Redding – a CIA assassin with a price on her head from one of the world's most deadly arms dealers. Because her boss suspects that a leak at the CIA blew her cover, he sends her to hide out in Sinful, Louisiana, posing as his niece, a librarian and ex–beauty queen named Sandy-Sue Morrow. The situation was resolved in Change of Fortune and Fortune is now a full-time resident of Sinful and has opened her own detective agency.

Ida Belle and Gertie – served in the military in Vietnam as spies, but no one in the town is aware of that fact except Fortune and Deputy LeBlanc.

Sinful Ladies Society – local group founded by Ida Belle, Gertie, and deceased member Marge. In order to gain membership, women must never have married or if widowed, their husband must have been deceased for at least ten years.

Sinful Ladies Cough Syrup – sold as an herbal medicine in Sinful, which is dry, but it's actually moonshine manufactured by the Sinful Ladies Society.

CHAPTER ONE

WEDNESDAY WAS THE DAY I FOUND OUT THAT CHICKENS ARE into Easter as much as religious folk. I suppose it made sense given all those dyed eggs. In a cannibalistic sort of way. But the rabbit has always gotten all the attention for that holiday. I assumed it was because they were cute and fuzzy and looked better wearing bows than chickens did. And people and pets looked cuter wearing those rabbit-ear headbands than they would wearing chicken-ear headbands, since they didn't have much ear to speak of. I supposed people could wear a chicken comb headband, but I don't think it would hit the cute mark.

So ultimately, the chickens were the forgotten workhorses for the event.

Well, them and church ladies. I was fairly certain that not a single event, or food and activities for those events, would exist in the South without church ladies.

I was far too young and uncouth to be considered part of that group, but since I had a good back and knees, I was drafted to help set up for the big Easter egg hunt. So I hauled a bunch of tables and boxes of food, set up chairs, and dumped a million bags of ice into coolers. I was not allowed to partake of the decorating part of things for obvious reasons, and I only lasted a couple minutes with the hiding-the-eggs job because the ladies accused me of making it too hard and too dangerous for the kids to retrieve the eggs.

I thought the top of the swing set and in branches a good thirty feet up seemed insignificant compared to what Jesus had accomplished, but apparently, I was wrong. And I figured placing them under the merry-go-round and seesaw just tested timing and reflexes, but I was outvoted. On the plus side, I suspected no one would ever ask me to babysit.

So I finished my pack-muling tasks and then grabbed a bottle of water from the cooler in the back of Walter's truck, pulled out another lawn chair, and sat down next to Walter, who had fled as soon as the pink and yellow baskets had been retrieved from vehicles. Apparently, his obligation ended with hauling things as well.

"Why are they using plastic eggs?" I asked.

"The critters made off with the real ones," he said. "It was back about ten years ago. The ladies got everything all set up for when they let the kids out of the Easter program at the school. There was a lot more women helping back then so they were done early."

"Did a bunch of them move away?"

"Yes. If you count moving into Sinful Cemetery. Anyway, the kids wouldn't be turned loose from the craft fair for another hour, so the women all headed home for a bathroom break and to put on the Crock-Pot or whatever else they needed to get up to, figuring they'd come back just before the kids were let out. Well, the whole park was overrun by foxes. They were fighting over the eggs and marking their territory. Have you ever smelled fox urine?"

"Good God. Yes."

He nodded. "Then you know what was up. They had to

close the whole park for a month until the smell lessened. We had a bit of a spring drought that year, so no rain to help. It was so bad some of the people with houses across the street moved out for a bit. The kids got one look at their failed hunt and started crying, and so did the church ladies. It was a huge mess."

"So no more real eggs."

"Only if you're indoors. That's the law. And if you're going to have more than a dozen boiled eggs inside, it's illegal to leave your doors or windows open, even if you have screens."

"Of course it is. I suppose the kids prefer the plastic eggs with candy in them anyway. Seems like the fun is in the hunting part, although it's not much of a challenge the way they set it up."

Walter laughed. "Easter isn't supposed to be an episode of *Survivor*."

"It would be a lot more interesting if it was."

"You and Ida Belle think a lot alike. You'll notice she doesn't have a basket."

I glanced over at Ida Belle, who was issuing orders to the women—mostly in direct opposition to Celia, which was probably on purpose. "She's not allowed to hide either?"

"No. Back when there weren't as many kids and we held the hunt at the Catholic church yard, she put an egg full of hot dog weenies in Father Abraham's robes. Then she let Farmer Frank's hounds loose. They chased Father Abraham around that yard until he climbed right up the cross and clung there."

"That's an Easter look for a priest. But who was Father Abraham?"

"Way before your time. Might have been born around the year the one in the Old Testament was."

"How old was Ida Belle?"

"At least thirty. Father Abraham had made the mistake of

having words with her about wearing blue jeans to hide the eggs, and she decided to let him know how she felt about it. He was wishing for a pair of blue jeans himself after he shinnied up that cross. Old Doc Hadley had to pull splinters out of places he didn't even want to talk about. Both of them retired a week later."

I started laughing. I'd assumed she'd been a kid when she'd done it, but knowing she'd been my age made it even more hilarious.

"So now Ida Belle's banned from dealing with the eggs," Walter said, grinning. "She always was a pistol. You remind me a lot of her."

"I can see why."

His smile faded some. "How is Carter doing? I know he can't talk about all this legal mess you're preparing for, and I get that the less other people know the better. But I'm worried about him."

"He's been working on documentation for Alexander. We all have some things to consider, but Carter's got a lot more to process than the rest of us."

"You think he's wondering about his service?"

"Yes."

Walter sighed. "That boy has nothing to feel guilty about. He was trained to do a job, then ordered where and how. He trusted the people giving those orders to be honorable."

"I know. But when you break everything down, the whole world is still controlled and run by humans. And humans are so fallible."

He gave me a curious look. "I imagine you've had your share of skirting the line on things. The CIA isn't exactly known for being choirboys. But you seem to be taking it a lot better than he is."

I shrugged. "I think I have an easier time compartmentalizing things than Carter does. I can separate what I did from who I am. I'm certain I played roles in others' hidden and likely personal agendas, but I don't know and don't want to know. I did my job and did it well. My conscience is clear."

Walter nodded. "Carter could take a few lessons from you on letting things go."

"If Carter wasn't questioning himself and everything else, then he wouldn't be the man we both love. I wish it wasn't so hard for him, but I don't see any point in asking him to change. He'll figure out how to balance it eventually, just like he did when he first came out of the Marines."

"This is a lot worse than back then, I'm afraid."

"I know. But all we can do is be there for him if he needs us. I'm paying attention, Walter. If he tips over a line, I'll be the first one to call in reinforcements."

"I know you will, and it makes me feel a lot better knowing someone who understands what he's dealing with is watching out for him. All the same, this whole investigation is a crock of bull. If they put me on the stand, I'm going to be an old man with sketchy memory."

"It's a hard defense to refute. But don't worry about it. Alexander will get everyone squared away. You have a meeting with him on Friday, right?"

"Yeah. Said since he needed to chat individually with all of us, that's why he's coming to Sinful instead of all of us hauling into NOLA. But between you and me, I think he's really wanting lunch at Francine's."

"I can't say that I blame him."

"Me either, which is why I offered to have my meeting with him there. Don't have much to say anyway, as I don't know anything, right?"

The ladies appeared to have wrapped up the egg hiding and were heading for their cars. Walter and I figured that was our cue, so we folded our lawn chairs, and I was just about to go toss mine in the bed of the truck when I heard yelling, ridiculously loud and completely out of place squawking, and barking.

I whirled around and spotted a frantic horde of chickens running, flapping, and sort of flying for the park. Behind them were two bloodhounds, mouths full of feathers, clearly intent on catching something to eat. I said a quick prayer of thanks that Rambo wasn't one of them and looked over at Walter.

"That's Skinny Lawson's hounds," he said.

About that time, a man I recognized as Skinny—whose physique didn't exactly fit his name—ran down the street, leashes dangling from his hand. He waved his arms in the air and yelled at the hounds, but they weren't remotely interested in stopping their fun.

"Looks like you're on hound-catching duty again," Walter said.

The chickens descended on the park in a giant wave of noise and feathers, and the ladies started running, trying to escape the frantic birds. Some dropped their baskets as they fled, trying to fend off the chickens with their arms as they ran. Others stumbled and fell, resorting to holding the baskets over their heads to protect themselves from the chickens' claws. I saw Gertie standing stock still in the middle of the mess, like a heroine in some weird, dark fantasy movie. But before I could figure out what she was up to, Celia, in a move that only she or Gertie could manage, spun around, ran headfirst into the tetherball pole, then flopped face down in the dirt.

Ida Belle had locked in on the hounds and was running toward them, attempting to cut them off. I launched off the sidewalk and angled toward them, figuring if the three of us could converge on them at the same time, we might be able to get the hounds secured before the Easter egg hunt turned into a death that no one was going to be resurrected from.

My speed was somewhat limited as I had to keep one hand over my face as I went. The chickens would run and then launch upward in their panic, and their claws scratched my arms. I was within a couple feet of one of the hounds and about to make a dive for him when the chickens suddenly changed trajectory. The birds and the dogs were way quicker turning than I could manage, so by the time I slid and pivoted, I had lost ground. The hounds were only inches from conquering their prey when I heard someone whistle.

I looked over and saw Gertie standing on top of the slide, holding a sub sandwich in her hands. She cocked her arm back like an NFL player and let the sandwich fly. If this had been the Super Bowl, she would have been named MVP. The sandwich landed right in front of the charging hounds, and they skidded to a stop, and each latched onto one end of the sub in a quick tug-of-war.

The sandwich game gave me enough time to catch up, and I grabbed one of the hounds while Ida Belle managed the other. A couple seconds later, Skinny came staggering up, looking as though he was about to have a heart attack from all the running, and weakly extended his arm with the leads before bending over to wheeze. Ida Belle and I secured the hounds as Skinny sank to the ground.

Gertie gave a giant whoop, but it was a little too much celebrating while perched on top of a slippery slide. One foot went a little too far over the edge, then she fell onto the slide and took off down the steep slope, shooting off the end and crashing into a giant Easter bunny display as she went. I heard a bang and froze, then sprinted for her, afraid she'd just shot herself or someone else with something in her deadly handbag.

The giant blow-up rabbit was whistling and deflating as I

7

ran up, and I could see a hole in the center of the head. Gertie had landed in a patch of straw and was covered in what looked like pink glitter.

Good. God.

"You had a glitter bomb in your purse," I accused. "And you shot the rabbit! Why isn't your safety on?"

"It is," she said as she struggled to sit up. "The pin from the bomb must have flown out and hit the rabbit. If it had taken a bullet, that rabbit would have been scattered across the Gulf of Mexico."

"You're carrying the Desert Eagle again? No wonder you fell off that slide. That thing weighs a ton, especially with everything else you probably have in that bag."

I extended my hand and helped her stand, then stepped back while she brushed hay and glitter off. No way did I want to be picking that stuff out of my hair for the next week.

"I'm going to have to switch to a smaller caliber," she said.

"It would definitely be kinder to your shoulder."

"It's not that. I can only fit a six-inch sub in there with the Eagle."

"Well, good Lord, there's a crisis that needs addressing."

I shook my head and looked over at Ida Belle, who'd helped Skinny secure the hounds to a park bench. He'd managed to pick himself up off the ground and was now slumped on the bench, his face so red I was afraid he might need the paramedics. The dogs had gulped down the sandwich and were now straining so hard to get loose and back at the chickens that they were slowly pulling the bench across the grass.

Ida Belle saw me look over and threw her hands in the air.

"It's going to take a tractor to tow these hounds out of here," she said.

"We've got to get rid of those chickens," I said.

As I turned around, a cry went up with the rest of the ladies. The ones who'd been trampled were at least in sitting position, which was a good sign. Except for Celia. She'd hit that pole so hard that I had no doubt she'd knocked herself out. And if there had been any doubt, it was completely eliminated by the scene in front of me.

The chickens had discovered the poorly hidden eggs and were roosting on them. Roosting chickens were now scattered throughout the entire park with church ladies shrieking in dismay.

Except for one chicken, who had taken a particular liking to Celia's hat and had taken up roost there. I couldn't really blame it since the hat was made of straw and had a ring of eggs around it. To a chicken, it probably looked like a five-star resort. But this chicken wasn't just roosting—it was currently working on getting out a real egg. I assumed the stress had worked it out of the poor bird. As soon as the egg plopped out onto Celia's hat, it was like it flipped a switch on Celia's head to On. She threw her arms up over her head, frantically waving to get the chicken off her head.

But the chicken wasn't having any.

That egg had been hard earned and the chicken wasn't letting it go that easily. Celia pushed herself onto her knees, then grabbed the pole she'd run into and pulled herself into a standing position and started spinning around and waving her hands again, but the chicken had dug in for the ride, plopped down hard on its prize.

Desperate to be rid of the bird, Celia leaned forward and pulled the hat off her head. The startled chicken squawked and flapped so hard trying to get away that it flipped the hat over and kicked it into Celia's face.

Where the egg broke.

CHAPTER TWO

GERTIE STARTED LAUGHING SO HARD SHE DOUBLED OVER then sank onto the ground, unable to contain herself.

I looked over at Ida Belle, who'd stepped up beside me, her cell phone out, recording the entire thing.

"No one writes better fiction than what we have here in real life," Ida Belle said. "Let's see AI whip that scene up."

"Post a pic with Celia and that chicken on her head and people will swear it's fake," I said.

"People who aren't from southwest Louisiana will," Gertie said, struggling to catch her breath. "I'm so glad you got that recorded. I think I lost my phone going down the slide."

"Where was it?" I asked, because her purse was right there beside her.

"In my bra."

Ida Belle shook her head. "You need to get a smaller purse and a smaller bra. That way, you won't lose as much and you're less of a threat. As soon as Celia has a shower and some time to get over that whole egg in her face thing—which is the epitome of irony—she's going to have a fit over that rabbit. She donated it herself."

"The bigger problem is all these chickens," I said. "If you guys still plan on kids hunting eggs, you need to get them out of here."

Ida Belle lifted one shoe and I saw the smear of brown on the bottom. "I think the park is going to be off-limits until after the rainstorm tonight. Chickens tend to 'cut loose' when they're panicked. If kids come home covered in poo, the parents will not be pleased."

"Well, we can't leave them here," Gertie said. "There's coyotes all over those woods. It will look like a massacre tomorrow if we don't get them out. Who do they belong to?"

"Good question," Ida Belle said. "Let's go find out."

We headed for the park bench where Skinny was now lying down, his eyes closed. Walter, who'd quietly observed the entire mess, clearly enjoying himself, was standing over him and staring—probably trying to figure out if he was still breathing.

"Are you all right?" I asked as we approached.

"I think so," Skinny said. "I just needed a minute. All that running. And the stress."

"You might be up for a relapse when the owner of those chickens finds out your hounds got after them," Walter said.

"This isn't on me," he said. "Someone opened my back gate, but those chickens were already loose. I let the dogs out for their afternoon constitutional like I always do, and the next thing I knew, I looked out the front window and there's a flock of chickens running past my house. I figured it wouldn't be a problem because it's not like a hound is going to clear a six-foot fence, and even though they're good diggers, they couldn't have dug their way out that fast."

"So what happened?" Ida Belle asked.

"I don't know. I just saw them bolt into the front yard. I

pulled on my shoes and ran after them as fast as I could, but I could hear my gate banging as I went."

"You sure you didn't leave it open yourself?" Walter asked.

"I never use the thing. It was probably the neighbor's kids. They're always hitting their ball into my yard, and I've told them a million times not to go in there, but they don't listen. Guess I'm going to have to put a lock on it."

"Probably a good idea," I said. "But the bigger question is where the heck did all those chickens come from and why are they parading down the streets?"

"They came from the south past my house. Only guy up that way with that many chickens is Flint Parsons."

Walter whistled and Ida Belle frowned. "I was afraid you were going to say that."

"I've never heard of him," I said.

"You never do," Skinny said. "*Until* you do, and then he'll be stamped in your mind forever."

Since that statement applied to so many Sinful residents, I was almost afraid to ask, but curiosity always got the better of me.

"So what's his deal?"

"He's a prepper," Ida Belle said. "With strong feelings about people as a species."

I waited. So far, he didn't sound that bad.

Ida Belle noticed my expression and laughed. "He thinks the earth is flat and that Christ returned a couple decades back and forgot to whisk him up. That would be up in the spaceship. Flint lives in a big clearing in the woods and pretty much refuses to leave his property because that's where he built a landing strip for when they send a rescue unit for him. He shoots at anyone who trespasses, much to law enforcement's dismay."

I nodded. "Jesus in a UFO is a new one. Maybe he's been sneaking some of Nora's stash."

"If only that was the answer," Ida Belle said. "But I'm pretty sure he's not on anything at all except water. He thinks manufacturers are poisoning us."

I put my hands on my hips and blew out a breath. "So do we send up smoke signals to the Unabomber so he can come collect his chickens? Because it sounds like delivery isn't an option."

"Definitely not," Skinny agreed.

"How old is this guy?" I asked.

"About one thousand eighty-two," Skinny said. "He was old when I was a kid, and that was more years ago than I'm going to mention."

Since Skinny was every bit of sixty, that gave me a good idea. "What about Sheriff Lee? I assume Flint knows him, right? And probably thinks he's still sheriff. He wouldn't shoot at him, would he?"

Ida Belle brightened. "That's a good idea. Let me give him a call."

She pulled out her phone and dialed Lee. "It's Ida Belle. I need some help with some chickens. No. I'm not eating chicken. Put in your hearing aid!"

She waited a minute, then explained the situation, then shoved the phone back in her pocket. "He's going to saddle up and ride out there. Flint responds better to horses. He thinks motorized vehicles are the devil. Except for his truck, which is as old as him. He had it blessed."

"This guy just gets better every time you talk about him," I said. "In the meantime, what do we do about the chickens?"

Ida Belle shrugged. "They're all roosting quietly now. No point in stirring them up until we have a place to put them."

She looked over at Skinny. "But it's probably best if you get out of here with those hounds."

The thought of facing Flint Parsons was like a jolt with defibrillator pads. Skinny came up off the bench and practically ran out of the park, pulling the reluctant hounds behind him. Walter glanced at the retreating Skinny, then back at the chickens.

"I'm going to head into town and follow Sheriff Lee to the edge of the woods," he said. "At least if there's gunfire, I can call for backup."

Then he retreated as quickly as Skinny had.

All the church ladies were still collected in the park, staring at the chickens as if they could will them off the eggs, so I followed a reluctant Ida Belle back over to them.

"What are you going to do about this mess?" Celia demanded.

Ida Belle raised one eyebrow. "I see. Now that there's a problem, you're no longer in charge? Typical. The chickens likely belong to Flint Parsons."

There was a collective intake of breath so big that I saw some of the chickens' feathers move.

"Sheriff Lee is going to see if they're his chickens. If they are, he'll come retrieve them. I'm sure he doesn't want them roosting in the park any more than we do."

"What about the kids?"

"Everyone take out your call list and notify the parents you've been assigned that we have to cancel for today. If we get rain overnight, then we can do it tomorrow."

Celia bowed up. "That is completely unacceptable."

"Well, if you've got a better idea, I'm all ears," Ida Belle said. "We could let the kids run, slide, and wrestle for eggs in masses of chicken poop, or we can move the whole thing to your house. What's it going to be?"

"I want Flint Parsons and Skinny Lawson arrested."

"Of course you do," I said. "Stop wasting law enforcement's time. You know good and well they're not arresting anyone for this. I swear to God, just hearing you speak makes me dumber."

Several of the ladies let out strangled laughs, then all tried to look as though it wasn't them. But I could still see their shoulders shaking.

"Who's going to pay for that rabbit that Gertie destroyed?" Celia continued. "That's destruction of private property."

"I'll replace it," Gertie said. "With better quality. You're the only person I know who celebrates Jesus on a discount."

Celia's face turned red, and she started to sputter like an old boat motor, but she was stopped from replying by a truck backfiring. I looked over to see an ancient pickup truck with a camper cover on the back stop in the middle of the street. When the man climbed out of his truck, I could only assume this was Flint Parsons.

Five foot two...now. He was probably four inches taller before all of his discs and cartilage turned to dust. Maybe a hundred pounds of man but at least twenty pounds of gear on the military belt he wore. At least there was some muscle in there to haul all that weight. He looked old enough to have babysat Sheriff Lee. No threat at all in a fight, a footrace, or sanity competitions, but if the collection of guns, knives, and grenades on his belt was any indication, he was a match for Gertie's purse.

He stalked into the park and glared at everyone. "Well, isn't this just perfect. They're all out here among you heathens. I'll have to rebaptize every one of them or they'll lay possessed eggs."

I leaned toward Ida Belle. "This guy is great."

Celia's eyes widened and although I didn't think it was possible, she turned even redder and looked more offended than she had before. "Heathens? This is an Easter celebration for the children of this town."

He waved a hand at her. "Get out of my way. And you owe me for that egg you're wearing. Shame it was wasted on the likes of you."

"Why have you been hiding him?" I whispered.

Ida Belle stepped forward before Celia said something that had Flint reaching for his waistband. "Hello, Mr. Parsons. I'm sorry about the chickens, but we don't know why they're here or how they got here. We're happy to help you get them rounded up. Did you bring cages?"

"You're not touching my birds with unclean hands. I know who you are. Your mother was a sinner and you're no better than her."

Ida Belle smiled. "Everyone but Jesus is a sinner, Mr. Parsons. But we'll leave you to it."

She grabbed Gertie and dragged her toward the road.

"Do we have to go?" I asked as I followed.

"We can watch from the road," she said. "At least half the things on that utility belt of his won't reach that far. And I saw Gertie's purse hand twitching."

"I was just going to give him a flash of my new sexy underwear," Gertie said. "I figured he'd have a heart attack and then we could fry up all those chickens."

"There's a thought," I said, and stopped walking and turned around. "Hey, Mr. Parsons—you want to just wring those chickens' necks here in the park? They'll be easier to transport that way."

He glared at me and shook his head. "Those are layers, not fryers, you moron."

I barely managed to hold in my grin before turning around.

The church ladies apparently decided if we were leaving the park, it was a good idea, so they trailed after us. Then we all stood huddled on the road, watching as Flint gathered the birds as if he was carrying precious cargo and put them in the back of his truck. They didn't protest and remained calm, which I guessed was a testament to his treatment of the birds, but I had a feeling people didn't get half as much concern.

It took him a good thirty minutes to gather up the chickens, and he drove off without so much as a backward glance. The church ladies had used the time to call the parents and let them know the egg hunt had been postponed. Celia had called the sheriff's department demanding that Carter come out to the park so she could press charges on Gertie, Parsons, Lawson and his dogs, and the chickens.

Myrtle had texted me that she'd told Celia that Carter was too busy to deal with nonsense, which explained why Celia was standing there glaring at her cell phone. I had a feeling she was headed straight to the sheriff's department when she left the park, so I texted Carter with a warning to clear out for a while.

Once Flint's truck was out of sight, the ladies inched back into the park, staring in dismay at the filthy eggs and baskets.

"We can't use these eggs," one of the ladies said. "They've got poop all over them."

"They're plastic," Gertie said. "They'll wash."

"But people will know!" one of the ladies complained. "Everyone is going to hear about what happened today. They'll expect new eggs."

"We have a whole case of them at the church," Ida Belle said. "Just ask Pastor Don to get them out of the storeroom. Problem solved."

The ladies shuffled a bit, clearly still uncomfortable.

"What about the candy inside?" one of them finally asked.

"What about it?" Ida Belle asked. "It's inside a plastic egg and wrapped. Take it out and put it in the new eggs."

Celia stepped forward, hands on her hips. "I'm a godly

woman, and I refuse to allow those lambs of God to eat tainted candy."

"I'd like a vote on the use of the words 'godly' and 'woman' when referring to Celia," Gertie said.

"The Catholics provided the candy," Ida Belle said. "Do you have more?"

A couple of the women nodded. "Probably just enough to refill the eggs."

"Then I suggest you get to it," Ida Belle said. "But don't you dare throw that candy away. Your silly notions don't make it any less viable. I'll take it for myself unless anyone wants to share?"

Most of them shook their heads.

"Good. Then stuff it all in a bag, and I'll pick it up later," Ida Belle said. "We have plenty of extra grass for the baskets for the displays. I am not going to replace the baskets. We don't have the stock or the time to get more, and the kids will be bringing their own to hunt with. Besides, they're plastic. Clean them and get over it or toss them out and the Catholics can buy new ones for next year. Waste is a sin."

She gave Celia—the godly woman—a hard stare when she issued that last sentence, then turned around and walked off.

Gertie and I hurried behind her.

"You don't even like that candy," Gertie said. "What are you up to?"

"I'm going to sneak into the Catholic church next week and dump it all in the God's Wives stash that I know Celia keeps there."

I laughed and held my hand up to high-five her.

"That woman will be down at the sheriff's department as soon as she leaves here," Ida Belle said.

I nodded. "I already sent Carter a warning."

Gertie put her hands up. "Well, looks like our afternoon just opened up. Any ideas?"

"Hot tub and beer?" I asked.

"I thought you'd never ask," Gertie said, and rubbed her rear. "I think I broke my butt."

"Don't you need to get another giant rabbit?" I asked.

"I already have one. Jeb and I wanted a backdrop for these Playboy Bunny pictures—"

"No!" Ida Belle said. "And don't you dare let Celia and her crew know what things that rabbit has witnessed. She'll have Father Michael perform an exorcism on it."

I laughed. All in all, it had been a good day so far. No dead bodies—not even a chicken—no phone calls about the military's investigation, and I'd gotten to meet one of Sinful's hidden gems. As far as normal days in Sinful went, this one was fairly innocuous.

I spoke too soon.

CHAPTER THREE

A CAR I DIDN'T RECOGNIZE WAS PARKED IN FRONT OF MY house when we pulled up. Since it was a basic blue Honda Accord, it could have been a rental or new to someone I did know, but as we pulled into the drive, a woman stepped out.

Thirtyish. Five foot six. Trim build. Good muscle tone. But the worried look on her face reduced the threat factor. This woman had something serious on her mind.

I glanced at Gertie and Ida Belle, who both shook their heads. Interesting. She'd obviously come to find me, knew where I lived, and yet wasn't from Sinful or related to anyone who was.

"You think she has something to do with the military investigation?" Gertie asked.

"She doesn't walk like she's military," I said.

"Or an attorney," Ida Belle said. "Besides, Alexander would have told you if he'd hired help, and the others aren't allowed to talk to you."

"Well then, let's go see what this is about," I said, and climbed out of Ida Belle's SUV.

The woman approached as we exited the vehicle.

"Fortune Redding?" she asked and extended her hand. "My name is Kelsey Spalding. I'm sorry for accosting you this way at your home, but I got your name from Jenny Babin. I'd like to hire you."

"Jenny?" I said, a bit surprised.

Jenny Babin had been caught up in our last investigation, although it was technically an unofficial one, and she had come dangerously close to being arrested for murder. She'd ultimately been cleared but had left Sinful as soon as she was released and hadn't so much as glanced back.

"Yes," Kelsey said. "I work with her at the hotel. I'm the head chef. Jenny found me crying one day and my situation just spilled out. She told me a little about what had happened to her and how you'd unraveled it all. She said if anyone could sort out the truth, it was you."

I shuffled a little, feeling a tiny bit guilty since it was my investigation that had gotten Jenny almost arrested in the first place, but she didn't know that. And since I'd ultimately cleared her as well, I supposed it had all worked out just fine.

"Okay," I said. "Why don't you come inside. These are my assistants, Ida Belle and Gertie. I assume you're okay with them listening as well?"

"Of course. Jenny said you had fierce local support. I think you're going to need all the help you can get. I'm afraid my situation is as hopeless as I am desperate."

"Then let's go see what we can do."

We headed inside to the kitchen and Gertie poured us all up some tea. Kelsey seemed nervous, and I noticed her hands shook as she lifted the glass. She barely glanced around the room, instead alternating staring out the window or picking at her cuticles. I noticed so much skin was missing on some of the fingers that they'd been bleeding. This woman was definitely stressed.

"Where do I start?" she finally asked.

"Wherever you want," I said. "I need the whole story, either way, so tell it how it will be easiest to understand. There's no time limit. Our afternoon has just cleared up."

Her shoulders relaxed a tiny bit, and she nodded. "Okay. Then I guess I should start at the beginning. That's all the way back to high school just about."

"I've got underwear older than you," Ida Belle said. "You'll be fine."

Gertie grimaced. "You really should get some new underwear. Elastic can't last that long."

"It does if you don't gain weight and stretch it out."

Gertie gave her the finger and Kelsey relaxed a bit more, Ida Belle and Gertie's banter having the intended effect.

I gave her an encouraging smile. "Since you're not drawing Social Security yet, and Ida Belle's volunteered her underwear information, I'm sure your story will be fine no matter how far back you have to go."

She took a deep breath and slowly blew it out. "Okay, here goes... I met my husband the summer after high school. I was waiting tables in one of the restaurants his family's firm holds as an investment. He was home from college until fall—he was a junior at Harvard."

"Law?" Ida Belle asked.

"No. Finance. His family was grooming him to take over their investment firm so they could retire early. They're big travelers and never liked staying in one place much. Anyway, we started dating and I figured it would all end when he headed back to college, but it didn't. He went back in the fall, I started culinary school, and we kept the relationship going long distance."

"A hard thing to do, especially at that age," Gertie said.

Kelsey nodded. "I think it worked because we were both so

busy with our education. We didn't have a lot of time for hanging out with friends and meeting other people, so the temptation to try someone new wasn't really there. When he graduated the next year, he came home, and we took up full force. And to be honest, that's when things got harder."

Ida Belle raised one eyebrow. "The rose-colored glasses were gone after summer but having been separated all that time, you still didn't really know each other."

"Exactly," Kelsey agreed. "Brett is a good man in many ways, but he's also very rigid. Mostly because he never thinks he's wrong."

"We got that part when you said he was a man," Gertie said.

She laughed. "I suppose there might be some truth to that, as my son is often the same."

"How old is he?"

She sobered and her expression shifted to sad and serious. "Ten, and he might not make it to eleven."

"What's wrong?"

"He has a birth defect that causes kidney issues. He needs an organ transplant, or I should say *another* organ transplant. He had one transplant already, but it failed, and the odds of him getting pushed up the list a second time are next to none."

"And you and your husband aren't a match?" I asked.

She shook her head. "We were both tested before he went on the list. I'm not a match. And Brett's not his father."

A flush crept up her face, and she stared down at the table.

"I take it Brett didn't know?" I asked.

"No. Neither did I. Benjamin—Ben—looks so much like Brett. I just didn't think..."

"But obviously, it was a possibility."

She nodded. "We had broken up. Brett wanted to get married, but I wanted to finish culinary school first and get established in a full-time position as a chef before I even thought about planning a wedding or being a wife. But he was older than me, done with school, and his career was already planned. He was far ahead of me in life and either couldn't or didn't want to see things from my perspective."

"Which was?" I asked.

She thought for a moment, then blew out a breath. "Brett didn't have any real climbing up the work ladder to do since he was being presented with his family's company on a silver platter. He didn't want to accept that getting that foot in the door is the biggest challenge for most young people establishing a career, and it would be for me as well, because I wasn't interested in being handed a job. I wanted to earn my title and position."

"And your wanting to delay marriage until you finished your education and secured a job on your own caused him to break up with you?" Ida Belle asked.

"It was more of a split because of a fight—one of many, but I was tired of them, and he was tired of not getting his way. He'd been getting more and more antsy about it all, especially since I refused to live with him, too."

"That's very old-fashioned of you in such a throw-caution-to-the wind society," Gertie said.

She smiled. "Obviously, it wasn't about saving myself for marriage or even for appearances. I just didn't want the distraction, and I knew he would be one. Given the business and its clients, Brett spent several nights a week at some party or event. There was no way I could handle that kind of schedule and finish school, and he would have wanted me to attend."

Ida Belle shook her head. "I guess he was more concerned with what *he* wanted than what you did. Spoiled? Controlling? Entitled?"

"Those all play a role, for sure," she agreed. "Added to that, he was getting pressure from his parents. I'm certain they never liked me—probably thought I wasn't good enough since I didn't come from money or a society family. I think he believed getting married would shut them down."

"But as long as he was still single, they'd keep trying to push off someone they thought was better suited," Gertie said.

"That's it exactly," Kelsey said. "I also knew he didn't want me to work, and we certainly didn't need the additional salary. He would have preferred I spend my time catering to him. And even if I insisted that I needed to work for *me*, his viewpoint was that his family's firm owned several restaurants. It's not like I had to finish at the top of my class and then go begging for a chance like all the other culinary graduates with no connections. But I didn't want to work at a restaurant his family firm controlled. I wanted to do it myself, and I didn't want to deal with the resentment that would come from being shoved into a job because of my relationship with Brett."

"Smart," Ida Belle said. "Because that's exactly how it would have gone."

"Anyway, we kept arguing over it and he finally said that if I wasn't going to marry him then there was no point in us continuing. I just wanted to be left alone to finish school, so I agreed, and we went our separate ways."

"Still couldn't have been easy," Gertie said, "even though it was the right decision."

"It wasn't. By that time, we'd been dating for almost three years—two in person and one with him away. I understood his position, but I didn't feel like he'd ever made the effort to understand mine. I was completely down about the whole thing, of course, so my roommate and a couple other friends insisted on taking me out for a night on the town. We popped in and out of a bunch of bars in the French Quarter and finally ended up at the casino. By the time midnight had come and gone, we'd all had way too much to drink and two of them had headed home already. My roommate tried to get me to leave, but I didn't feel like going home and staring at the ceiling like I had every night before. So I promised her that I'd take a cab home and took a seat at the bar counter. That's where I met Ryan."

"And Ryan is Ben's father?" I asked.

"Definitely. I've never been the kind of person to sleep around. For three years, I'd only been with Brett, and after Ryan, it was only Brett again, so there are no other options."

"Was he another customer?" Gertie asked.

"No. He was the bartender. He was about my age, cute, and clued right into my confused and depressed state. He asked me what I wanted to drink, then asked me what was wrong. I dumped everything on him. He was a really good listener. Turned out, he'd been having relationship problems as well. He and his longtime girlfriend had recently separated, and he'd moved out. I stayed at the bar, talking to him, until the bar closed. We were the only two people in there by then."

"And you went home with him?" Ida Belle asked.

"No. But it was a one-night stand. God, I feel so embarrassed admitting that. When we left the bar, he asked me if I was hungry and said we could grab something to eat and keep talking. I didn't want to leave either. It had been so long since a man listened to me—really listened—so I took a chance and kissed him. I figured if he wasn't interested, he'd push me off and we'd both go our separate ways, but he didn't. He got big discounts on rooms when the hotel wasn't busy, so he got a room and we headed up."

She shook her head and frowned. "When I woke up the next morning, I almost screamed. I didn't know where I was or who the strange man in bed with me was. Then it all came flooding back in, and I was so humiliated. I grabbed my clothes and dressed on the way to the door. I left and never saw him again. That day was my birthday, and Brett came to see me and apologized. We talked everything out, found some middle ground, and got back together. A month later, I found out I was pregnant."

"And you never worried that Ben might not be Brett's?" Gertie asked.

"The thought definitely flickered through my mind while I was pregnant, but when Ben was born, Brett was so excited to be a father and actually invested, you know? And Ben looked like Brett's baby pictures. Brett's mother was always going on about it, so I let it go, figuring the possibility was so slim that it wasn't worth considering."

"So I take it Brett and Ryan look a lot alike?" I asked.

"Yeah. They do," she admitted. "I guess I have a type. Anyway, Brett and I got married. His parents made him president of the firm and started traveling most of the year, handling what little business they still personally oversaw from other countries. I managed to finish culinary school and graduated right before Ben was born. I stayed home with him the first year and then started working part time after that—still not for a restaurant connected to Brett. I found a chef who was willing to work with me part time until Ben was in school and I could start working full time."

She raised her chin a little. "I'm a really good chef. As soon as I went full time, I moved up quickly and was a head chef at a top-tier restaurant within two years."

"That's impressive," Ida Belle said. "We've eaten at the hotel recently, and the food was excellent."

"Thank you. The owner is a great boss. Of course, I'm completely biased in saying that as he's the first person I've worked for who let me have complete creative control."

"Seems like a smart move on his part," Gertie said.

She nodded, then frowned. "So fast-forward some years and both of us are clicking along just fine in our careers and Ben is doing great. He's such a wonderful kid. I know every parent says that, but in Ben's case, it's really true. As ill as he is, he's never once complained, never cried, never raged against God. I've done all that and more."

"And your marriage?" I asked. "Now that certain things have been revealed?"

She sighed. "To be honest, it wasn't exactly a storybook romance before Ben got sick, either. My kid is perfect, but my husband is far from it. We've been drifting apart for years, and that's assuming we were ever solid to begin with. Brett is a great father but not a good husband. Unless being controlled is your thing, and it never was for me. But I allowed too much of it because of the pregnancy and then once Ben was born, I wanted to be able to stay with him without having to rush off to work right away. But I never intended for that to be my sole existence."

"I take it Brett would have preferred you not go back to work?" Gertie asked.

"That's putting it mildly. It's been a source of contention between us ever since I walked out the door in a chef's coat. Don't get me wrong—I get it on some level. His parents are… uninvolved, I guess is the politest way to put it. They almost seem like they don't even like him very much. They returned to the United States for only two days after Ben was born and have only seen him a handful of times since then."

"Sounds like Brett wants the perfect family so badly that he's destroying any chance of having it by trying to control everyone," Gertie said. "That's sad for all of you."

Kelsey nodded. "He stopped the digs and snide comments a long time ago, but I have no doubt his feelings are the same.

I often wondered what would happen when Ben was old enough to start becoming his own person, separate from Brett's will."

She choked and had to take a drink of water as her eyes filled with tears. "Now I don't even know if he'll ever get old enough to start that battle."

My heart clenched and I prayed I could help her.

"I take it you need me to find Ryan?" I asked.

She shook her head. "I already found him. I didn't know his last name, but I went back to the casino, praying that a longtime employee would remember him. I got lucky. The housekeeping manager had just started part time back then, and she remembered him because he always walked her to her car when she got off and he was coming on."

I frowned. I hoped Kelsey didn't want me to try to convince Ryan to give up a kidney. That was a job better suited for a therapist or maybe a priest. "So you know his full name and where he lives? Then what's the problem?"

"His current residence is Angola prison."

CHAPTER FOUR

GERTIE SUCKED IN A BREATH AND IDA BELLE'S EYES widened. I felt a rush of the same despair that must be coursing through every square inch of the poor woman in front of me.

"For what?" I asked.

"Murder."

My heart sank. It couldn't have been any worse.

"Who did he kill?"

"His girlfriend."

I was wrong. It was worse.

"Tell me everything you know."

She nodded. "It's not a whole lot. He was from Mudbug, and she was from Magnolia Pass, which is where they lived, so I guess that's why it wasn't really covered in the NOLA papers. The Magnolia Pass cops won't give out any information, but I found a couple of brief statements online given by other residents and matched what they said with what little I got from the court records. Basically, Ryan and his girlfriend had broken up a couple weeks before and he'd moved out of the house they shared. He'd been living in a motel up the highway just outside of Sinful...one of those sketchy places."

"I know it."

"Anyway, he said he'd been calling her, but she wasn't answering, and he knew she wasn't working that day, so he went over to the house. He claimed he wanted to talk—to patch things up. But he found her stabbed to death in the kitchen."

"He still had a key to the house?"

She nodded. "And the cops found the murder weapon in the dumpster at the motel. It had his fingerprints on it."

"No forced entry?"

"No."

I shook my head. "I don't know what you want me to do. This sounds like an open-and-shut case. Short of having video of the actual crime, the prosecutor could have phoned this one in."

She leaned forward in her chair. "But that's just it. The medical examiner gave a specific window for her time of death —between 2:00 and 4:00 a.m.—the night he was with me in the casino hotel in New Orleans."

"Holy crap!"

"You've got to be kidding me!"

Ida Belle and Gertie both spoke at once. I just sat back and whistled.

"You're positive it was the same night?" I asked.

"Absolutely, 100 percent certain of it, and my friends will confirm it as well," she said. "When you do something so out of character, you tend to remember it in excruciating detail. Plus, it was the day before my birthday, and the night before I got back with Brett. I have plenty of reasons to be absolutely certain that I've got the date right, and Ryan Comeaux did *not* murder his girlfriend."

"Is it possible he left the hotel after you fell asleep?" I asked. I knew it was a really long shot, but I had to think like a prosecutor, and that's the first place they'd go.

"I suppose it's possible, but the thing is, we didn't go to sleep until after 5:00 a.m. We had sex a couple times, ordered champagne and food from room service, then had another round of 'dessert.' I know for certain it was after five when we finally went to sleep because I checked my phone for messages and sent a follow-up text to my roommate so she wouldn't freak out the next morning when she woke up and realized I'd never come home."

"But surely Ryan told the cops the same thing," I said. "Why didn't they come see you then for an alibi?"

Her shoulders slumped and she sighed. "Because I didn't give him my real name. I used my middle name and never told him my last name. I didn't tell him anything about me that could allow him to identify me after the fact. He knew all the sordid details of my relationship, but nothing that would have allowed him to track me down. It was a one-night stand. You don't plan on keeping in touch."

"What about your friends?" I asked. "Somebody had to settle up the tab. The cops didn't try to track you by credit card receipt?"

She smiled. "Four hot young women in tight clothes—we never reached for our wallets all night."

I nodded. "Did you go to the police with this information?"

She threw her hands in the air. "Of course! When I read the date and time in the court documents, I went straight to the police station in Magnolia Pass and asked to talk to someone in charge. They gave me some dude who looked like he hadn't done any work besides eat doughnuts for ten years—and I'm not stereotyping. There was a half-eaten box of doughnuts next to his keyboard and he was covered in chocolate drippings and powdered sugar."

"And he did nothing?"

"He took my statement and my information and said he'd give it to the ADA. I called back after a week, and he said he'd sent it over and if the ADA hadn't contacted me then it was obviously because he felt there was nothing to pursue."

I shook my head. "An innocent man doing life for a crime he didn't commit isn't worth pursuing? Good Lord!"

"I know. So I marched down to the ADA's office and refused to leave unless he spoke to me or they called the police and had me hauled out of there. They left me waiting for hours, but he finally gave me five minutes of his time. He surfed his phone while I talked."

"Wow. Just wow," Gertie said. "One would think he'd be working to redeem his reputation given how sketchy it is at the moment, but he's just doubling down."

"I'm beginning to think he's not capable of being a decent human being," Ida Belle said. "Or of actually doing his job."

"I don't have any other experience with him, but I agree," Kelsey said. "When I was done, he asked if I had proof that Ryan was with me that night. Since it was just the two of us in the room, sans a film crew or Peeping Toms, the answer was no. So then he asked if anyone could verify that I left the bar with Ryan and checked into the hotel, but I don't have proof of that either. We shut the bar down, and Ryan got the room with his discount. I didn't even go to the desk with him. I waited by the elevators, and good Lord, even if I had, who the hell's going to remember that after ten years?"

"Hotel records?" I asked.

"Don't go back that far."

I blew out a breath. I didn't doubt that Kelsey was telling the truth, but given her reason for needing access to Ryan, I could see where a prosecutor could make a mockery of her story.

"What about the prison?" Ida Belle asked. "Have you tried talking to them—explaining the situation? I've heard of inmates being able to donate bone marrow and organs to relatives when they were the only match."

"I tried but got nowhere. Ryan isn't listed as the father on the birth certificate, so without a DNA test to prove he's Ben's father, the warden won't even talk to me."

"And unless the warden allows it, you can't get a DNA test," I said. "The very definition of the runaround. So what do you want me to do? I know some people who are usually owed favors from a certain element. And I have a killer attorney. One of them might be able to get you audience with the warden."

She shook her head. "It would all take time. His assistant told me that the warden is booked for the next three months, if you can believe that. So unless your friends have dirt on him that would put him on the other side of those bars he manages, waiting on him to budge might be too late."

"Then I don't know what you want from me."

"I want you to find out who murdered Lindsay. Jenny said you had a way of finding out every secret that was never supposed to be revealed. I thought she was exaggerating, but then she told me about those women you found out in the swamp and how that organization had been hidden there trafficking women and drugs for decades before you blew it all wide open in a matter of days."

Kelsey frowned. "And she told me about everything that happened with her husband and his brother. She said if you hadn't put it all together, they might never have known about the body buried under her deck, and she might have ended up like Ryan...in prison for a murder she didn't commit."

I shook my head. I wanted to help her. A man was in prison for a crime that I was 99.99 percent certain he didn't commit, and the worst part was, that wasn't even the most pressing issue. A young boy's life depended on the father who didn't even know he had a son. I'd taken on cases that seemed impossible, but this one was dire on so many levels. Failure would literally ruin multiple lives and end at least one.

"I want to help you," I said. "You can't even imagine how much, but there is so little to go on. And even if I could prove Ryan's innocence, it would take time to get his conviction overturned, even with my attorney working on it, and trust me, there exists none better."

"I get it," she agreed. "But if you can get enough for your attorney to pressure the ADA, then that would give me leverage with the press, right? And that might be enough to push the warden into giving us medical access until the whole thing can be sorted."

"You already have leverage with the press by virtue of having a terminally ill child whose only hope is his biological father," I said. "Why not try that route first? It would be faster."

"I spoke with top reporters for the newspaper and local television, but they all said the same thing—it's my word against a ten-year-old conviction. And this is still the Bible Belt, and this bunch of hypocrites will see my one-night stand as proof that I'm a floozy and an unreliable witness. They all wanted to help, but they can't stick their necks out over a story that I can't corroborate in any way. Add to it that I was drunk, I never told Ryan he was the father, I'm married to another man who never knew Ben wasn't his and, well..."

I sighed. "They'll be saying if you were that drunk, then it might not have been Ryan."

She nodded. "Or worse. It might not *only* be Ryan. Anyway,

I have to live and work in this city. My kid, if he ever gets better, has to live here. With my marriage on the rocks, I can't afford to lose my job over bad publicity."

"Surely Brett would support you and Ben," Gertie said.

"Ben, sure. He still sees Ben as his son, but I'd be cut out completely. Brett has access to plenty of money, but it's all protected in trusts. I can't touch it in a divorce."

"But Brett could use it to get full custody," Ida Belle said.

"That's my biggest fear. I don't care about the money for myself. I know people say that all the time, but I swear, in my case it's true. I didn't even know who Brett was when we met, and I went out with him thinking he was an average college student off for the summer and working for the company who owned the hotel."

"And attending Harvard?" Ida Belle asked.

She smiled. "He didn't tell me the school until we'd been going out for weeks, which was when I realized the hotel staff treated him with a lot of deference for someone who was supposed to be doing a summer internship in accounting. I'm not saying that having money is a bad thing. I'm just saying it's not everything."

I nodded. "This is what I don't understand. If Brett still considers Ben his son, and wants to save him, why isn't he using his family money and connections to get access to Ryan?"

Kelsey huffed. "He says he's tried. That he can't even get the warden to take his phone calls and he got the same runaround on appointments that I did. And I hate to say it, but at this point, I don't know that he believes me either. He certainly doesn't trust me. I never told him about that night until all this came out with Ben's tests."

"Why would you?" Gertie asked. "You didn't owe him a

minute-by-minute itinerary of the time you were apart. Did he go out with other women while you were broken up?"

"Most definitely. A couple of them relished shoving it in my face for months after we got back together. Until I started showing. Then they finally gave up."

"Well, there you go," Gertie said.

"I don't need Ryan's case overturned right away," Kelsey said. "Although in the long run, that's exactly what I want to see happen. But right now, I just need enough evidence to create a public outcry. One so big it forces the people who can make this happen to do their jobs."

"Evidence on a crime that happened ten years ago," I said. "Where no one but you can alibi the convicted, and where the only likely witness to the actual crime is the killer. Do you know how much of a reach that is?"

"No more than the things Jenny told me you've done. You did figure out that body was under her deck, and it had been there for decades."

Gertie nodded. "Did you know that Fortune found a body in her own backyard the day she arrived in town?"

Ida Belle snorted. "Like that's some big feat. Do you have any idea how many bodies are dumped in the swamp? Instead of sportsman's paradise, the state motto should be 'we can disappear you.'"

Kelsey managed a small smile, but I could see how much effort it was. "I have money to pay you. I'm not asking you to work for free. In fact, I insist on paying you. This is your job. I don't cook for free. Please. I think you might be my last hope."

I blew out a breath and nodded, and Kelsey's shoulders slumped with relief.

"But," I said, "I'll do a contract and take a retainer of two thousand. Then I'll spend four or five hours pushing this. If I don't come up with anything worth pursuing after that, we'll revisit everything. But you have to understand that I can't find evidence if it doesn't exist."

"I'm just asking that you try. If you can't find anything, then I'll attempt the press again. Or start my own online campaign."

"It's not the worst idea," Ida Belle said. "Social media cuts through a lot of the BS systems in place."

"Let me go get that contract," I said and headed out, feeling uneasy about the entire thing.

I didn't have a problem taking the case, per se. Quite frankly, even if she hadn't agreed to my terms and we'd parted ways with no agreement, I still would have poked around. It was just the way I was wired, and with a young boy's life on the line, the stakes were particularly high. But I was worried that this might be the first time I couldn't come up with anything. Finding witnesses that could even place Ryan at the hotel in NOLA with Kelsey was going to be a needle in a haystack under the best of circumstances, but in a transient tourist city at a busy casino, it would take a miracle.

After Kelsey left, contract in hand, I headed back to the kitchen and slumped into my chair. Ida Belle and Gertie glanced at each other, then both looked at me, clearly concerned.

"I know what you're thinking," Ida Belle said. "That if you can't solve this, that boy's going to die, and an innocent man is going to waste away in prison. And you're not wrong, but neither of those is on you because you didn't cause this. Trying to fix it and failing still doesn't make any of it your fault."

Gertie nodded. "You're Ryan and Ben's best chance. If you can't figure it out, then I can't imagine anyone else could either."

"I know that should make me feel better," I said.

"But it doesn't," Gertie said. "I get it. But all we can do is try, right?"

Ida Belle nodded. "So where do we start?"

"I'd like to run the whole thing by Alexander, of course. He might have some ideas on budging the immovable warden. It wouldn't kill the man to allow a DNA test, and if positive to allow the tests to see if Ryan's a match for the organ donation. If he's not, the entire thing might be an exercise in futility."

Gertie shook her head. "That's not true. Even if Ryan can't save Ben, he'll die in Angola. He's already spent a third of his life behind bars, but he's got a long, long time to go."

"So I take it you two believe her story? And that she's certain on her dates?"

They both nodded.

I drew in a deep breath and slowly blew it out. "So do I."

"Then I guess we approach it like every other case," I continued. "From the beginning. Let's start with, do either of you know Ryan Comeaux or his family?"

They both shook their heads.

"There's plenty of Comeaux in Louisiana," Ida Belle said, "but his name's not coming to mind as someone's grandson or anything. If he's still got family in Mudbug, it must not be a big one."

Gertie nodded. "If we knew any of his family, we'd have heard about all of this."

"What about this Magnolia Pass?" I asked. "Where is it?"

"A little off the highway between Sinful and NOLA," Ida Belle said.

I frowned. I'd never heard of the place, which meant it was far enough off the highway that it didn't have signs directing people that way.

"Why does a town that small have their own police department?" I asked. "Why wouldn't it fall under the sheriff department's jurisdiction, like Sinful and Mudbug?"

"Magnolia Pass is small," Gertie said, "but it's got old-money families who fund it and run it like their own little country."

"I've never even heard of it, and it's right up the road," I said, still amazed.

"The reigning families in Magnolia Pass prefer to keep it hidden," Ida Belle said. "That's why there's no signs on the highway, no advertisements for tourists, no hotels, no encouraging people to visit. They're insular and want to remain that way. People who want growth and change leave."

Gertie nodded. "The richest and oldest family there are the Beeches."

I groaned. "Ryan's girlfriend was Lindsay *Beech*. What are the odds that she *isn't* related to them?"

"Less than zero," Ida Belle said. "But it gives you another angle on motive. Where there's money, there's always the potential for problems."

"True," I agreed. "But if this place is as insular as you're describing, and Lindsay's family basically owns and runs it, then we're never going to get people to talk to us. Including the cops."

Ida Belle nodded. "*Especially* the cops."

CHAPTER FIVE

CARTER OFFERED TO BRING DINNER TO MY HOUSE THAT night, so after Ida Belle, Gertie, and I made plans for the next day, they headed out and I hit the shower. What was supposed to have been a quiet afternoon in the park had become a workout I wasn't planning for. And it took two washes before I didn't smell like chicken feathers, but it was probably my imagination.

Carter brought chicken-fried steak and didn't even bother to take it into the kitchen. He just plopped it on the coffee table and went to grab us a couple beers. So we chowed down in the living room, and he told me all about his afternoon.

"Walter said Flint darn near shot Sheriff Lee," Carter said. "He claimed Sheriff Lee was trespassing."

"I guess, technically, he's right, since Lee isn't the sheriff anymore, but Flint doesn't know that. How has he been here this long and no one's taken a round from him?"

"He has horrible aim. And since he's got to be eight thousand two years old by now, I can't imagine his vision is all that great."

"A bad shot and poor vision is still walking dynamite."

43

"True. But Lee yelled at him for a bit and he recognized his voice. Almost panicked when he heard his chickens were loose. Didn't believe him so he made Lee come look with him."

"Obviously they were his, since Mr. Personality showed up at the park to collect them and tell us all we were going to hell."

Carter grinned. "Sounds right. Anyway, there was a big cypress tree behind his coop that had fallen. Roots tore a hole in the back of it, so the chickens had decided to take a stroll."

"That's a heck of a stroll from where Flint lives to the paved roads."

"My guess is something got after them, and they took off down the dirt road toward town."

I nodded. "Then Skinny Lawson's hounds got after them and ran them into the park."

"Flint was beside himself saying they probably won't lay for a week."

"One of them has no anxiety issues. She laid one right in Celia's hat—while it was still on her head."

"Oh, I've seen the video."

"It was even more glorious in person, especially when she smacked her own face with it."

"I almost wish I would have been there, but then she would have been harassing me to arrest the chicken."

"And Gertie."

"Oh yeah, the rabbit. I heard all about that too. Why wasn't her gun on safety?"

"It was. She was carrying the Baby Eagle. Pieces of the rabbit would have been in Mexico if that thing had gone off."

"So what destroyed the rabbit?"

"Glitter bomb. I guess the pin went through it."

"I'm going to talk to Marie about making a new law that Gertie can't carry a purse."

"You'd have to insist on no bra as well."

His eyes widened a bit and he looked slightly horrified but wisely chose to leave the conversation off there.

"Did you talk to Skinny about his faulty fence?" I asked.

"Oh yeah. No way I was letting Celia get one up on me. If Skinny had a fence problem, then I was going to make darn sure it was rectified before Celia made it by there to get evidence for her assault-by-dogs-chasing-chickens claim."

"And was his fence faulty?"

"Not a single square inch. I didn't figure it would be. Skinny's serious about his hounds. They've won awards and been written up in hunting magazines. No way he'd risk them with something as stupid as not maintaining his fence."

"He said it was probably the kids next door. Said he's told them not to go into his yard, but they don't listen."

"They might now. I had a cop-to-boys chat with them. I could tell as soon as their mother opened the door that they were the culprits."

"Why weren't they at the celebration at school with all the other kids?"

"Homeschooled. They tended to disrupt classes and spent most of their time in detention, so they were asked to leave. It was clear they thought the whole thing was hilarious."

"I see. Then what could you possibly say to them to turn them from their juvenile delinquent ways?"

"I told them it wouldn't have been so funny if Flint had shot those dogs going after his chickens."

"How old are these kids?"

"Ten and twelve."

"Isn't that kind of harsh?"

"Better to hear it in theory than to see it in person.

Besides, they hunt. They know the score. Sobered them up right quick, and they promised to knock on Skinny's door and ask for their ball. Or better yet, go play in the park where they can't lose the thing over the fence."

He gave me an amused look. "I'm surprised you look that upset at me for coming down on some kids."

"I'm not upset about that. Sounds like they needed a wake-up call. I'm more worried that they're allowed to hunt."

He laughed. "If you worried about everyone in Sinful who has a gun they have no business owning, then you'd never stop worrying. Gertie's accidental discharges probably total more than the rest of the citizens combined, and I don't see you cutting back on the time you spend with her."

"Touché."

"Speaking of the terrible twosome, what did you guys do after the big chicken event? Sit in the hot tub and drink?"

"That was the plan, but then I caught a case."

"What case?"

I told him. When I was done, he shook his head. "That's bad business all the way around. You think she was telling the truth?"

"Yes. But beyond that, why would she lie? Why hinge your kid's life on a felon convicted of murder unless that's the truth?"

He nodded. "Where are you going to start?"

"The beginning. If there's one thing I've learned since I moved here, it's that nothing is surface deep. Everything and everyone has a beginning and an end and one always factors into the other."

"So background, with an attempt to suss out potential witnesses."

"That's the idea." I shook my head. "I know it's a long shot

—the whole thing is in more ways than one—but I have to try."

He put his arm around me and kissed me gently on the lips. "Of course you do. Let me know if I can help. In any authorized way, of course. We've got enough legal problems without me going rogue here and adding to them."

"Did you know Ryan or know of him? Or the case?"

"No. He would have been too young for my crowd."

"And the murder?"

He shook his head. "It sounds vaguely familiar, but I was already in the Marines by then."

"So if you heard anything, it was probably from your mother or Walter."

"My mother would be my guess. Walter isn't much of one for gossip. Taking it in, absolutely, but he doesn't share a lot."

"Much to the dismay of Sinful. I bet Walter has all the good gossip. The General Store is basically like the Swamp Bar without all the booze, drunks, wet T-shirt contests, and well... maybe it's not like that at all."

Carter laughed. "The store's not, but Walter is kind of like bartenders in shows where everyone comes around and talks their ear off. I wouldn't hold my breath on a wet T-shirt contest down there though."

"Why not? He could make a great marketing play. A big selection of mirrored sunglasses for the men and wrinkle cream for their wives for all that frowning they'd do. Or maybe just go straight for Bibles and the conversion angle."

He snorted. "If a bunch of loose women started wet boob dancing in the General Store, my guess is he'd have a run on lightning rods, not Bibles."

"True. I'll give your mom a call in the morning, then. See if maybe she knows someone who's related to or knows Ryan or his family well. I did some checking online but couldn't run much down. And unfortunately, you don't have jurisdiction so I can't even launch a useless plea for case files."

"NOLA?"

"Magnolia Pass. I've been informed by Ida Belle and Gertie that the entire town is run and pretty much owned by the old, rich families there, but they don't really know much else about it."

He frowned. "I know the police captain. He's a joke. A prop for the Beeches. They've been the overlords there for years now."

I sighed. "Then I guess it's not going to help matters that Ryan's girlfriend was Lindsay Beech?"

He whistled. "Holy crap. You've really stepped in it with this one. Cops don't like PIs to begin with, but if you prove the local cops got this wrong, and the real killer of a Beech has gotten away with it, then the Beeches won't hesitate to clean house."

"So their jobs and reputations are on the line. They have absolutely zero reason to want this investigated."

"That pretty much sums it up."

I sighed. "What does it say about our justice system that people would rather be presumed right than proven wrong?"

"A whole lot of things I don't want to consider given that I'm trying to run my small piece of the parish. Here's a thought though—Detective Casey might be able to help you. Your client claims they were in the casino hotel with the convicted. That might be enough for her to pull the case files over. At least you'd know if they bothered to check out the story, because I'm sure Ryan told the cops where he was that night."

I nodded. "I'd be surprised if they looked beyond the stacked bunch of evidence they turned up quickly and easily."

He frowned. "Yeah. I don't like it when things are too easy."

"Because it smells like a setup."

He nodded and looked out my front window. I knew where his mind had jumped to—the mission in Iran. I still didn't know the details—couldn't know them—but I had put enough together to know that while it wasn't necessarily a setup, it was now a cover-up. Carter was never meant to return home. I believed Colonel Kitts intended him to take everything he knew about the bungled mission to the grave.

A very sandy grave.

———

I WAS UP EARLY AND HOPING THAT EMMALINE COULD provide me with a lead. Since I knew she always had coffee around 7:00 a.m. on her front porch, so that all the early risers would stop by and give her the latest gossip, I dressed and headed over there about ten minutes past. I was hoping to kill two birds with one stone—ask about my case and answer any questions I could about Alexander and Carter and the upcoming interviews we all had the next day.

Ever since we'd heard about the DOD investigation, I'd been checking in on Emmaline regularly. I knew she was worried about Carter, probably even more now that she'd realized his emotional issues were far worse than his physical ones. A broken bone was a lot easier to deal with. And now the legal issues had thrown a whole other kink into things. Emmaline was going to be questioned, and I knew she was stressed about it, so I tried to see her more often to help curb some of her worry.

Mostly by lying about my own level of concern.

But since nothing could be accomplished by worrying, and

I was already doing enough for everyone, I figured stretching the truth fell under the good deed rules. I was pleased to see her out front with her coffee when I pulled up, and even happier when she lifted her hand and smiled when she saw me. She rose as I walked up and gave me a quick hug.

"I just finished a fresh pot. Let me go pour you a cup."

I had already had three so far that morning, but I was also a firm believer that one could never really have too much caffeine. Much to Ronald's dismay. He was always harping on me about what everything I consumed would do to my skin. Then complaining even more when nothing bad seemed to happen.

Emmaline returned with a refill for herself and a new cup for me, and we sipped silently for a few seconds. But I knew she was just itching to ask me about Carter, so I decided to offer information before she was forced to ask.

"Carter and I had dinner last night," I said. "He seems good. Better."

She gave me a hopeful look. "Really? You're not just saying that to make me feel better?"

Of course I would, but that wasn't the point.

I shrugged. "Wouldn't do much good, I guess. You're his mother. You'd know if I was lying, right?"

She didn't look convinced. "I don't know that I would, to be honest. Carter was always a hard one to read. All that 'still water' and stuff. Happy and mad were easy to spot. He's pretty black-and-white when it comes to those, but when he's struggling to come to grips with something, he just goes silent and has that faraway look. He had it when his father died, and then when he first came home after leaving the Marines, and now again."

"He's processing a lot, but I think he'll be fine. We all will. Alexander is the best attorney in the country, and that is definitely no lie. By the time he's done with this, Kitts will be court-martialed, and Carter will get a medal."

Emmaline nodded, but the worry etched on her face didn't lesson. "I struggle with thinking that if I knew what was going on, then I could help more, but I know that would only make things worse as far as me being called to testify."

"Are you ready for your meeting with Alexander tomorrow?" I asked, hoping that shifting Emmaline's focus from Carter's state of mind—something she couldn't control—to her testimony—something she had complete control over—might ease some of her tension.

"Yes. And I've spoken with him several times on the phone. Not long conversations, but it didn't take long for me to figure out he's brilliant."

I nodded.

She gave me a small smile. "And he's so eloquent. I know attorneys are supposed to be, and he'd have to be with the heights in his career that he achieved, but his speaking voice is so nice. I can see why he comes across so well with juries."

I noticed a tiny blush creep up her face and stared.

"You looked him up," I said. "And you think he's hot."

"No! I would never. Okay, I looked him up, but that's only because I wanted to know about the man who has the future of so many people I love in his hands."

"Uh-huh. And what did you think of his 'hands'?"

"They're very 'hand'-some?"

I laughed. "Alexander is a good-looking man. There is no doubt. And I'm sure that helps him with juries, but he could be a toad and he'd still win. His mind is even better than his looks."

"So you think he's good-looking, too?"

"I'm not blind, so yeah. Obviously, he's out of my age range, but he's the perfect age for you."

She placed her hand over her chest and shook her head. "Oh, I'm not interested in dating him."

"You haven't met him yet."

"That's not it. I'm not saying I never want another relationship. I'm just not pursuing one."

"But if one happens to fall in your lap, then why not give it a go? I definitely wasn't pursuing a relationship when I met Carter. Hell, I was trying to hide from him."

She smiled. "It's just not a good idea. He's your attorney, and Carter's and Harrison's. Isn't that some sort of conflict?"

"He's not *your* attorney, but I get what you're saying. Besides, you might meet him and think he's all wrong."

"Do you think so?"

"Heck no. My guess is you're going to meet him and wonder why the hell he's still single."

"So why *is* he still single?"

I laughed. "I have no idea. I'm not exactly 'girl talk' material. The only interaction I had with Alexander in the past was about cases. I admire and respect him, and I'm in awe of the things he does in a courtroom, but I know very little about his personal life."

She nodded, but I noticed a tiny bit of disappointment. "There wasn't much online either. Except about his court wins, of course."

I grinned. "I can't imagine he'd allow much else to be known. He strikes me as a very private person."

Emmaline threw her hands in the air. "You're a private investigator, for Christ's sake. Aren't you supposed to be nosy about everything all the time? And Lord knows, you can read people like a book, so give me Fortune's CliffsNotes thoughts on the man."

I considered this for a moment. "I think he comes from money. I know he made a ton of it, but he's got this air and polish about him that says exclusive private schools and rubbing elbows all his life with the rich and powerful. He's always impeccably dressed and nothing comes off the rack—not even the designer clothes rack. He has expensive taste in automobiles, and they always look like he just drove off the showroom floor. He was a regular guest at every important event in DC—you know, the kind where you bring your checkbook for donations—but I never saw pictures of him with a date."

"Good God. You don't think he's gay, do you?"

"No. I think he's discreet. If someone rated the status of a relationship, I think he would have been happy to have her on his arm." I shrugged. "Who knows? Maybe he had that one true love that got away and no one else has ever measured up? Maybe he's destined to be lonely and sad, pining over that one lost love and he'll die without having moved on."

"You've been watching movies with Gertie again."

"She watches. I mostly nap, but I guess some of it seeps into my subconscious. But I actually came over here this morning because I just took on a case that I'm hoping you can help me with."

"Me? I don't see how, but I'm happy to try."

I explained the situation to her and when I was done, her eyes were misty. "That poor woman. I can't even imagine how desperate she must be, and up against a system so cruel that it doesn't care about a boy's life."

I nodded. "Carter said all this went down when he was already in the Marines, but he thought you mentioned it on one of your phone calls. Either you or Walter, but he was betting it was you."

She frowned. "I probably did. I have a vague recollection of it. Of course, since Ryan no longer lived in Mudbug, there wasn't much gossip and less than zero press. In fact, I remember thinking about it a year or so later and going online to see what the outcome was. I'm afraid I won't be much help."

"I don't really need facts. I can run those down as much as possible myself. What I'm hoping for is a connection. Do you have any idea who his friends and family are? Someone I could talk to in order to get some background on him?"

Her eyes widened and she looked excited. "Yes! I don't know why I didn't remember when you first mentioned his name, but Ryan has a relative right here."

"In Sinful?"

She nodded. "Hank Comeaux is his cousin."

"Really? That's great."

Hank "Hot Rod" Comeaux was a local tuner and a friend of Ida Belle's. She'd bought her SUV from him, and he'd done all the engine work and a bunch of other extras that we mostly didn't tell people about. Since he and Ida Belle had bonded over their love of fast cars, I figured he wouldn't have a problem talking to us.

My morning had just taken a sharp upturn.

CHAPTER SIX

I wrapped things up with Emmaline and headed back home for breakfast. I knew Ida Belle and Gertie would appear when they were up and about, especially since they knew we had a case, so I didn't bother to text them. They were as anxious as I was to get going on this one. They strolled in just as I finished putting my dishes in the dishwasher and I noticed Gertie was limping slightly.

"Did that fall down the slide get you?" I asked.

"Oh no, that was nothing," she said. "Jeb came over last night and we had our own version of an egg hunt with these little marshmallow eggs. If you lick them, they stick right on your skin—"

"No!" Ida Belle said.

Gertie rolled her eyes. "You've been up for at least four hours. Don't give me that too-early-for-that crap."

"I could have been up for the last hundred years and it's still too early. In fact, put me down for the next hundred life-times is too early. Now I'll never be able to eat marshmallows again."

I laughed, but she did kinda have a point. "Guess what I

found out from Emmaline, via a recommendation from Carter?"

They both gave me expectant looks.

"Ryan has a cousin right here in Sinful."

"Who?" They both asked at the same time.

"Hot Rod."

"No kidding?" Ida Belle asked, perking up. "That's good news. If Hot Rod knows anything, he'll share it, especially if it means helping his cousin."

"You're assuming he likes his cousin," Gertie said. "What if Ryan is a big ole douchebag? I mean, it's not like Kelsey really knows him."

"That's a valid point," I said. "Ryan being a less-than-stellar guy is certainly a possibility, but we've all agreed he's not a killer, so we'll just tackle what we might actually be able to fix."

"Are we headed there now?" Ida Belle asked.

"He's definitely first on my list," I said. "Carter also suggested I talk to Detective Casey and see if she could possibly swing case files given that my witness lives in NOLA and claims that's where they were that night. It's flimsy, but it might work. Assuming Casey is okay with helping us."

"I think she will be," Gertie said. "She strikes me as someone who would hate an innocent man sitting in prison."

Ida Belle snorted. "She strikes me more as someone who would be even more hacked off knowing the real criminal was walking around scot-free."

I nodded. "I'll text her on the way and see if she has some time to meet with us after we talk to Hot Rod. What time do we have to be back for the redo of the egg hunt?"

"Two o'clock," Ida Belle said. "We just need everything in place before the kids are let go from the arts and crafts fair at two thirty, but the ladies can start without me."

"If you're not there, Celia will take over," Gertie said.

Ida Belle grinned. "I'll send Nora to fill in for me."

I laughed. Nora was Sinful's resident free spirit. She had invented drug paraphernalia years ago and regularly cashed in huge royalty checks. It gave her the money and the freedom to travel the world, looking for the best high. She also spent most of her free, semi-lucid time inventing new drugs to try.

Carter pretended to know absolutely nothing about her, but Gertie was always ready to play lab rat for Nora's latest invention. I had to admit that given some of the injuries Gertie had sustained while being Full On Gertie, Nora's concoctions had seemed to have miraculous effects. But I didn't care if I was missing a limb. No way was I putting something from Nora's stash in my mouth.

"Do we need to call Hot Rod and make an appointment?" I asked.

Since he wasn't a potential suspect—at least I didn't think he was—I saw no benefit in the unannounced drop-ins that I was so fond of. And the man was running a business. He might have an angry customer ready to pick up this morning and he still needed to put bulletproof plates on the side mirrors or something.

"Nah," Ida Belle said. "If he's got an emergency going, he'll tell us. The beautiful thing about Hot Rod is he doesn't have much of a filter. Well, except in his engines."

I grinned. "Then let's go see what he knows about Ryan."

I sent Detective Casey a text on the way to Hot Rod's place, but I didn't expect a quick answer. Casey was a homicide detective, so she could be surveilling, arresting, booking, questioning, or shooting someone. But hopefully, she'd have some time soon. The case files would be a good way to figure out other angles of investigation, especially since I was already expecting to see huge holes. I'd gotten the names of Kelsey's friends, but hadn't called them. They'd already gone home by the time Kelsey hooked up with Ryan, so all they could do was confirm the day, which I wasn't really questioning. But they'd be needed if I got enough evidence to launch a retrial.

When we pulled up, Hot Rod was in front of his garage, climbing out of a bright green car. Ida Belle took one look at the vehicle and let out a sigh so dramatic it belonged in *Gone with the Wind*.

"Do you know what that is?" she asked, her voice reverent.

"An old car that's probably so fast it gives you whiplash in neutral," Gertie said.

Ida Belle shook her head. "How are we friends?"

"If you listen to my marshmallow story, I'll talk about cars."

"There is no car on the face of this earth that's worth that exchange."

Hot Rod had looked over and grinned when he'd seen us pull in. He waved at the car as we climbed out. "What do you think, Ida Belle? Owner's picking her up in an hour. Eight hundred horsepower on the dyno."

"I think you're a genius," she said. "But I'm not sure I would have modified a Hemi 'Cuda."

"He's got more money than he knows what to do with," Hot Rod said. "Wanna see inside?"

"Why are you wasting time asking?"

He popped open the hood and the two of them leaned over as Ida Belle exclaimed over things I didn't understand and Hot Rod explained even more things I didn't understand. But I figured interrupting this conversation was akin to a toddler bounding into their parents' bedroom during sexy time.

No one appreciated the toddler.

Gertie seemed resigned to the entire exchange. She sat on the front bumper of Ida Belle's SUV and pulled a breakfast croissant out of her purse.

"I have half a doughnut too," she said as she offered me some of the croissant.

"I've already had breakfast."

"This is second breakfast," she said. "Didn't you watch *Lord of the Rings?*"

"You know I did. You made me."

"Don't pretend you didn't like it."

"There was a lot of killing of the bad guys. I liked that, but their wardrobes seemed awfully burdensome, especially for all that running, climbing, and fighting they did."

She nodded.

"And I'm not living in a tree root or underground," I said. "Especially underground."

She raised one eyebrow. "You get locked in a basement at some point?"

"Buried alive, but that's another story."

She shook her head. "Most days, I'm amazed that you're a walking, breathing, mostly normal person. Then I hear more snippets of your past and you kinda scare the crap out of me."

Hot Rod closed the hood of the car and Gertie shoved the croissant wrapper into her purse. "Looks like we're up."

Hot Rod waved at his shop. "Ida Belle says you guys need to talk to me about something important. I have cheap coffee, bottled water, and canned sodas. Can't offer anything else, I'm afraid."

"Actually," I said as we followed him into his office inside, "we're hoping you have information."

The office was small and only had two other chairs, so I perched on a credenza on the back wall and Gertie and Ida Belle sat across the desk from Hot Rod.

"So what are you wanting to know about?" he asked.

"Not a what," I said. "A who. Your cousin Ryan Comeaux."

His eyes widened. "Lord, that's a shot into the past. Why do you want to know about Ryan?"

I told him. By the time I was done, he had popped up and was pacing the four-step space available behind his desk. Finally, he stopped, shook his head, and banged his fists on the desk.

"I knew that boy never killed anyone," he said. "Told the cops there was no way. Told his attorney, the judge, the jury, and everyone else who would listen. No one believed me. And now ten years later, this woman is stating outright there's no way he did it and no one is listening to her either. I don't understand."

"The system doesn't like when they got it wrong, especially if the people who conducted the original investigation believe Ryan was guilty."

Ida Belle nodded. "It's bad for promotions and in the case of attorneys, it's bad for political aspirations."

Hot Rod gave us a look of dismay. "Doesn't anyone care about the truth anymore?"

"I do," I said. "That's why I took the case. And for that boy."

Hot Rod shook his head. "I've got a second cousin...Ryan is a father. And he doesn't even know it. This is the biggest dang mess I've ever heard. Ask me for anything. You need money? I'll sell my own car for your fees."

"I'm already on retainer with Kelsey," I said. "What I need from you is information about Ryan. If there's one thing I've learned since I started investigating, it's that very few things happen over a small space of time. People are a product of their genetics and their experiences. Knowing more about the people involved helps me come up with potential defenses and other suspects. Both help get cases overturned."

He nodded. "I see what you're saying. That makes sense

and it's smart, but then you're probably the smartest person in Sinful. How about I start with that day and work backward. Then you can ask me for more anytime you need it."

"That day?" I asked.

"The day the cops found Lindsay dead. I saw Ryan that morning."

We all stared.

"You're kidding?" I said.

"Nope. He stopped here on his way to their house. He told me they'd split up a couple weeks before and he'd been staying at the Bayou Inn. I got on to him because he'd have been welcome to stay with me, but I think he was embarrassed about them breaking up and wasn't ready for people to poke at him about it."

He sighed. "I wouldn't have done that, you know. I don't get in a man's business concerning money, religion, or his lady."

"Smart," Ida Belle said. "So what prompted him to stop by and fess up that morning?"

Hot Rod slumped back into his chair, looking a bit uncomfortable. "He said he'd messed up big. That he'd spent the night with some girl he picked up in the bar during his shift. Said he knew it was a mistake—he really loved Lindsay—but he didn't know how he was supposed to face her after what he'd done."

I leaned forward. "Wait. He told you he was coming home from the casino where he'd spent the night with another woman?"

He nodded.

"Did you tell the police that?" I asked.

"Of course! But they wouldn't listen. They said they had all this evidence, and he could have just as easily killed her the night before, then stopped by here and told me all that stuff to try to create an alibi."

"But you believed he was telling the truth?" I asked.

"'Course I did. He had no reason to lie to me. I get what they're saying about the whole alibi thing, but I don't buy it. Look, I hate to speak bad of Ryan, but the truth is, he's a simple sort. They were making him out to be some master criminal, and I just don't see it. Besides, it's not much of an alibi anyway."

I nodded. "When the police found the murder weapon with his prints on it in the motel dumpster, I'm guessing they didn't bother to dig any deeper."

"They didn't," he agreed. "Hell, that knife came from Ryan and Lindsay's own kitchen. Of course his fingerprints were going to be on it."

I groaned. Good God. Could this investigation and trial be any more of a farce?

"Did he have an attorney? Why wasn't all of this brought up?"

"He had the public defender, who was about as useful as a fart in a hurricane. I didn't have much money back then and no credit either. And Ryan didn't have any other family still living. I tried to scrape up some funds, but I couldn't afford anyone good."

I sighed. "I'm really sorry, Hot Rod. Do you still keep in touch?"

"Yeah. I'm the only person he has left. He calls me every Thursday night when he has phone privileges, and I put money in his inmate account every month."

He frowned. "I don't think he's doing good, though. I went to visit every month the first few years and the last two times I was there, he had bruises on his face. Then he asked me to stop coming. Said it was too depressing and he'd rather just talk on the phone. I wasn't happy about it, but I can't make the man see me if he doesn't want to. Lately, he sounds worse than he ever has. I know it ain't Disneyland, but it sucks hard, especially when I know for a fact he didn't do this."

"Have you ever talked to anyone about an appeal, now that you have a bit more money?" I asked.

"Sure. First thing I did when I started putting back some money was talk to one of those bigwig attorneys in NOLA. But he said it was harder to get a conviction overturned than it was to avoid it in the first place. And without anything new to go on, he thought it would take a lot of money and time, and we'd all just end up disappointed in the end."

"So he didn't want to do it because he didn't think he could win," Gertie said. "Sometimes I dislike attorneys as much as I do politicians."

Hot Rod nodded. "'Bout once a year, I head into NOLA and try again with someone new. But I just get the same song and dance." He sat forward, looking a bit more animated. "But now I've got that evidence they wanted. The girl he was with. That should be enough, right?"

"Maybe," I said. "But the first thing the prosecutor will point out is that Kelsey would say anything to save her son."

Hot Rod cursed. "So what do we do?"

"You tell me everything you can about Ryan and Lindsay and the original investigation and trial. Let me handle the rest of it. And the next time you talk to Ryan, ask him to put my name on his visitation list."

"You think I should contact another attorney?"

"I've already got one. He's the best in existence and has zero desire for a political career. If he thinks I've got enough to make this happen, then he'll handle it."

"I can't tell you how much I appreciate it. If you could get him out of there before...I don't know. I just have a bad feeling. I'm afraid he's given up."

I nodded. I did too.

CHAPTER SEVEN

WE SPENT AN HOUR WITH HOT ROD, AND BY THE TIME HIS customer arrived, I thought I had a good idea of what kind of person Ryan was and some idea about how the entire investigation had been handled, or mishandled. Everything I'd learned about Ryan only helped confirm his innocence. I was well aware that Hot Rod had a huge bias, but the fact that he'd spoken to Ryan the morning after he'd spent the night with Kelsey confirmed that she wasn't iffy on the date and that their night together was definitely a onetime deal.

As we were leaving, I got a text from Detective Casey saying she was available in about an hour, if we could make it to NOLA by then. I texted her back and set up a meet at a favorite café of hers.

Gertie clapped her hands and bounced on the seat like a grade-schooler. "Beignets!"

I couldn't disagree with her on that one. The café did have very excellent beignets, and I was as likely to turn down a beignet as I was a funnel cake. Casey was already seated when we walked in and had secured a table in the corner with no one else around. A young woman popped over to get our order as soon as we sat, and we all ordered rounds of coffee and a large plate of beignets. It wouldn't be enough, but the tabletop was only big enough for one at a time.

"So?" Casey looked at me, one eyebrow raised. "I never know whether to be excited or scared when you want to talk, but my curiosity won't let me say no."

"This time, it was actually Carter's idea that I speak to you."

"Now I'm even more intrigued. Carter doesn't seem like the kind of guy who'd sic you on me if it wasn't important."

I laughed. "Definitely not. I've caught a new case—a cold case—and it's a doozy with high stakes."

"Tell me."

So I did. She listened intently to everything we knew, and when I was done, she frowned and leaned back in her chair.

"You weren't lying," she said. "That's a seriously crap situation."

"What do you think? If I'm reaching because I feel sorry for this woman, let me know."

She laughed. "I've never pegged you as the type to let your emotions override the facts. Hell, I wasn't completely convinced you had any besides justified anger and a healthy dose of boredom. But to answer your question, I don't think you're wrong. Everything points to an innocent man going down for murder. I don't like it. But then you already knew I wouldn't, or you wouldn't have called me."

"You're kinda an easy read on some things as well."

She nodded. "I've crossed paths with the police captain in Magnolia Pass a few times."

"You don't sound impressed," Ida Belle said.

She snorted. "Captain Cantrell...who NOLA PD refers to as Captain Kangaroo."

"I hope that's because he's useless and not because he likes to play with little kids," I said.

"The Beeches would never have anyone in charge who was a threat to kids, but he's a threat to anyone who isn't a Beech. He's the laziest person in the parish and lacks the skills to be a decent human being, much less a cop. He's bought and paid for, and that's the worst kind of person who can wear a badge. You've got a serious uphill battle here."

"So they'll slam the door in my face as soon as they see me coming," I said.

She shook her head. "They slammed those doors, locked them, and boarded them up as soon as they railroaded this guy into prison. There is no way in hell Cantrell is going to let you make a mockery of his investigation by proving he was wrong, especially when the victim was a Beech and the perp wasn't a local. It's the perfect answer to a horrible situation as far as the Beeches and Cantrell are concerned."

"So how do I get my hands on the police reports? I don't figure they did much of anything, but it's hard to build a counterargument when I don't know what I'm working against."

She nodded and stared out the window, tapping her finger on the table. "Give me some time. Carter was smart to send you my way. Since the witness puts the accused in NOLA at the time of the murder, I might be able to pull the case files over. I'll speak to my captain about it. He hates Cantrell and would love to take him down a notch or ten. I'll just tell him I have a source—I won't tell him it's you."

"I appreciate it, but if this blows up—which things I'm involved with usually do—I don't want you in trouble with your captain."

She grinned. "Don't worry about me. When I was on surveillance last week, I got pics of him with a stripper in one of those places cops should never be in unless they're looking for a suspect. He has four kids and a wife who's never worked a day in her life. He can't afford a divorce."

I raised one eyebrow. "You'd blackmail your captain?"

"Of course not. But if he ever threatens me with my job, I'll play that card without hesitation."

She rose from the table. "He should be in the office by now, which is where I'm headed. I'll say I had a tip and run the story by him. If the records request comes from him, Cantrell won't try to drag his feet on it. He doesn't want scrutiny by the NOLA PD and knows refusing to give us those records would bring it on twice as hard as handing them over."

"Let's just hope he sends them unabridged and unaltered," Gertie said. "He wouldn't be the first to 'misplace' paperwork when it suited his interests."

"Unfortunately true," Casey said. "I'll get the court transcripts as well and at least you'll have a comparison of facts introduced. But I guarantee you, by sheer incompetence alone, those police files are going to be seriously lacking."

"I figured as much, but I've got to start somewhere. What are the odds that any of the Beech family will speak to me?"

"I don't really know them except by reputation, but I wouldn't count on it."

I nodded and she headed out.

"Another round of beignets?" Gertie asked.

"Might as well," I said. "Then I want to head over to Magnolia Pass and get a feel for it—check out the rental that Ryan and Lindsay shared—maybe see if we can find a neighbor who remembers something. I looked up Lindsay's immediate family last night and made a list. She's got a brother and sister still living on the family estate. Parents are deceased, so I won't be able to play that emotional card."

"Maybe the brother and sister will be upset that the real killer got away," Gertie said.

Ida Belle snorted. "There's money involved. For all we know, one or both of them is the killer."

I nodded. "But if they are, they might be willing to speak to me thinking it will throw me off the scent."

———

MAGNOLIA PASS WAS PRETTY. I MEAN REALLY PRETTY. Sinful has a certain charm about it and the downtown area is always neat and well kept, but Magnolia Pass looked like a Disney village. Main Street was a long row of brick buildings, each with colorful awnings. Out front were park benches, and you couldn't walk three steps without being able to touch a huge planter of flowers or shrubs. And right down the center of the street was an enormous median with huge magnolia trees all in a line.

"I can see where the town got its name," I said as we drove down the street. "Those are some seriously big trees."

"I came here back when I was a kid for some sort of charity thing," Gertie said. "I remember one of the old church ladies saying that the trees were planted when the town was founded. That was probably a hundred years ago or better. They sure are pretty."

I nodded and checked the notes on my phone. "Take a right up here and then the second left. Their rental is the third house on the right."

Ida Belle followed my instructions and then pulled to the curb in front of a picturesque cottage that was just as cute as Main Street.

"Nice digs," Gertie said. "It's small, but historic, and I'm betting the rent wasn't cheap, even ten years ago. Is it still a rental?"

"Yeah. And running twenty-five hundred a month. For 1,100 square feet."

She whistled. "That's even more than I was figuring."

"How can anyone afford that?" I asked. "I didn't see any big businesses when we drove in. What do these people do for a living that they can afford that kind of rent? Because if rent is that high, then buying isn't going to be a bargain either."

"I imagine a good portion are trust-fund babies," Ida Belle said. "Descendants from the old families. The Beeches own a lot of real estate in NOLA. Office buildings, apartments, and the like. Bought back when everything cost nothing, and I'm guessing they own it all free and clear. Raymond Beech, Lindsay's father, started the investment first to handle their own assets and then figured why not make even more money doing it for other people."

"So what you're saying is that there are a lot of people living here whose ancestors made good investments decades ago and they don't need to work."

Gertie nodded. "That goes for homes as well. People's grandparents and parents bought here years ago, and the homes are passing down with a clear title. It's only a thirty-minute drive to NOLA, so anyone career-minded but wanting to live and raise kids well outside of city surroundings would probably find it worth the drive for the quality of living the town offers."

"True," I agreed. "Heck, it was an hour's drive from my apartment in DC to the office and it was only eight miles."

Ida Belle shook her head. "I could never live in a big city. I'd end up turning Gertie and her purse loose on it."

"I didn't know any better at the time, and for the most part, was out of the country. Not like I had to commute to the office every day, but I totally agree. Especially now that I live in Sinful and have seen a different lifestyle, I totally get why people would make the commute for this."

I was staring at the house and contemplating my next move when someone knocked on Ida Belle's window. It took all the control I could muster not to pull my weapon, but I managed to stop with my hand over the hilt of the gun and get a good look at the older woman standing next to the SUV, hands on her hips.

Ida Belle rolled down the window, and once the woman could see us, she gave us all a critical once-over, then relaxed.

"Can I help you?" she asked. "You were just sitting here, and I thought maybe you were lost."

She tried to sound casual, but there was no way she'd marched over here to help. She'd been afraid shenanigans were going on, and she was going to make darn sure it didn't happen in her neighborhood. I had to respect her gumption. If we'd been a carload of bad guys, she wouldn't have stood a chance with that rolling pin she was holding.

"I apologize, Ms...."

"Abrams," she said curtly. "Hester Abrams."

"Ms. Abrams, my name is Fortune Redding. I'm a private investigator, and I'm looking into Lindsay Beech's murder."

She looked confused. "Why? That boyfriend of hers was sent up to Angola and far as I know, he's going to rot there for what he did to that poor girl."

"I absolutely agree that Lindsay's killer should rot in prison, but there's an out-of-town witness who has just recently become aware of the murder and claims they had eyes on Ryan the entire night. So there's no way he could have committed the crime."

Her eyes widened and she slowly blinked. "Well, I don't even know what to say about that."

"I'm hoping people will say they'd like to make sure the right man is in prison."

She straightened and gave me a disdainful look. "Of course I want the right man in prison. I'm a Christian woman. I believe in punishment but only for the wicked."

"Of course. Do you live in the neighborhood?"

She nodded. "Live right there," she said, and pointed to the house on the right side of the rental. "Born in the living room. Never slept a night anywhere else."

"So you knew Lindsay and Ryan."

She looked up and down the neighborhood, then back at us and nodded. "Best you come inside. I don't want people wondering why I'm standing out here talking to you like this. If you look like visitors, people don't get to flapping their gums when they ought not to."

We climbed out of the SUV and followed her inside and then took a seat in her kitchen while she poured up iced tea.

"I'm just wondering," I said. "Why would people talk about you speaking with us on the street? And why does it bother you so much?"

She put the glasses on the table and pursed her lips as she sat. "The Beeches are important people around here. And if that Captain Cantrell got it all wrong, then it's going to be bad. I don't want anyone knowing I was involved."

I nodded. "You said you've never spent a night away from home, so I assume you were here that night? Can you remember it?"

"I remember it like it was last night. Most horrific thing I've ever been exposed to personally, you know?"

"And did you see or hear anything?"

"Not a thing. I had my cocoa at eight like I always do and watched my shows. Went to bed around ten. Slept right through the night and didn't know a thing was happening until the sirens came around the next morning."

I frowned. Lindsay had been stabbed to death, and one would assume she'd fought back and screamed while it was happening. These homes were old and close together. Even the soundest of sleepers would usually have been awakened by a woman literally screaming bloody murder. And Ms. Abrams didn't seem remotely deaf.

"Do you take anything to sleep, Ms. Abrams?"

"I just told you I had my cocoa. Caffeine and chocolate are my only vices. I've been blessed with decent sleep."

"But you didn't hear anything—not a call for help or a cry of pain? I'm just thinking given how she was killed..."

She gave me a grim nod. "I've thought about that—probably more than I needed to—but it doesn't change the facts. That night, for me, was just like any other night." She sighed. "My bedroom's on the far side of the house, and I usually have my fan running. I wish I had heard something. Maybe if I'd known what was happening, I could have gotten her help."

"Had you ever heard anything next door before that night? I'm trying to get an idea of how well the houses are constructed."

"Oh, they're solid. Built back when things were made to last, not fall apart right after your warranty is up. But they're certainly not soundproof. I'd heard them arguing before that night. On more than one occasion. There was arguing a couple nights before. I told Cantrell that too."

"What time was that?"

"Must have been eleven. I forgot to refill my water before I went to bed, and the kitchen has that window facing their house. Sound can travel through it some."

"What were they arguing about?"

She frowned. "I couldn't make it out really, but I know it

was loud given that it was traveling between two sets of windows. It was raised voices but muffled. I think I heard the words *house* and *money*, but I wouldn't swear to it."

"And before that?"

She nodded. "Most of them have been the same as that night and I couldn't really hear what they were arguing about. But one time was different. I have a bit of asthma sometimes—probably the only thing that will wake me up—and I stepped outside to get some fresh air and allow my inhaler to work. Then I could hear things better, and they were definitely arguing about moving."

"Were you friendly with Lindsay?"

"Of course! We were neighbors, and that still means something in a place like Magnolia Pass. But we weren't exactly exchanging life stories over coffee. Bit of a generational gap there, and with me being an old spinster, I don't exactly have any words of wisdom for those dealing with the foolishness of men."

"Here, here!" Gertie said.

Hester looked over at her. "You never married?"

"No, and have no plans to," Gertie said. "Ida Belle didn't give up the ghost until last year. But in her defense, the man had been waiting for her since the crib. I guess she finally figured she could trust him."

"Hmmm," she considered and looked over at me. "What about you? You're about that age where women start thinking about settling down and having babies."

I choked on my tea and grabbed my napkin to cover my mouth. "No. Not married. And absolutely zero plans for babies. I have a cat and I barely manage to live with him."

She gave me an approving nod. "Don't get me wrong, men have their uses. I have a couple who pursued me for a while. But when they realized I wasn't going to live my life taking care of them like their mothers, they went and found a willing subject."

"So did you have a career?" I asked.

"Of course I did. My parents weren't rich, and even though this house is paid for, God knows insurance, taxes, and maintenance go up every year. I was a nurse to the local doctor for forty years. Retired the same day he did when his son took over his practice."

"That's an excellent career," Ida Belle said. "I was a medic in Vietnam."

Hester stared at her, her expression a mixture of surprise and approval. "Good for you for serving. I was a little too young to make the trip, but if I'd have been old enough..."

Ida Belle nodded. "Gertie served too. Five of us friends from Sinful all joined at the same time."

"And you?" Hester asked me. "You said you're a detective. Were you in the military as well?"

"No. CIA."

She blinked and then chuckled. "Well, hasn't this morning gotten interesting. If someone would have told me that there were women vets and CIA agents living in these parts, I would have called them a liar."

She sobered a bit and shook her head. "But given all your collective experience, I have to assume you think Ryan is innocent or you wouldn't be here. At first, I thought someone had told you a good tale and you'd figure that out and be on your way. Now I find myself wondering."

"I'm certain my witness is telling the truth. It's someone who has no ties to Ryan other than that night, which is why they never knew what had happened until recently."

I was deliberately hedging on Kelsey being female and just how she knew for certain Ryan hadn't killed Lindsay. I didn't think a one-night stand would go over big with the morally upright and sketchy-on-men Hester.

"So this person came forward when they realized they could alibi Ryan?" Hester asked.

"Yes. But neither the cops nor the ADA seem to care that an innocent man is in prison and a killer is still walking free. So that's where I come in."

Hester pursed her lips. "I've never liked Cantrell. He does less than the absolute minimum required. If he was living anywhere but a town like Magnolia Pass, the place would have been in shambles after two days of him being on the job. His deputies are no better—his useless family members who couldn't be employed to make coffee in a fast-food chain, much less wear a badge."

"Then why is the town so peaceful?" I asked.

"Because that's how the founding families want it," she said. "If anyone gets out of line here, they make it impossible for them to stay. No job, fines, and I'm sure Cantrell wouldn't be opposed to trumping up charges on people if the families wanted them out of here. I can't say that I approve of the methods, but it makes for a nice place to live."

"Sounds like the Mafia," I said. "Minus the extortion. Is there anything else you can tell me about Lindsay and Ryan that might help my investigation? Any other neighbors hear them arguing or might have seen something that night?"

She shook her head. "Everyone here talked about it a lot when it first happened. The houses across the street have been occupied by the same people for years, but they were all asleep and their bedrooms are off the back. The house on the other side of Ryan and Lindsay's is a rental now. The man who lived there then passed a few years back. But he was deaf as a doornail and couldn't see two feet in front of him even with his glasses on."

I nodded and pulled out a business card. "I really appreciate you talking with us. If you think of anything else, just give me a call."

She took the card and studied it for a moment. "Sinful, huh? I've been there a time or two. Nice place. Not as nice as Magnolia Pass, but still a nice place to live."

"I like it."

She stuck the card in her pocket and gave me a tentative look. "You won't tell anyone I spoke to you, right?"

"If by anyone you mean Cantrell, then absolutely not. Nothing you've said would ever come up unless it somehow mattered in a retrial. And then you'd only be called because you were part of the first investigation. No one ever has to know you talked to me."

She gave me a nod and her shoulders slumped a little with relief. We thanked her for the tea and made our way out. When we were all back in the SUV, Ida Belle gave me a concerned look.

"Did you see how worried she was about that Cantrell?" she asked. "I don't care how nice or safe this place is, you shouldn't have to live with that kind of worry, especially about your local law enforcement."

"No way I'd live here worried that I might do something to hack off the Disney Village Mafia," Gertie said.

I snorted. "They wouldn't even allow you to lease here. All they have to do is google you and they'd know you'd never make it a day without breaking some rule. I thought Sinful was bad, but this place is a whole other level of weird."

Ida Belle nodded and looked around, frowning. "Deceptive in its beauty, but it's still a prison. What do you want to bet that all that arguing was because Ryan wanted to move?"

"Can't say that I blame him," I said. "Toe the line or be run out of town is bad enough, but living with one of the controlling families' daughters takes that to an entirely different level. He must have felt suffocated."

I looked out my window as Ida Belle pulled away. Pristine lawns with grass that looked as if it had been cut by a hairdresser, complemented by shrubs that were trimmed without so much as a dip in level or shape, and flowers blooming everywhere they could be placed. Colorful rocking chairs sat on most front porches. Homes without a single speck of peeling paint or a chip in a roof tile.

Amazing how some of the most beautiful things could also be the most deadly.

CHAPTER EIGHT

THE LADIES HAD ALMOST FINISHED WITH THE SETUP AT THE park by the time we got back to Sinful. Celia gave us a haughty look as we walked up.

"I guess you thought there was something more important to do than set up Easter for the kids," she said.

"We were working on trying to save a terminally ill boy," Gertie said. "Since all the kids hunting eggs aren't likely to die over dinner tonight, then yes, I think it takes priority. That whole resurrection thing only worked once."

Celia stared at us for a moment, waiting for the punchline, but when it was clear that Gertie was serious, she huffed and stomped away. Marie, our good friend and current mayor, rolled her eyes.

"She's done absolutely nothing but stand and complain the whole afternoon," Marie said. "Now she wants to act like she was here working. I think she's just mad that Gertie came through with the rabbit and it's even nicer than hers was. She wasn't expecting you to come up with anything on such short notice."

"Oh, I already had it," Gertie said. "You see—"

"No!" Ida Belle said. "Trust me, Marie, this is not information you want to know."

Marie laughed. "I'll take your word for it. I swear, that Celia could wear out a stone. I practically jogged hiding those eggs, but she huffed along behind me, nagging me about putting those chickens down or levying charges and fines on Skinny for those boys setting his hounds loose. There's just no point in dishing out logic to someone who only feeds on untruth and lives in a constant state of victimhood."

Marie blew out a breath. "I guess I best get off my soapbox before you accuse me of doing the same."

We all laughed, and Gertie patted her arm before digging in her purse.

"We all know how dealing with Celia is," Gertie said as she pulled out Easter bunny chocolates in pink foil wrappers. "Have one of these. It will make the whole day better."

Something about her tone had me clamping my palm over hers before Marie could take the candy.

"Where did you get that?" I asked.

"The store," Gertie said, but I saw her eye twitch.

"Uh-huh, and why is the wrapper uneven?"

"Fine. Nora fixed me up some special chocolate candies. My back was bothering me after that fall down the slide and then me and Jeb—"

"No!" Ida Belle said.

Marie gave the candy a wistful look. "Well, knowing Nora as well as I do, I guess I better pass on the candy."

"Spoilsports," Gertie mumbled before she unwrapped the chocolate and popped the entire thing into her mouth.

Ida Belle stared at her in dismay. "Good. God. Do you even have any idea what's in that?"

"Do you want me to ask?" Gertie asked. "Tastes like chocolate."

"Too late now," I said. "Give her thirty minutes, and she'll either be racing the kids to get to the eggs or face down in a basket. Then we'll know."

Gertie nodded. "The last time, she put painkiller in an energy drink. She said she was wanting the caffeine to counteract the drowsiness that the painkiller caused."

"How'd that work out?" Marie asked.

"Well, she accidentally loaded it up with speed instead of painkiller. I didn't sleep for two days, but I repainted the entire upstairs of my house and knitted forty-six sweaters."

"Good. God," Ida Belle repeated. "Do you have handcuffs? Maybe we need to secure you to a bench."

"I don't have them on me, but I got these cute pink fluffy ones with fake diamonds that loop around the bedposts—"

Ida Belle didn't even speak. She just lifted one hand and then walked off. Marie giggled.

"Where is Nora anyway?" I asked. "I thought Ida Belle called her in to fill her slot. To aggravate Celia, of course."

Marie nodded. "And Nora was every bit as successful as Ida Belle thought she'd be. But I thought it best to send her home after the egg hiding. She was...uh, rolling the grass from one of the egg baskets so she could smoke it."

"Hmmm," Gertie said, and gave the baskets a side-eye.

"Don't even think about it," I said. "We're about to be overrun with kids, and you've already eaten God knows what."

As if to reinforce my statement, the school bell echoed in the distance, and the ladies hurriedly unloaded the last of the treats, then shoved the containers under the tables where they were hidden from view under pink tablecloths with colorful eggs printed on them. In minutes, the kids would descend on the place as though it was the apocalypse and Easter eggs were the key to surviving it.

I said a hasty goodbye to Marie and practically sprinted for

Ida Belle's SUV. I had agreed to remain for the hunt just in case they needed some muscle, but no way I was going to attempt to corral kids. My methods of controlling people were the kind that got you a cell next to Ryan Comeaux.

The kids rushed into the park like NFL players into a stadium for the Super Bowl game, but with more shoving and yelling and less protective gear. Their parents hurried behind them at various speeds depending on their own physical conditioning. Some looked excited. Some looked terrified.

The church ladies stood in a row between the kids and their prey, forcing them all to stop in a messy huddle and then disperse out in a solid line parallel to the road. Several of them crouched down like sprinters and I was certain that if someone blew a whistle or even broke wind loud enough, they'd all trample the ladies to get to those eggs.

Ida Belle stepped forward and I noticed all the fidgeting ceased. Either they didn't want to risk being kicked out of the fun or they were all a little afraid of Ida Belle. I was going with both. She waved the church ladies off and followed them to the sideline, while the kids waited for the signal.

"Do you want me to fire off a starting round?" I asked Marie, who'd come to stand next to me.

"Good Lord, no! Ida Belle will handle it. Besides, it's against the law to fire a gun at an egg hunt, courtesy of the Great Egg Hunting Disaster of 1938."

"Don't tell me someone hit a kid."

"Nothing like that. A man fired rock salt into the trees where there was a ton of pigeons roosting. They all hightailed it out of the tree and over the people. I've seen pictures. Even fuzzy old black-and-whites capture the horror."

I cringed. I'd seen what kind of havoc frantic pigeons caused.

When the church ladies were all clear of the upcoming stampede, Ida Belle put her fingers in her mouth and whistled.

And they were off.

Several fell off the line, and some got to running faster than they were capable of and did some face-first sliding that professional baseball players would have envied. But for the most part, they scattered in every direction, rushing to find the plastic prizes. Two boys were in a tussle for an egg on top of the slide, and eventually one managed to shove the other down the slide and claim the prize.

Two girls raced for the same egg in the middle of the merry-go-round. When the older one got there first, she grabbed the egg and stood on the edge of the merry-go-round taunting the young girl. The younger one, in a move I had to appreciate for cleverness, gave the merry-go-round a hard shove and sent the other girl flying off backward. Then she scrambled around and claimed the dropped egg and hurried off before the older girl could retaliate.

"This is a little like *The Hunger Games*," I remarked. "Isn't Easter supposed to be all about peace and love?"

Marie grinned. "Well, they'd all love a piece of chocolate."

"How's your brother doing?" I asked.

Marie's brother was special needs, and she was his primary caretaker.

"He's as good as he's ever going to be. Seems happy where he is, though. He's especially fond of music and art class. I've asked him to come home with me on the weekends for visits, but he doesn't want to leave."

"That's a good sign. I'm glad you found a place where he feels he belongs."

"I heard what Gertie said about you helping that ill boy. If there's anything I can do, please let me know."

I nodded and started to reply when a series of repetitive

blasts went up in the woods behind the park. I looked over just as a flock of birds rose out of the trees surrounding the park and flew straight for us. I immediately jumped up and bolted into Ida Belle's SUV. Marie jumped in behind me and slammed the door, then we both stuck our faces to the window, watching the drama unfold.

"It's 1938 all over again," Marie said. "Lord help us all."

The birds—mostly pigeons—were clearly panicked, attempting to flee from what they assumed was certain death. But given that they'd never been the smartest of the bird family, they all appeared to be trying to find a place to land, but as they dipped down, kids and church ladies screamed, sending them back up, sometimes slamming into each other midflight. And they never failed to leave a 'deposit' as they made their retreats.

Ida Belle was the only one who'd remained somewhat collected, and she dashed for the table of snacks, yanked the tablecloth out from under the food and punch without moving anything so much as an inch, and covered the whole lot of it. Then she crawled under the table and sat down, which was the smartest thing she could have done. Some of the kids had taken the clever route of flipping their baskets over their heads as they ran for their cars.

The parents were as panicked as the birds as they twirled around, running into each other as they tried to locate their retreating children. Some of the church ladies spotted Ida Belle under the table and ran over, practically diving underneath to join her. Celia, of course, was standing in the middle of the hurricane of birds, flapping her arms like one of the panicked pigeons.

"Does she think if she moves her arms fast enough she's going to be able to fly?" I asked.

Marie snorted. "Maybe if there's a big gust of wind, she

could use her huge panties as a wind sock and they could carry her away. Hopefully to another parish."

I shook my head at the spectacle. "It's just like that old movie Gertie had me watch—*The Birds*."

Marie sighed. "I'll go down in history as the mayor who ruined Easter. The *second* mayor who ruined Easter. Who the heck is shooting in those woods?"

"That's not gunfire. It's fireworks."

"Are you sure—never mind. You would know. There's no way the location and timing were an accident. If I get my hands on whoever did this..."

"I have an idea where to start—the kids who live next door to Skinny. The ones who let his dogs out yesterday. My guess is they weren't allowed to come today and decided to get their revenge."

We watched as two moms fought over the giant stuffed rabbit, both trying to crawl underneath it.

"Isn't there anything we can do?" Marie asked.

"I could shoot them, but I'm guessing that would make things worse."

"The people or the birds?"

I laughed. "The birds, but you'd have the Easter Egg Hunt Pigeon Massacre on your résumé."

Marie groaned just as I saw Gertie dash from underneath the slide and into the middle of the park, wide open for dive-bombing.

"What the heck is she doing?" I asked.

Marie's eyes widened and she grabbed my arm. "Is she on fire?"

It seemed like a ridiculous question, but then I saw the flames shooting up Gertie's arm and realized she was, in fact, on fire.

Good. God.

She was running with a fistful of lit bottle rockets but at least had the forethought to put on a glove. Unfortunately, one of the fireworks must have gone off early and sent sparks backward because her sleeve was on fire, and the flame was shooting up her arm at an alarming rate. I jumped out of the SUV and sprinted toward her, just as she bounced to a stop and held her hand up in the air.

The bottle rockets shot out of her hand, sending a shower of sparks all around her as she bolted away. She'd managed a few steps before she realized that the fire on her sleeve was about to reach the end of the line, so she lowered her shoulder and launched into the stuffed rabbit. The two moms who'd been cowering underneath it jumped up and ran for their cars. The rabbit went up in flames as if someone had doused it with jet fuel.

I saw Ida Belle spring out from under the table and grab the punch bowl from beneath the tablecloth. She reached Gertie seconds before I did and threw the entire bowl of punch on her.

And me.

I yanked Gertie's sleeve completely off her shirt and threw it on the ground, then gave it a good stomping. One of Celia's crew ran toward the rabbit with a fire extinguisher, but it was pretty much a giant pile of ashes at that point. When she was about ten feet away, she stepped in a discarded basket, tripped, and set off the canister.

All over Celia.

I took one look at the giant glob of foamy white anger and sank onto the ground next to Gertie, laughing so hard I had tears in my eyes.

Gertie wiped the punch out of her face, and when she got a clear look at Celia and realized what had happened, she joined me. We both had red punch dripping down our faces, but we didn't even care. Ida Belle looked at Celia and grinned.

"You look like the Stay Puft Marshmallow Man," Ida Belle said. "And before you threaten to sue, that was one of your own ladies who doused you."

Celia dragged one hand across her face and flung the extinguisher foam at the three of us. "But it wasn't her that started all this."

"It wasn't Gertie either," I said. "Someone set off fireworks in the woods. Gertie was just retaliating to get those birds out of the park."

Celia glared at us, but it was impossible to take her seriously looking like she did. When Gertie started giggling again, I couldn't help but join in. Celia whirled around, slinging foam everywhere, and stomped off. The woman who'd doused her had disappeared and was probably hoping no one would tell Celia she was the guilty party.

"Are you all right?" I asked Gertie as I inspected her arm.

It was red but I didn't see any blistering. She'd gotten lucky. The fire had burned so quickly on the sleeve that it hadn't had time to scorch her skin badly.

"It stings some," she said, "but it doesn't look too bad. I'll get some aloe vera on it and hopefully it won't blister."

"The sooner the better," Ida Belle said. "Why don't you head to the SUV? I'll get the ladies started on cleanup and then run you home. I'm glad I have waterproof seat covers. Being friends with you is like having a perpetual toddler around."

"Don't worry about me," I said. "It's only a couple blocks and I can jog it. Saves you laundering one of the covers anyway."

I jumped up and extended my arm to help Gertie.

"This has been a heck of a day," she said as we headed for

the street. "I haven't had this much excitement since, well, yesterday."

I laughed. "I'm not sure religious folk meant for Easter to be this entertaining."

"It's not for Marie," Gertie said, and pointed to where Celia stood, dripping and flapping in front of our mayoral friend. "She'll be wanting fire extinguisher woman, me, the birds, and the fireworks manufacturer all arrested."

I shook my head. "God bless Marie. I don't know how she deals with her."

"She was married to Harvey. Marie looks all sweet and nice, but she could play chicken with a serial killer."

I grinned and opened the door to the SUV, then closed her in before jogging off. My house was only a couple blocks away, and I figured by the time I got home I'd be mostly dry. If not, I'd go in through the garage and ditch all my clothes there so as not to drip across my floor. I wasn't a fan of domestic duties, and mopping was definitely one of my least favorites.

As I jogged up to my house, I saw Ronald on his front lawn, pulling weeds. He caught a glimpse of me and headed my way, frowning.

"There was a situation at the Easter egg hunt," I said.

"Were you in a duel in the park?" he asked, staring at me in dismay. "I heard gunfire."

"Fireworks set off a pigeon explosion, but Gertie sent them back to where they came with her own stash."

He gestured up and down. "And this?"

"Gertie caught herself on fire and Ida Belle put her out with the punch. I was collateral damage."

He shook his head, then pulled out his phone and took a picture of me.

"What the heck was that for?" I asked.

"Because the next time I start complaining about how your

wardrobe is mostly cheap stuff from Amazon, I'm going to look at this to remind myself how you treat clothes. Even cheap cotton with loose threads, uneven seams, and sketchy dye deserves better."

"So what you're saying is my refusal to shop is doing the fashion universe a favor?"

"As much as it pains me to admit it, yes. Now hurry up and get in the shower before that blond hair of yours stays pink."

I gave him a wave and headed inside.

CHAPTER NINE

AFTER A LONG HOT SHOWER, I CHECKED MY HAIR, BUT IT appeared that the punch had all washed out. Thank goodness. I wasn't exactly a pink sort of girl and definitely not in my hair. I didn't even bother trying to wash the clothes. I just tossed them in the trash. That was the whole point of cheap clothes —you didn't have to fret over ruining them.

Carter had the late shift, so I wouldn't see him again until tomorrow morning when we all met with Alexander, and even if he hadn't been on duty, I had a feeling he would have been called anyway to deal with the second round of the Easter debacle.

All of that meant I was on my own as far as dinner went, which called for fast and easy. I had just finished putting together a peanut butter and banana sandwich when my phone rang.

Detective Casey.

I grabbed a bottled water and sat down at the kitchen table as I answered.

"I didn't expect to hear from you so quickly," I said.

"Well, I figured it was a time-sensitive thing, so I pushed it with my captain."

"I bet that made him happy."

"Oh, he's mad as a hornet, but not with me. He called that idiot Cantrell straightaway, but he was 'busy' and couldn't take the call. So the captain called back again a little while ago and told dispatch that Cantrell could either take his call or he'd drive over there and sit on his front porch."

"Ha. I'd like to see that."

"You and me both. Of course, Cantrell was suddenly available."

"Naturally. So did he make any headway?"

"Yep. He told Cantrell that he had someone alibiing his murder convict for the time of the crime and that he was pulling the case to NOLA as that's where the witness and the convict were when the murder occurred."

"Can he do that?"

"Not really, but Cantrell doesn't know the law. Cantrell can't find his butt with both hands. The captain said Cantrell was sputtering so much he sounded like a flooded boat engine. He tried to put him off, claiming he needed time to find the old files, but the captain pointed out that we'd all been required to go digital years ago and he expected an email with all of those case files in the next few minutes."

"And Cantrell sent them?"

"He did."

"Smart of the captain to ask for them right away. That didn't leave Cantrell any time to doctor them up."

"No, but your witness went there first, so they were tipped off. Hopefully, they thought they'd gotten rid of her and were too lazy to go back and attempt to cover up any gaps in their investigation. But like I said, there's sure to be holes from shoddy police work alone."

"You didn't tell the captain I was the source, right?"

"No, but if this moves toward a retrial, I don't see any way around it. But as it stands now, the captain's back is up over Cantrell's attitude, so he's asked me to poke around. I hope you don't mind."

"Are you kidding me? That's great. You have the authority to do things I can't."

"And you have the lack of rules and red tape to do things I can't. If the two of us can't figure this out, I'm not sure it's doable. I'll let you know if I turn up anything."

She disconnected and I pulled my laptop over and checked my email. I couldn't help laughing when I saw the mail from cantrellsucks in my inbox. I clicked on it and downloaded the files—the ones that Casey wasn't supposed to give me. I'd figured she was going to anyway, which is why I hadn't asked. Out of curiosity, I did a trace on the email and found it bouncing off a server in India. Clever.

I stored the file, labeling it *Insurance Documents*, and replaced the name of each individual file with a number. If I was ever compelled to give up my computer, people rarely wanted to comb through insurance stuff. It was the kind of folder people passed by.

I grabbed another water from the fridge, snagged some of Ally's cookies from my stash, and sat down to read. It took less than a minute for me to determine that Detective Casey had called this one—the file was severely lacking. Lindsay's father, brother, and sister all claimed to have been at home all night and as far as I could tell, no attempt had been made to corroborate that with household help. All three had stated that Ryan and Lindsay had been at odds. Hester Abrams had verified the fighting, and it didn't appear they'd questioned anyone else about their relationship.

The medical examiner was clear on the time-of-death

range, and it was fairly narrow given that it was inside and a controlled environment. Assuming Kelsey was telling the truth about her night with Ryan—and I still hadn't come up with a good reason for her to lie—then there was no way he'd killed Lindsay.

Which made the next bit the most interesting. Cantrell's notes said they'd received an anonymous tip concerning Ryan, and this person claimed they had seen him throw something into the dumpster at the Bayou Inn around 4:00 a.m., and that he'd had dark stains on his shirt. They'd searched the dumpster, found the knife with his fingerprints and Lindsay's blood on it, and arrested him. But they hadn't found the shirt and there was no indication they'd looked, nor had they tested for Lindsay's blood in Ryan's room.

Good. God. What a mockery of an investigation.

Ryan had given his statement, which matched what Kelsey had told me about that night. There was a phone call to the casino hotel, but there was no record of Ryan having rented a room. Cantrell hadn't bothered to ask for the security camera footage. Just verified the time Ryan had gotten off work.

I shook my head. Twenty bucks said the person working the front desk had either slipped Ryan a room card for free or pocketed the cash himself. It wouldn't be the first or last time hotel employees had hooked up their coworkers that way. But it created a huge problem as far as alibis went. I continued reading and found that Ryan had told them exactly what I'd thought—that a friend had given him the room card as a favor, but when questioned, that 'friend' had denied doing so.

I blew out a breath. Probably afraid of losing his job. But letting someone go down for murder seemed like taking things too far. I opened a new window and did a quick search on the front desk clerk, but he'd been killed in a bar fight a couple years back. So much for asking him to rescind his original statement.

I also made a mental note to visit the Bayou Inn tomorrow and have a chat with our friend Shadow Chaser. He wouldn't have been working there at the time, but I'd seen old boxes stacked everywhere in the motel storeroom. I might get lucky and find a person or two who were staying at the motel at that time.

I didn't like the 'anonymous' source thing. Never had and never would.

Now that I had pinned down the particulars on Ryan, it was time to put together a list of people who might have wanted Lindsay dead. Who benefited from her death? Who hated her? Who hated Ryan?

I had just closed my laptop and was about to move into the living room to collapse in my recliner and fall asleep to insignificant TV when my phone rang. It was Hot Rod. I answered as I headed out of the kitchen.

"Hi, Hot Rod. I take it you talked to Ryan?"

"Yeah, I did. Good Lord, that was one of the roughest conversations I've ever had. Bad enough I had to tell the man he's got a kid, but then have to follow that up with 'but he's dying, and you might be the only person who can save him.' The boy's got enough on him already and now this. I can't even imagine how torn up he is right now."

"Me either. Did he handle it all okay? I mean, as well as he could given the circumstances?"

"He was shocked—really shocked. He'd tried like the devil to find that girl after Lindsay was killed, but he just didn't have anything to go on. She never did say where she lived or attended school, so for all he knew, she could have been from out of state. He even tried calling culinary schools, but some random dude trying to track down a woman whose last name he didn't even know didn't go over with most of them."

"I can't imagine it did. The cops might have managed it, though, if they'd bothered to try."

"They claimed they made the effort, but I don't believe it."

"Me either." I couldn't tell Hot Rod that I had the police files because I didn't want to compromise Detective Casey, but I was certain Cantrell had never made an attempt to locate Kelsey.

"I even tried myself some...searched online for the name and 'chef' or 'restaurant,' but I never came up with anything either."

"You never would have. She gave Ryan her middle name."

"Crap. Well, I guess it accomplished what she intended in that some strange dude she spent the night with couldn't stalk her, but it would have been nice if he'd picked a woman with less security sense."

"Did you ask him to put me on the visitation list?"

"One hundred percent. In fact, it was the first thing out of my mouth. I said you have to put this name on your visitation list. It's beyond important. I made him repeat it several times during our conversation. He said he'd do it straightaway. I think you have to call and make sure it's updated, but once they have it all in the system, you should be good to go. They'll give you his visiting hours once you're approved."

"Great. I'll call tomorrow and see if I'm on. If not, I'll keep calling until I am. I'd like to get in to see him as soon as possible."

"Me too. I told him I was going next weekend whether he liked it or not—wish it could be sooner, but I've got car deliveries to make the next couple days and they can't wait. But I need to put eyes on him. That was a hell of a lot to put on a man in one conversation."

"Definitely."

"I really appreciate you doing this. I just wish there was something else I could do."

"You already did it. You added weight to Kelsey's story, and you told Ryan what was going on. I know that was a hard thing to do. Just leave the rest to me. I'm going to do my best to fix this."

"Your worst is better than most people's best, so I've got hope again for the first time in a long time."

I heard Hot Rod sniff before he disconnected and I flopped back in the recliner, letting out a huge sigh. I'd known from the beginning that this case was going to be hard from an investigative standpoint as well as an emotional one, but it was even worse than I'd imagined.

One life at stake. Numerous others potentially ruined forever.

———

THE NEXT MORNING, I WAS UP EARLY AND OFF TO GRAB A box of breakfast goodies from the bakery. Alexander was taking meetings with everyone at my house, except Harrison, who was on call in Mudbug, so Alexander would meet with him over there this afternoon, and Walter, who was meeting him at Francine's. Ally had already offered to put together some excellent treats for what would be a stressful morning for some of us. Back home, I made a pot of coffee and straightened up my office for Alexander to use. Everyone had an allotted time for their interview, but I figured people would probably overlap and we could use the kitchen and living room as the lobby and break room.

I'd asked Alexander to come a little early if he could. Since we were using my house and I was certain to be there, I was first up on the interview list, but I also wanted to run Kelsey's situation by him and see if he could turn any screws with the warden now that I'd pinned down a few things. It was just shy of 8:00 a.m. when I heard a knock on my door.

Alexander stood there in his steel-gray suit with light turquoise shirt and teal tie, grinning and looking like a Gen X Calvin Klein model for office wear instead of the cutthroat attorney he was. I waved him in and got him settled in my office, then grabbed us both coffee and a plate of the breakfast goodies and headed inside.

"What do you want to cover first?" he asked as he opened his laptop. "Iran or your new case?"

"Let's go with my case and get it out of the way."

I told him everything I'd learned, including the information from the severely lacking police files. When I was done, he leaned back in the chair and twirled his Montblanc pen between his fingers. I was pretty sure that was why he had the pen, as I rarely saw him write with it. After a minute or so, he leaned forward and stopped the twirling.

"First, let me say that I'm glad Kelsey brought this to you, which means it's on my radar, because when I 'retired' this was exactly the kind of work I wanted to do. I hate when regular people are railroaded by the system or people in a position to take advantage of them. Justice is my overwhelming passion."

I nodded. "I can appreciate that. I think it's why I decided to be a PI. It allows me to right wrongs but still be myself. Well, mostly myself. Besides, I had to have something to do, otherwise what would I do with all my time?"

"Get bored and rot. One can only spend so many hours at the gym or on hobbies, and since other people are often more work than they're worth, I don't lean toward a heavy social calendar."

I nodded my agreement.

"So this is what I think," he said. "First, I agree that it sounds like Ryan got railroaded, but if we take that as a fact, then that means someone set him up. Which points directly to premeditation. So whoever wanted Lindsay dead had a reason. And given your ability and the advantage you have of being able to color outside the lines, you ought to be able to turn that reason up."

"What about the warden? I'm going to call today and see if I'm on the visitation list. If I'm clear to go, I'll be there the first available slot. I need to talk to Ryan. He's probably the only person who's going to be able to fill out a suspects list for me. Everyone else assumes it was him and has moved on."

Alexander nodded. "People are always happy to believe a crime is perpetrated by the outsider. Makes them feel safer. When you talk to Ryan, tell him I'll be representing him going forward. I'll send the paperwork with you to turn in for me, but he'll need to add my name to the list as well. As soon as they've been alerted that he has new representation, I'll contact the warden and impress upon him the urgency of the matter and how it would look if a young boy dies because of his failure to allow something that already has a legal precedent."

"I really appreciate your help on this. If anyone can move the warden, it will be you."

"If I can't move him, the governor can. I won't play that card unless I have to, but if ever a situation called for escalating things, this is it."

"Why would the governor get involved?"

He grinned.

"You have something on the governor?"

"Honey, I have something on everyone who matters."

I laughed. Given the people he'd worked with during his career, that made sense.

"Well, then I guess we best start with what the military thinks they have on me," I said.

He nodded. "I have it on authority that Kitts has attempted to stall or outright bury the investigation. He miscalculated big-time. He thought he'd be able to shift blame onto Carter and the situation would die out, but the other members of the team are questioning things. Carter wasn't the only one who realized something was wrong. He's just the one who made the call to abort."

"Good. I'm glad he's not going to be flailing in the wind on that one."

"Nope. Kitts is hanging out there by himself. He's been unable to squelch the DOD investigation, and my understanding is they're focusing hard on him. Don't get me wrong, they're looking at all of you, but the reality is, this all starts and ends with Kitts, and as he's the only active military member involved, he's the liability they need to contain."

"So this looks good for us."

"It looks great for you. Couldn't be better. But there is no greater defense than preparation."

"I thought the saying was there is no greater defense than the truth."

He raised one eyebrow. "I'm a prosecutor. Not a priest."

"Then I better get to covering the details, so you can tell me how it really happened."

He grinned. "What I always liked about you, Fortune, is that you're a fast learner."

———

CARTER MET WITH ALEXANDER NEXT, AND I WAS BEYOND pleased to see that although he went into my office looking apprehensive, he came out looking relaxed and confident.

Emmaline was after Carter and gave him a long look before hugging him. I told Carter to give me a minute and headed in to make the introductions.

Alexander rose from the desk when I walked in and although he had a poker face that could hang with professionals or even the CIA, I saw his eyes widen by a millimeter when Emmaline walked in. She hesitated just a bit before stepping forward, and he gave her a genuine smile as he extended his hand.

"I know you're Carter's mother because Fortune gave me the schedule, but I have to say, you look far too young to have a son his age. It's a pleasure to meet you."

Emmaline blushed and managed to mumble a thank-you before Alexander gestured to a chair. I raised one eyebrow at him, which he completely ignored, and then headed for the kitchen, where Carter was leaned against the counter, drinking a bottled water.

"How did it go?" I asked.

"Very well. Great, in fact. That man has incredible tactical abilities. If he was running the military, we'd probably win every war in a day and by a phone call."

"They don't call him the Grim Reaper for nothing. I was pleased to hear that Kitts is the one getting heat on this, and that the other men say what you did—obviously not to the same extent, as you were separated after capture—but they're going to back up your claims, and that makes Kitts's accusations completely baseless."

He nodded. "I have to say it's a huge relief. I didn't really worry much about the other men because they always have the 'following orders' defense. But I've been worried about you and Harrison. Kitts was pushing hard to shift focus onto the three of us."

I wrapped my arms around him and gave him a soft kiss on

the lips. "Don't worry about me. I'm former CIA. We have lives like a cat. Besides, what they know and what they can prove are two different things. What's the worst they can come up with—that we went to Dubai on fake passports? Given our pasts, that's just good common sense, whether it's legal or not. And a federal judge is not going to punish us for lying about our identity to take a vacation, not given our previous professions."

"No one in the know will believe you were on vacation."

"Of course not, but they also can't prove we ever set foot in Iran. And that's the bottom line."

"What about your father?"

"What about him? It's not like they can call him in for questioning."

He snorted. "It would be fun to see them try to subpoena a twice-dead man, but I meant what are you going to say when they ask you about him?"

"Nothing. I was never there. And as far as I know my father is dead. I have the official letter from the CIA telling me as much—two of them, as a matter of fact—and Director Morrow is prepared to say the exact same thing."

"So who do you think he's working for?"

I shrugged. "The CIA, the military—hell, for all I know, he might be doing it just for fun."

"He's awfully dialed in."

"Did I ever tell you what the other agents called him?"

"The Prophet?"

"Close. The Omniscient."

"Seems perfect."

I nodded. "The truth is, no one knows where he gets his information. Even the CIA was in the dark. Given that I've had the same job, I can only assume that he has a million important connections, all of whom owe him."

Carter pulled me close to him and gave me a squeeze. "I'm glad he called in a marker over me."

I leaned my head on his shoulder. "Me too."

———

EMMALINE WAS GIGGLING LIKE A SCHOOLGIRL AS ALEXANDER escorted her out, even walking her to her car and opening the door for her. Ida Belle and Gertie had just arrived a couple minutes before, and we were all sitting in the living room, watching it all play out. When Alexander stepped back inside, we all gave him the one-raised-eyebrow stare, which he promptly ignored.

"Ida Belle, you can come on back," he called as he hurried out of the room.

"You know he's calling me back first because he thinks I won't quiz him on it," Ida Belle said as she got up.

"Will you?" I ask.

"Heck, yeah!"

Gertie grinned as she headed off. "Wouldn't that be a match?"

"It just might be, but it will have to wait until all this is over. Alexander would never compromise a case by getting involved with a client."

Gertie sighed. "I know. So I'll just hope this whole mess is over soon."

"It sounds good. I haven't filled you in because I know he will, but Kitts is on the defensive, and it looks like he's run out of favors. The DOD seems to be focusing all their energy on him."

"That's good news for the rest of us."

"Definitely. Not that you and Ida Belle had to worry about it. No one wants to believe you could take part in a mission. If they only knew about Ida Belle's shooting ability and your illegal explosives collection, they'd have to rethink it all."

"Well, this is one of those times when I'm happy to play a woolly-headed old woman. The prosecution doesn't want to put me on the stand. I'll have them so annoyed by the time they get me out of that chair, you'll all be trying not to laugh. And Ida Belle has grumpy old lady sarcasm down to a science. Hell, she was an expert at it when we were in grade school."

I laughed. "It will be fun to see, though. Assuming it even gets that far. And while I'd love to see Alexander in action, I'm really hoping it doesn't come to that because I don't want Carter to have to take the stand and lie."

Gertie sobered. "And is that what he plans to do?"

I nodded. "It's the only way to leave me, Harrison, Mannie, and my father out of it. And at the moment, Mannie isn't even on their radar. Carter doesn't want to put him there."

"Lying never did sit right with him," Gertie said. "Even when he was a boy. You always knew there was something he didn't want to tell you when he avoided you like the plague. I guess we'll just have to see how it plays out, but I don't see a man like Kitts getting stripped of his medals and pension without a fight."

"Me either."

"So what's up with our case?"

"Plenty. As soon as you finish up with Alexander and he's gone, I'll fill you guys in. But we've got some things to do this afternoon."

She clapped her hands. "I love investigating. It's better than knitting, fishing, and baking. But it's not better than sexy time."

"Probably more dangerous though."

"Well, that depends. Last week—"

"No," Ida Belle said as she walked back into the living room.

"That was fast," I said.

She nodded and motioned for Gertie to head back. "He refused to talk about Emmaline, gave me the rundown on Kitts, and then I showed him my Ida Belle-on-the-stand act and he just laughed and waved me out. Gertie is even worse. She's made those door-to-door religion people fake sudden illness to get away."

Sure enough, Gertie was back within minutes and Alexander looked very pleased.

"Stop worrying," he said to me. "I've got this so in the bag, I almost feel sorry for the other side. Put all your energy into this new case and let me know when you get to visit Ryan."

"Thanks, Alexander. I really appreciate everything. Are you sure you won't let me pay you? There's a lot of us to handle."

"Are you kidding me? I should be paying you for the opportunity. I've been wanting a go at Kitts for years. I'll be in touch as soon as I know anything more."

He gave us a backward wave and headed out.

"I think I love him," Gertie said.

I nodded. "I'm pretty sure we all do. So what do you say we take his advice? Let's head to the kitchen for sandwiches and I'll bring you up-to-date on the case. Then we've got some people to talk to."

Gertie clapped. "Road trip!"

CHAPTER TEN

W<small>HEN</small> <small>WE</small> <small>WALKED</small> <small>INTO</small> <small>THE</small> B<small>AYOU</small> I<small>NN,</small> M<small>ANNIE</small> <small>WAS</small> behind the counter with Shadow Chaser, who looked relieved to see us. I barely kept from laughing because if Shadow was happy I had walked in the door, then he must be terrified of Mannie. Mannie gave us all a big smile.

"Are you ladies here to harass my manager?" he asked.

"That's never what we set out to do," Gertie said. "But sometimes, there's unintended consequences."

He chuckled. "Well, I'll get out of here and leave you to it. Shadow, get those reports to me. I'd like to get started on the room updates next month if possible."

Shadow's head bobbed up and down and a single bead of sweat ran down his face even though it was easily sixty-five degrees in the office. Mannie winked at us and headed out.

"So Mannie's your boss now," I said. "That's cool."

Shadow sank into his chair, looking as though he was about to pass out. "It figures you're friends. He looks like he kills people for a living."

"Not since he left the Navy. I mean, he's killed people since then, but as far as I know, he hasn't been paid to do it."

He paled. "So what murderer have I rented a room to this time?"

"Well, it was ten years ago, so unless you were working the desk in middle school, I think you're off the hook on this one."

"Thank the baby Jesus. Then I'm almost afraid to ask what you want."

"This one will be easy. That room in the back with the fifty million dusty boxes... I don't suppose those are records from when the old manager was here."

"You mean the guy who fought computers like they were the Germans in World War II? Yeah, that's exactly what it is. I started trying to clear them out, but there's credit card numbers written on a lot of it and I'm having to go sheet by sheet. When the serial killer you're friends with found out, he told me to find a company to pick the whole lot up and shred it. They'll be here next week."

"Looks like we're just in time. I don't suppose you mind if we go through the papers then?"

He waved a hand at the door to the back room.

"You don't want to know why we want to see them?"

"Absolutely not. The less I know about the things you do, the better."

I nodded. "I get that a lot."

"I can't imagine why. Now, if you'll excuse me, I have to put those numbers together for my boss. I don't want to be found lacking in case he gets the urge to kill someone for free again."

We managed to wait until we were in the back room before we started laughing.

"This whole businessman thing that Mannie has going is kind of sexy," Gertie said. "It's nice if a man can get your engine revving, protect you from an assailant, and do your taxes."

"I'll stick to doing my own protecting and taxes," Ida Belle said.

Gertie raised her eyebrows. "But you caved on that engine thing, or you wouldn't have married Walter."

"Why are you assuming I waited until I was married for engine work?" Ida Belle said. "You don't assume that about Fortune."

Gertie hooted. "Do tell?"

Ida Belle shook her head. "Not now. Not the last time you asked. Not the next time you ask. What exactly are we looking for in this mess?"

"Receipts for the night that Lindsay was murdered. If we can find someone who used their real name, I'm hoping to find a witness who saw someone other than Ryan toss that knife in that dumpster."

"That's a long shot," Ida Belle said. "But I guess it's an angle we should cover."

"You never know," Gertie said. "This motel has given us some good leads before."

She grabbed a box with the correct year on it and plopped down on the floor with it between her legs. As soon as the box hit the floor, a cloud of dust went up in the air and she started coughing.

"We should have brought masks," Ida Belle said and sighed as she hefted another box off the stack.

Thirty minutes later, we were all coughing and sneezing. Gertie threw her hands in the air.

"It's amazing how many famous people stayed here that night," she said. "JFK, John Wayne, heck, even Elvis. I'm surprised the paparazzi weren't camped in the parking lot."

"If those three were here that night, the paparazzi, ten priests, and at least eighty of those ghost-hunting YouTubers would have been in the parking lot," Ida Belle said.

Gertie shook her head as she looked at the last sheet. "And they put John Lennon in the room next to Elvis. That's just rude."

I sighed and grabbed another handful of invoices from my box. "Hey, these are from the right night at least."

I dug through the box and pulled out everything with the date, then divvied them up. "Pull out anyone who looks like a real person."

We'd pulled out six receipts that seemed normal, including Ryan's, when Ida Belle whistled. "Guess who was staying here that night?"

"Who?" Gertie and I both asked at the same time.

"Kenny Bertrand."

"Cool," I said. "Get a pic of that receipt in case he needs reminding, but I'm guessing he'll remember given what happened while he was here."

"Why would Kenny be staying at the motel?" Gertie asked. "He has a house."

Ida Belle shrugged. "Maybe he ordered a new bed and sold the mattresses the day it was supposed to be delivered and the furniture company totally screwed him on delivery."

Since her description was very specific, I had to assume it had happened to her before, but given her tone, I wasn't about to ask. Kenny staying here that night was a good find. It might amount to absolutely nothing, but on the plus side, he was trustworthy and not overly dramatic.

"I found one too!" Gertie said, waving a receipt in the air. "Father Michael stayed here that night. I'm not sure I even want to know why."

"I think our best bet is to avoid asking why and just see if they saw anything," I said. "If either one of them was up to no good, then us asking about it might make them clam up on everything."

"I'm more concerned that Father Michael drove all the way out here," Ida Belle said. "The last time I saw him sober was about fifteen years ago, and he'd had surgery, so that one was forced on him."

I flipped over the last of my receipts and wiped my hands on my jeans. "That's all of mine."

"Me too," Gertie said.

Ida Belle nodded. "How did we do?"

"Five real names total, but three are common. Only two that we know."

"To be honest, that's better than I thought we'd do," Ida Belle said.

We dumped the receipts back into the boxes, stacked them up, then headed for the front desk. Shadow Chaser looked up and wrinkled his nose. We probably smelled like an attic that hadn't been touched in a couple decades.

"Did you find your murderer?" he asked.

"Oh, the accused is already in prison," I said. "We're trying to get him out."

His look of dismay was priceless. "Why would you—you know what, I don't even want to know."

"Relax. He's innocent or I wouldn't even be here."

"How can you be sure?"

I raised one eyebrow, and he waved a hand at me. "You're right. Sorry. I don't know what I was thinking. Well, I hope you free the innocent and catch the guilty and all of that. Now, if you don't mind, I have to get on these spreadsheets before I become the next reason for police tape around here."

We headed out smiling, and when we hopped in the SUV, Ida Belle laughed. "That kid is going to have a heart attack working with Mannie."

"Fortune didn't help matters with all those killing people jokes," Gertie said.

"Those weren't jokes," I said. "They were accurate statements. Besides, a little fear might have him doing a better job rather than playing video games on his shift. I want Mannie to succeed. I know he's still associated with the Heberts since it's their properties he's managing, but it looks better for him to have a visible and socially acceptable job, especially in regard to his relationship with Ally."

Gertie smiled. "You old softy. You're a good friend, Fortune."

Ida Belle nodded. "So what now? Are we headed back to Stepford Pass?"

"Ha," I said. "Accurate. And yes. I want to talk to Lindsay's brother and sister."

"You think they'll agree to that?" Gertie asked.

I shrugged. "Only one way to find out. But if they refuse to talk to someone who says their sister's killer is still out there, I'd have to wonder why."

"Have you heard anything from Kelsey's husband?" Ida Belle asked as she pulled away.

"No," I said.

I'd left Brett Spalding a message the day before, telling him I'd been retained by Kelsey and would like to speak with him, but so far, he hadn't returned the call. I hadn't heard anything from Kelsey either in regard to Brett, so I assumed he was mulling the whole thing over.

"If I don't hear from him by this evening, I'll call again," I said. "If he refuses my calls, then we'll just dip over to NOLA and track him down."

Gertie sighed. "I get that he's mad over Ben not being his biological son, but he raised the boy. And if another man—who never meant anything to Kelsey anyway—could save the boy's life, why hasn't he returned your call?"

"He's rich," Ida Belle said. "Rich people often assume money can solve everything. And he's a man. He wants to think he can fix this."

"You think he'd try to buy the boy an organ on the black market?" I asked.

"It's crossed my mind," Ida Belle said. "He wouldn't be the first to do so."

It was an angle I hadn't considered yet, but it made perfect sense for someone like Brett—plenty of money and issues relinquishing control. Add that to desperate parent and you had a combination ripe for illegal activity. And that might be why he was avoiding me.

Magnolia Pass looked as if it had been polished and vacuumed ahead of our arrival. I stared at the sidewalk as we drove down Main Street, trying to find a crack or a piece of gum, but couldn't find so much as a wayward leaf.

"Do they not have wind in this town?" I asked. "Seriously. Nothing is out of place. It looks like a painted Hollywood set."

"It gives me the creeps," Gertie said.

I nodded. While I wasn't necessarily creeped out by the place, I definitely thought it was all a carefully crafted facade. I directed Ida Belle to the Beech estate—and it was a real estate, not one of those neighborhoods calling themselves such. I'd gotten all the pertinent information online. The main house looked like a palace and there were five other residences on the fifty acres the Beeches called home. I figured the homes were occupied by staff and maybe older relatives, or perhaps they'd been intended for the kids when they got older and wanted more independence.

Their mother had died in a car accident when Holly, the youngest, was only five. Lindsay was the oldest and nine years older than Holly. Jared was in the middle and two years younger than Lindsay, so Holly had been a late baby. Their father, Raymond, had died five years ago. Jared and Holly both lived in the main home.

Jared and Holly were now thirty-two and twenty-five, and neither appeared to be married or even have significant others. The only other people listed as living on the estate were household employees. I'd found a good amount of information on Jared as he was the head of the Beech's investment firm and was a regular at charity events, but I'd found very little on Holly. She didn't seem to be enamored—or perhaps, tasked—with fulfilling charitable obligations like her older brother, and the few pictures I found of her were as a girl and she always appeared to be avoiding the camera. Socially awkward perhaps.

Jared had attended Yale and acquired a business degree, but I couldn't find any reference to Holly having attended college or public schools. I assumed she'd been in private schools. There was also very little online about Lindsay. I knew she'd graduated with top honor from Yale with dual degrees in finance and mathematics but couldn't find anything else. None of the Beeches had social media.

An enormous wrought iron fence with spiked top and stone columns surrounded the estate and the entrance was a couple miles from downtown. As we pulled up in front of the gate, a security guard stepped out of a stone building next to the gate and approached the vehicle.

Early forties. Five foot ten. A hundred ninety pounds. Good body tone and no flaws except that he worked security for the Beeches. He was strapped and didn't look overly friendly, so I'd keep my guard up. So to speak.

"Name and appointment time, please," he said as he flipped a sheet on a clipboard. I saw a list of names on the paper.

"We don't have an appointment," I said and passed him a business card. "I'm a private investigator and have information about Lindsay Beech's death that I think would interest her siblings. I'd like to speak to them."

He frowned. "The Beeches only see people by appointment. You'll need to call Mr. Beech's assistant to get on his schedule."

"There is an emergency that makes this conversation time critical. A young boy's life depends on it. I'm not trying to be dramatic, but that is the crux of the matter."

He flickered his gaze over to Ida Belle and Gertie, clearly confused by the combination of the three of us and what I was presenting to him.

"If you could just call Mr. Beech and ask him if he'll see me?" I asked. "I promise I won't take up much of his time."

He was clearly reluctant to make the call, but he must have finally decided that I wasn't going to go away easily.

"Give me a minute," he said and stepped back in the building. Through the window, I saw him make a phone call and talk to someone. I hoped it was Jared and not another staff member and that Jared was either curious enough or afraid enough to let me in. I saw him put the phone down and stand there, staring out the back window, then after a minute or so, he picked up the phone again. A couple seconds later, he headed back to the SUV.

"You have ten minutes with Mr. Beech. He has other appointments today and that's the only time he can spare. Follow the road directly to the main house. The butler will let you in."

He pivoted and headed back into the building, and the gate began to open. As we drove past, he stared straight ahead, his jaw set, and never even glanced our way.

"Mr. Personality," Gertie said.

"He looks pissed off that Jared agreed to see us," Ida Belle said.

"Maybe he got his butt chewed out for calling," Gertie said.

Ida Belle parked on one side of a porte cochere that was so big it could have easily covered six vehicles beneath it, and we headed for the door. I rang the bell and took in the absolutely massive wood and iron structure. It was a double door, and each side stood at least twelve feet high and five feet wide.

"Maybe they were planning on parking cars in the foyer," Gertie said, noticing my scrutiny.

"Or moving in their beds fully assembled," Ida Belle said. "These doors probably cost as much as a new boat motor."

"They are rather impressive," I said, and then the door swung open.

Seventy if he was a day. Six foot four. Maybe a hundred forty pounds. Weak wrists peeking out from under the heavily starched dress shirt. No threat in a physical way, but he still represented the troll at the bridge.

"Hello," I said. "I'm Fortune Redding. Mr. Beech agreed to see me."

He lifted his head so that he had a better view of me looking down his nose, and I knew it was intentional. I'm sure I didn't look appropriate or important enough to speak to a Beech, and I probably smelled a little dusty. Well, he'd get over it.

Without a word, he turned around and I took that as an order to follow him. He walked across the entry and opened a door and stepped back, gesturing with one gloved hand for us to enter. Then without speaking, he closed the door behind us.

"He was actually wearing gloves?" Gertie said. "It's like no one has a calendar. People don't wear gloves in the house anymore."

"Clearly, Jeeves thinks we're beneath him," Ida Belle said. "Is this a drawing room?"

I looked around. "I don't see any art supplies."

"No. It's an old term," Ida Belle said. "It's where you'd put company to meet. Usually a room at the front of the house that you only used when speaking to someone you didn't know well enough to let into your personal spaces."

"So this is the lobby," I said. "Got it."

It was a nice room. Big with tall ceilings, lots of bookcases, and walls of wood with ornate patterns and scrolling. The furniture looked uncomfortable, and I walked over and plopped down on one to test it out.

Yep. Definitely uncomfortable.

"Let me guess," I said. "If your butt goes to sleep, you won't stay as long."

"You've got it," Ida Belle said.

The door opened, and I stood back up as a younger man walked in.

Early thirties. Six foot two. A hundred ninety pounds. Good muscle tone. Nice tan. Perfect fingernails and not a sign of a callous. Definitely not a guy who worked outdoors even though he spent plenty of time there. He wouldn't last two seconds with me in a fight, but his name and money were clearly a threat to the people of Magnolia Pass.

He scrutinized the three of us as he approached, but he showed no sign of apprehension, just confusion. "I'm Jared Beech. Security told me you want to speak to me about Lindsay."

"That's correct." I gave him my business card. "I'm representing a client who was with Ryan Comeaux on the night Lindsay was murdered. She was with him the entire night."

He shook his head, clearly skeptical, and I honestly couldn't blame him. "I don't see how that's possible. I think you've been duped. Obviously Ryan is attempting a retrial and has paid someone to come forth as a witness."

"I can see why you might think that, but I'd like to tell you why I believe her, and why I believe that whoever murdered your sister is still out there while an innocent man is in prison."

CHAPTER ELEVEN

"WHAT ARE YOU SAYING!" A VOICE SOUNDED BEHIND ME, and I turned around as a young woman slipped through a rear door. She looked so much like Jared that I had to assume it was his sister Holly.

"This doesn't concern you," Jared said to her. "I'll take care of it."

"If it's about Lindsay and Ryan, it absolutely concerns me," she said. "I'm not a child, Jared. And you're not my father."

She strode over and stuck her hand out. "I'm Holly Beech. Who are you, and what do you know about my sister?"

Jared looked irritated but didn't try to dissuade her again. He motioned toward the uncomfortable chairs. "Perhaps you'd like to sit and explain what all this is about."

So I did. When I got to the part where Kelsey had gotten pregnant from her night with Ryan, Holly jumped up and glared at her brother.

"I told you Ryan didn't do it. I told you it wasn't *possible*, but no one believed me."

Jared cut his eyes at her, and the tension between them was

palpable. But within it was something else—fear. "You were just a child, Holly. You didn't know anything about their real lives."

"I did too!" she said. "You just wanted to believe the worst about him because he didn't have money and status. You're a snob, just like our father."

"Yes, I am. And he's the reason you live in a mansion, wearing designer clothes, and never have to get a job. There are worse things to be. If this woman got pregnant by Ryan, then why didn't she contact him?"

I continued to explain the situation—Kelsey's reunion with her then-boyfriend, who she married, and that they'd assumed the boy was his because they looked alike. When I got to the situation with Ben's medical issues, Holly's face fell.

"Oh my God!" she said. "That's awful. He's just a little boy. And the only person who can save him is Ryan."

Jared sighed. "Which is a damned good reason for her to lie about being with him that night. Don't you see that, Holly? She needs access to Ryan to save her son. That's all this is about."

Holly bit her lip, obviously not wanting to side with her brother but unable to counter his argument. "She's sure her son belongs to Ryan?"

"There are only two options, and her husband is not the father. She met Ryan at the hotel while he was tending bar. She's absolutely certain of his identity."

"Then she got the date wrong," Jared said. "And she's lying, hoping to get her son the help he needs."

I shook my head. "It was the day before her birthday and her friends agree on the date as well. During the range of time when your sister was killed, Ryan was in a hotel room with her in New Orleans. I have to tell you, I'm a former CIA agent, and one of the first things we learn to do and learn it well is to determine when people are lying. She's not lying. I would stake my reputation on it, and that's saying a lot."

His eyes widened a bit when I mentioned the CIA and then he frowned. "Even if all of this was true, what do you want from us? Lindsay no longer lived at home and mostly tried to avoid all of us. We hadn't seen her for at least a week before she was killed, and that was here for a family meeting."

Holly nodded. "Which meant our father told us how disappointed he was in our life choices over an awkward and long dinner."

Jared gave his sister a look that said he clearly didn't appreciate her talking about her father that way. "Lindsay left in the middle of dinner. That's the last time any of us saw her."

"You didn't speak to her at all after that night?" I asked.

"By phone, twice, but she refused to do what father wanted, which was for her to break it off with Ryan and take her proper place in this family. I tried to talk some sense into her because father was making noise about cutting her out of the will, but she didn't care. She said she loved Ryan and intended to stick it out with him."

"What about you, Holly? Did you see her after that dinner?"

Holly shook her head. "I was only fifteen. Lindsay worked a lot in the city and then she had Ryan. No one really wanted to hang out with me."

"Did you talk to her on the phone?"

"No. Lindsay was really smart. We didn't have a lot in common. I was really immature back then."

Jared smirked and it was clear he thought Holly was still immature.

"There you have it, Ms. Redding," Jared said. "Neither of

us know anything about that night. So I ask again, what is it you expect us to do?"

"Tell me who wanted your sister dead," I said. "If Ryan didn't kill her—and I don't believe he did—then someone else did."

Jared's eyes flashed. "Not me, if that's what you're suggesting."

"I'm not suggesting anything. I simply want to figure out who killed your sister so that a little boy doesn't die because a man was railroaded into a murder conviction."

Jared turned his hands up in the air. "I wish I could help. I can certainly sympathize with her situation, but I don't know anything about what happened. I was here all night, as were Holly and our father. We didn't know anything about it until the next day when the police showed up. I didn't even know Lindsay and Ryan had split until the police said something about him living at a motel."

"You can bet our father didn't know either, or he would have been gloating about it," Holly said.

Jared sighed. "All that protesting and angering the man the week before, and Lindsay wasn't even living with Ryan anymore. Seems a complete waste. If she'd simply admitted the relationship wasn't working and moved back home, she might still be alive."

"How did your father take it?" I asked.

"He was devastated, of course," Jared said. "Lindsay was firstborn and had the business acumen most like our father's, although that was probably the reason they butted heads. But he had big plans for her."

"Plans that didn't include Ryan. Just how angry was he when she stormed out of dinner?"

A blush crept up Jared's face and he stiffened. "If you're

suggesting our father killed his own daughter over an ill-fated romance, then you don't know anything about the man. There were a million ways he could have gotten rid of Ryan Comeaux. He was simply hoping that Lindsay would wake up and realize she was throwing her life away and make the right choice. All he had to do was wait and Lindsay would have come around."

"And if she hadn't?"

Jared shrugged. "Father would have eventually gotten the outcome he wanted."

Holly smirked. "He always did."

"Did Lindsay have any friends that I could speak to?" I asked. "People she might have confided in about her relationship with Ryan?"

"Mandy Reynolds—Amanda—was her bestie," Holly said. "They were always thick as thieves. But Mandy always had her own drama, so I don't know how much attention she paid to someone else's."

Jared cut his eyes at Holly, clearly giving her the signal to stop talking, and rose from his seat.

"I'm sorry, Ms. Redding," Jared said. "But I'm going to have to bring this conversation to a close. I have a committee meeting for a charity event we support. I wish you luck with your investigation, but I'm afraid what you've told me hasn't changed my opinion in the slightest. I have always believed Lindsay finally acquiesced to our father's wishes and broke it off with Ryan, and he killed her. There is no point in searching for a monster under the bed when he's already in prison. The evidence suggested nothing different. Now, if you'll excuse me."

He left the room without so much as a backward glance. The butler, who must have been standing outside the door, just waiting for the opportunity to show us out, indicated with a single gloved hand and an extremely superior and pleased expression that we were to make our exit.

I pulled out another card and handed it to Holly. "If you think of anything that can help, please let me know."

She gave the card a wistful look, then looked back at me. "You really don't think he did it?"

"No. I don't."

"I don't either," she said quietly, then she whirled around and fled the room through the back door where she'd entered.

We headed out and drove off the estate, the security guard giving us a glare as he opened the gate to let us out.

"Boy, we're not popular here," Gertie said.

"I didn't figure we would be," Ida Belle said and looked over at me. "So what did you think?"

"Snooty, arrogant, weird—all of which I sort of expected—and their father definitely sounds like a raging narcissist."

"But?"

I shook my head. "I don't know. Jared didn't appear to be lying about not seeing Lindsay after that dinner, but then he showed almost zero change in expression or emotion over anything except a potential insult to his father. No change when I suggested Ryan hadn't killed his sister. Not even a flicker when I told him a ten-year-old boy's life depended on this."

"If he's a chip off the old block, then it might be impossible to get a read on him," Ida Belle said.

"The sister didn't seem normal, either," Gertie said. "But she was completely different from Jared. He's all stiff and formal and she's clearly a very immature twenty-five. Her behavior is more like an adolescent than an adult."

"She never grew up," Ida Belle said. "Was probably told what to do every second of her life and never learned to navigate any of it herself. She'll live in a permanent state of childhood with a complete lack of responsibility, all her needs and wants met."

I frowned. "Something about her was off. More than just her maturity level. She was adamant about her belief that Ryan was innocent, even though she admitted she wasn't close with her sister. And did you see that look Jared gave her when she said she'd never thought he did it?"

Ida Belle nodded. "My guess is Holly had a crush on her sister's boyfriend. That would explain her supporting Ryan's innocence as well as her claims that she and her sister weren't close. She was a lot younger and was probably a pest."

"Gertie nodded. "Most of us had crushes on inappropriate boys when we were young. And given that Ryan was much older and living with her sister, that would have made things even more tenuous. Holly is very awkward at twenty-five years old. When she was fifteen and her life was still completely controlled by her father, I imagine she was far worse. Pest is probably a charitable description of her back then."

I pulled out my phone and looked up Amanda Reynolds. "I want to talk to that bestie. If anyone will know what was going on with Lindsay and Ryan, and who else had a vested interest in Lindsay dying, it would be her."

Mandy's name came up immediately, and I scrolled through the data, looking for personal information. "She still lives in Magnolia Pass. Married to Sebastian Perkins."

Gertie sighed. "Guess who the second-oldest family in Magnolia Pass is?"

———

IT WASN'T DIFFICULT TO LOCATE MANDY'S HOUSE, OR I should say, the *other* estate in town. It was north of downtown, like the Beeches' property, but just a bit farther east. I figured we'd encounter another huge gate and a security guard, and I was right. At least this one was a much older man and looked friendlier.

Seventies or better. Five foot ten—probably used to be six foot tall, but now he stooped. Most of his cartilage had been long gone since a previous generation. Zero threat, even with a weapon. By the time he got it out of a holster, aimed, and pulled the trigger, I could have already acquired the weapon and knit a sweater. And I didn't even know how to knit.

"Hello," I said and passed a business card over to him. "I'm a private investigator and would like to speak to Ms. Perkins, if she's available."

He wrinkled his brow as he read my card. "You're that gal from Sinful, right? The one that rescued all those women in the swamp?"

"That's me."

"What do you want to see Ms. Perkins about? I'm not being nosy. She's going to want to know in order to decide whether she'll talk to you, especially with you being an investigator and all."

"It's about Lindsay Beech. I have good reason to believe that Ryan Comeaux is innocent."

He shook his head. "That was a bad, bad time here in Magnolia Pass, and especially for Ms. Perkins. Her and Lindsay had been friends from the crib. It took her a long time to get over Lindsay's death. I don't know that she'd want to go back to that place."

"Even if the real killer is still roaming around free?"

He frowned. "How sure are you that he didn't do it?"

"Ninety-nine percent."

"You were CIA, weren't you?"

"Yes."

He nodded. "I was a career Navy man myself before I

retired and came to work for the Perkinses. Give me a minute."

He stepped back in his building and a couple minutes later, popped back out. "Ms. Perkins will talk with you, but you'll do well to go easy on her. She was in a bad way for a long time. Mr. Perkins won't take kindly to anyone causing her grief all over again."

"I'm not here to make trouble. I just want information. If Ryan is innocent, I assume she'd want to know who killed her friend as well."

"I expect she would. Good luck."

He stepped back inside and opened the gates. This estate was beautiful but looked a lot more approachable than the Beeches'. It wasn't as grandiose and ornate. The main house was plantation style, with huge magnolia trees lining the drive and tons of azalea bushes in between. It looked like a place people actually lived and raised a family—granted, a huge place that people lived and raised families in, but it still had a homey feel where the Beeches' house had screamed pretentious.

I wondered if we would encounter another disapproving butler, but when the door opened, I assumed we were looking at Mandy Perkins.

Early thirties. Five foot six. Trim figure. Excellent muscle tone, but all derived from the gym. I seriously doubted she could fight, but she might be good with a weapon. This was Louisiana. Her anxious expression made her emotional disadvantage clear.

"Mandy?" I asked.

She nodded as she motioned us inside. "You have information about Lindsay's murder? Is that true?"

"Yes. Can we sit? I'd like to explain everything to you if you have time."

"Ha. I have nothing but time. No career. Never managed

to get pregnant. I spend more time trying to think up things to do to occupy the hours than I do actually doing them."

We followed her across the foyer to a room that I assumed was their version of a drawing room. But this one was light and airy and contained overstuffed couches and chairs in white with bright, cheerful pillows matching the colors in the floral art on the walls.

"This is really pretty," Gertie said. "I love the pillows."

She smiled and looked pleased with the compliment. "I do all the decorating. Even did the embroidery on the pillows and painted the florals on the wall."

"That's impressive," I said. "Do you sell your work?"

The pleased expression fled and was replaced by one of slight annoyance. "My husband doesn't want me to work."

Ah. So that's where the attitude came from. Nothing to do with us and everything to do with a controlling husband.

We all sat, and she perched anxiously on the edge of a chair. "So you think Ryan is innocent? Why?"

I told her everything. She listened intently, never once interrupting, barely blinking. When I got to the part about Ben, she lifted her hand over her mouth, and I could tell she was very troubled. When I was done, she shook her head.

"Wow," she said. "That's a lot. And your client is absolutely positive about the day?"

"Without a doubt. It was the day before her birthday, and she'd just had the big breakup."

Mandy nodded. "Definitely the sort of things a young woman remembers in detail, especially if you end up pregnant."

"I want to know about Ryan and Lindsay's relationship," I said. "Starting with—do you believe he killed her?"

She huffed. "I never wanted to. He never seemed like the type, and their relationship seemed great until her father started pressuring her about it. I never once heard Ryan raise his voice to Lindsay, even about her father, and God knows, I have. He was a horrible man."

She shook her head. "I guess I finally had to believe it because the police had the evidence, and he was convicted. I didn't have anything to contribute to the contrary, so what was I supposed to do?"

Gertie nodded. "And your best friend had just been killed. It was a lot to deal with, and you were a young woman yourself."

She stared down at the floor for a minute and picked at a loose thread on her shirt. Finally, she looked back up at me. "I had a complete breakdown. They hospitalized me for a while. My parents got me into therapy as soon as I got out, but I was so distraught I don't think I heard a word she said. The drugs they gave me made me feel nothing at all, which I guess I needed at the time, but how can you work through something when you feel nothing? I think I would have been fine after some time passed, but my parents were afraid..."

"That you'd harm yourself?" I asked gently.

She nodded. "Lindsay was more than my best friend. We'd practically been raised together. We were like sisters. I have never loved anyone like I loved her, not even my husband."

She darted a quick glance at the door, as if to make certain no one was listening, and I had to wonder if Mandy was afraid of her husband.

"Can you think of anyone who would have wanted to harm Lindsay?" I asked.

She leaned forward and locked her gaze on mine. "That's what it really comes down to, isn't it? If Ryan didn't do it, then someone else did. And all this time, he's thought he got away with it. Have you ever read *Sleeping Murder* by Agatha Christie?"

I shook my head.

"One of my favorites," Gertie said.

"Mine too," Mandy said. "There's a man who tells the woman who is starting to remember a murder she saw when she was a child to 'let sleeping murder lie.' The amateur detective—who's a senior woman with a great understanding of human nature—agrees to help the woman even though she believes the man has given her good advice. Neither take it, of course, or there would be no story, but it makes one think."

I nodded. "She's not incorrect. Are you worried that someone will come after you?"

"No. Because I don't know anything. But what if someone else does? Someone who isn't capable of protecting themselves like you are? And I'll admit that bothers me, but not as much as the fate of that poor little boy and his mother."

She stopped talking and gazed out the window, and I could tell she was rolling something around in her mind, trying to make a decision.

"Lindsay was having problems at her job," she said finally.

I frowned. "She worked for her father, so that's not a big surprise."

She turned back around to look at me. "No! Lindsay refused to work for her father. She worked for an investment firm in New Orleans. She was brilliant with numbers. I mean, really brilliant. Her father tried to play it off with other people, saying that it was better for her to get experience working at an organization where she had to make her own way instead of starting and finishing at a place where everyone knew she'd be in charge one day. But I never bought it. He was mad as hell about it and that was his way of saving face."

Interesting. When Holly had commented that Lindsay worked in the city, I'd assumed she chose to manage properties and clients there in order to avoid her father and Jared. But this added a whole new layer to things.

"Was her father causing her problems with her job?"

"I think so. She lost a client account—an old one that she'd been entrusted with. Her boss had come down hard on her and she was really upset. The client ended up moving all his investments to her father's company."

"Did she make a mistake on something?"

Mandy frowned. "She wouldn't tell me exactly what happened, but I can't believe she made a mistake that would have cost them a long-term client. She was so meticulous. I assumed that her father had poached the client—probably offering a big reduction in fees—so that the owners would suspect her of only working there to funnel clients over to Raymond's firm."

Ida Belle whistled. "That would definitely be a problem."

"How much money are we talking about?" I asked.

"I'm not sure exactly, but the hedge fund she worked with doesn't take on a client with less than ten million to invest. I think Lindsay said nine figures, but I can't remember exactly. It represented a loss of millions in fees over several years."

"Not to mention the other clients he might have convinced to leave or never invest with them," Ida Belle said.

"Good Lord, I can't even count that high," Gertie said. "Is that a hundred million?"

Mandy nodded. "At least."

I shook my head, having trouble not with the incredible numbers, but with a father who would deliberately sabotage his daughter in order to control her life so completely.

"Do you think one of the owners of her firm killed her?" I asked. "That seems extreme, even for millions of dollars. I'm sure they already had plenty."

She shrugged. "I'll admit, it doesn't sound overly plausible, but then, I always assumed it was Ryan. No one ever asked if I knew someone who might be holding a grudge against Lindsay. Not until now."

I nodded. "Could Raymond have done it? If he felt she was never going to fall in line?"

Her eyes widened. "Lord, I would hope not. He was a nasty human being and a horrible father, but that's a big leap to killing your kids for not going along with your plans for their lives."

"Especially if you had the ability to manipulate them back into line," Gertie said.

"What about Jared?" I asked. "He wasn't firstborn, but he's the only son. And he seems to think his father did no wrong. So why wasn't Raymond's focus on his son?"

Mandy smirked. "Because Jared doesn't have even half the ability Lindsay did. Lindsay was that scary kind of smart. Even when we were kids, she'd talk about things that I still wouldn't understand today, much less when we were six. She'd never met a book she didn't want to consume, and she remembered everything. She was brilliant all the way around, but when it came to numbers, she was practically a savant."

"And she was using her superpower to make someone else money," I said.

She nodded. "The pressure from every side was awful. Her job wanted perfection and to use her for what she could do for their business and their clients. Her father wanted to do the same and was angry that he couldn't. Jared practically came out of the womb jealous because he would never measure up to her."

"What about Holly?" I asked.

Mandy shook her head. "She was just a kid when Lindsay died, but I've never thought she was quite right. She's immature for her age, and that makes sense in one way because she's never had to be an adult, but I've always thought there was more to it than that."

"She claims she never believed Ryan killed Lindsay."

"That's true, but Holly also had a crush on Ryan," she said, confirming Ida Belle's theory. "Lindsay just ignored it because of Holly's age, but it was so obvious that Holly wanted to be like her sister. She dressed like her, cut her hair like her, and it was apparent to anyone with vision that she was crushing on Ryan."

"How did Ryan handle it?" Ida Belle asked.

"He was polite, of course, and respectful, but I doubt he was ever alone with her. I think he was smart enough to know better. Like I said, I think there's more going on with Holly than just immaturity."

"Do you think she could have killed Lindsay?"

"No!" Mandy looked shocked at the suggestion. "She was just a kid. She couldn't even drive a car. And her mind doesn't work well on complex things. Never did. She'd have never gotten away with it."

I nodded. I understood why Mandy felt that way, but I'd seen children commit some pretty heinous crimes, and all while convincing everyone around them that they were completely different. Sociopaths were often born, and they were very clever. It could be that Holly was a bit off normal or it could be that she was simply playing a role so that people had zero expectations, giving her unlimited freedom. She wouldn't be the first to figure that one out.

Mandy glanced at her watch and jumped up from the couch. "It's almost time for my husband to come home. I don't want him to find you here."

I could practically feel the tension coming off her in waves and I rose. "Won't your security guard mention it?"

"No. He knows how my husband can get. As long as you're

clear before he gets here, he won't say a word. I wish I could help you. I hate that a little boy's life is on the line, and I hate that Ryan is in prison when it sounds like he didn't do it. I always liked him. And he always treated Lindsay right. I hope you figure all of this out."

"One last thing—what was the name of the firm Lindsay worked for in NOLA?"

"Spalding Financial."

CHAPTER TWELVE

I MANAGED TO CONTROL MY SURPRISE AS I PULLED A CARD from my pocket and handed it to her. "Tuck that away somewhere. If you think of anything else, give me a call or email. Whatever works best for you."

She nodded, looking relieved that we were prepared to leave. We hurried behind her to the door and wasted no time climbing in the vehicle and clearing out of the estate. The gate was already open when we got to it, and the guard gave us a wave as we drove past. I couldn't help but notice that he looked relieved as well.

What the hell kind of hold did Sebastian Perkins have over his household?

It was almost as if we'd been waiting to drive off the property to speak because once we'd turned onto the main road, we all started talking at once.

"Mandy is afraid of her husband."

"Do you think Lindsay's father got her killed?"

"Lindsay was working for Brett Spalding's company?"

The last statement was mine and Ida Belle and Gertie both paused and then started exclaiming all over again.

"That's a hell of a coincidence," Ida Belle said.

I nodded. "I don't like it, but I can't come up with any good reason for Brett to have targeted Lindsay that way. It couldn't have been good for his business to have an employee murdered."

"I wonder why Kelsey didn't mention it," Gertie said.

"She didn't even know Ryan's last name at the time," Ida Belle said. "Why would she know his girlfriend's? And it doesn't sound like she was ever in the know on Brett's business dealings, nor did she want to be. With the news coverage being so minor, she might not have put it together."

I pulled out my cell phone. "I think we need to ask her, though."

I dialed Kelsey and she answered on the first ring. I knew she hoped I'd have information that would help her and felt bad that I was calling to ensure she hadn't been withholding critical data, but I often had to 'vet' my clients. Everyone had something they were hiding.

"Hi, Kelsey. I'm interviewing people today and an interesting item came up. I need to ask you some questions about Brett and his family."

"Okay," she said, and I could hear the disappointment in her voice.

"What is the firm's name?"

"Spalding Financial."

"That's what I thought. Okay, back when you and Brett first got back together, did he ever mention an employee who was killed?"

"I think so...yes, a young woman. Brett said she was supersmart and a big loss. I remember he was working a lot of overtime until her accounts were reassigned, but I don't know anything else about it. I'm afraid between school and my drama with Brett, I didn't have the bandwidth to pay attention to much else. Is it important?"

"It might be. That employee was Lindsay Beech."

Kelsey sucked in a breath. "No...there's no way...that's, that's just weird."

"So when you were trying to track down Ryan, you never came across a mention of Lindsay working for Spalding Financial?"

"No. There was very little personal information on either of them. I only found two articles total. Both of them mentioned she was from a prominent family from Magnolia Pass. Ryan never went into details about her either, just that her father was wealthy and was putting a lot of pressure on her about work. And the court documents never mentioned her place of employment. I guess I just assumed she worked for her father, if I assumed anything at all."

She was silent for several seconds. "You don't think... There's no way Brett could have known, right?"

"That the man you slept with was the same one who was convicted of killing his employee? Short of him having you under surveillance that night, I can't see how. But I also don't like the connection. It's messy and convoluted."

"I don't like it either. Do you want me to ask him about it?"

"No. But I'd like to speak with him myself. I'm going to call him again and figure out a way to get him to meet with me."

"He knows I've hired you and thought it was a waste of time, of course, but if he thought speaking to you gave him a say in anything, then he'd probably talk."

"Then I'll give him a call and pitch it as how he can help. Also, there was an incident that happened at the investment firm right before Lindsay was killed. She made a mistake on a big account and the man moved his funds to her father's business. Did Brett ever mention anything about losing a major account to a competitor?"

"No. But he rarely talked to me about work. He told me an employee had died, but even then, he never gave me details. Just enough to explain why he was working so many more hours. I hate to ask, but did you figure out anything else?"

"Not yet. But things are in motion. My attorney is going to put some pressure on the warden about the DNA test. And Ryan's cousin informed him about Ben and asked him to put me on the visitation list. As soon as I'm cleared, I'll go there. Hopefully, he'll be able to provide me more to go on."

"You mean suspects."

"That's what we need."

"Thanks, Fortune. I know this is a real long shot, but I think I made a good decision. You've already turned up more in two days than the police did during the entire investigation."

I disconnected and dialed Brett Spalding. "Head to NOLA," I told Ida Belle. "If he doesn't agree to talk to us, we'll just hunt him down."

Brett's assistant answered and gave me the usual runaround about an appointment, but when I explained that I was the investigator his wife had hired and needed to talk to him as soon as possible so he could provide me with direction on the case, she went silent and then asked for a brief hold. I was a little surprised when she popped back on and asked if we could meet him at a café in the French Quarter in an hour.

"That was easy," Ida Belle said.

I nodded. Almost too easy.

WE ARRIVED AT THE CAFÉ THIRTY MINUTES EARLY, BUT THE food looked great, so we decided to grab a table and order lunch. There was a large circular booth in a back corner surrounded by a half wall with plants on top. I wasn't foolish enough to believe it actually provided any privacy, but as long as Brett felt it did, he might not be afraid to speak openly. Since he had suggested a meeting place outside of his office, I assumed he didn't want his employees knowing about me or what I was up to.

Fried shrimp and French fries were the lunch special, so we all ordered it, figuring it would be the quickest thing to get. The fry on the shrimp was excellent and our server had just cleared our plates off the table when I spotted Brett walking in the door.

Midthirties. Six foot two. A hundred ninety pounds. Clearly devoted to the gym but not a hint of callous on his hands. Expensive suit. Slightly irritated expression. Dangerous because of his money and connections.

He spotted us in the corner, and I lifted a hand. I figured he'd already googled the heck out of me and knew what I looked like. As he stepped our direction, I realized the man who'd entered the café behind him was with him.

Midthirties. Six foot even. A hundred seventy pounds. Probably worked out at the same gym. Definitely used the same hand lotion. Wearing a suit that probably cost more than my Jeep, and I was pretty sure that was an Hermès tie around his neck because Ronald kept thrusting pictures of one in my face. No threat except to a charge card.

Brett frowned as he approached our table and gave Ida Belle and Gertie a quick glance. He was probably wondering why I brought my grandmothers to an important meeting. I rose and extended my hand.

"Fortune Redding. These are my assistants, Ida Belle and Gertie."

He raised one eyebrow. "You use seniors to run your business?"

"Do you know anyone nosier or with more dirt on people than seniors?" I asked.

"Touché," he said as he and the other man sat on the two ends of the booth. "This is my best friend and right-hand man, Devin Roberts. He's been around for everything important in my life, so he might be able to fill in gaps if my memory isn't on point. I've had some trouble concentrating lately."

"I'm sure everyone understands why," I said. "I'm so sorry about what you and Kelsey are going through. I'm going to do everything I can to help Ben."

"By trying to set a killer loose?" he asked.

"I don't believe he killed her," I said. "But then, you could probably tell me more about that. She was *your* employee. Something you never told your wife, even after she figured out who Ben's father was."

A flush crept up his face. "*I'm* Ben's father. Biology doesn't trump doing the actual work, day in and day out."

"It does when you need a kidney," I said.

His jaw flexed, and I could tell he was beyond enraged that with all his assets and connections, he was at the mercy of another man to save his son. A man who had indulged in a one-night stand with his wife. It was also clear to me that whatever Brett might feel for Kelsey at this point, he loved his son.

"I know this has to be the most awful thing you've ever endured," I said, "but this is about saving Ben. I'm going to suggest you concentrate only on that one thing for now because it's the only thing that matters. When Ben is healthy, you can unravel everything else and make decisions about your marriage and anything else you might want to change."

He stared at me for several seconds, then finally gave me a single nod. "What do you want from me?"

"I want to know who wanted Lindsay dead."

He shook his head. "I have no idea."

"No idea at all? Even though she cost your firm millions in fees and a client even more? Even though she was constantly going against her own powerful father's wishes?"

Brett remained silent and Devin stepped in.

"Her father was a real jerk," Devin said. "But we didn't know him except by reputation. The only time we were around him in person was events, and trust me, we tried to avoid him as much as possible at them. It was obvious why Lindsay didn't want to work for him."

"And the mistake she made on the account?" I asked. "No one was mad enough to want her punished for it? What about the investor? How much did he lose due to her error?"

Brett gave me an incredulous look. "Are you really suggesting that the client, a man for whom that loss was like pocket change, would kill someone over a mistake? That's ridiculous. He simply did what all clients do if you lose their trust—he changed firms."

"But he wasn't the only loser. You lost millions in revenue and likely, it was a slam to your reputation. Why didn't you fire Lindsay?"

"Because you don't just go firing your best employees without investigating first," he said.

Interesting. There wasn't anything to investigate about a mistake. But if it was intentional...

"You wondered if she did it on purpose in order to feed accounts to her father," I said.

He broke eye contact, and I could tell he didn't want to admit Lindsay might have swindled them, but he wasn't convinced it didn't happen, either. Finally, he looked back at me.

"I don't know what really happened," he said. "We were

looking into the matter but then she was murdered. An investigation became not only pointless but tasteless as well."

"And when all of this about Ben came up and your wife tracked down Ryan, why didn't you tell her that you had a connection to Ryan's presumed victim?"

"Because it wasn't relevant. I didn't kill her. I didn't even know about Kelsey and her sordid night with a murderer. If I had and I was going to kill anyone, why wouldn't it be him? Lindsay had nothing to do with that and probably would have been as upset as I was to find out."

I shrugged. "Perhaps. But you have to admit, the way it went down solved all your problems. You got rid of a potentially problematic employee and got revenge on the man who slept with your future wife."

His jaw flexed, and I could tell that he was seething underneath the controlled demeanor. Brett Spalding did not like reminders of things he couldn't call the shots on.

"I suppose in hindsight, it looks like I came out the big winner," he said finally. "But how did I know my wife had rebound sex with a guy from a bar? How did I find out who he was and that he was Lindsay's ex, and somehow also make it over to her place to kill her and then frame him, all in the span of a couple hours? And framing him meant I also had to know that he was living in a motel and not at their home."

He shook his head. "For me to know any of that, I would have had to have been following Kelsey and see her go into a hotel room with him. And if I'd seen any of that, then I would have known he had an alibi, and it would have been foolish to attempt to frame him. I'm a lot of things, Ms. Redding, but a fool isn't one of them."

I nodded. "But someone did it. And they got away with it. Unless you think Kelsey is lying and her fling with Ryan was more than a one-nighter."

His jaw flexed again, and he rose from the table. "This discussion is over. I don't know anything that can help you. I'm working with my own attorneys to get access to Ryan in order to save my son. If he's really not some psychopathic murderer, then he won't let a child suffer, right? But trying to prove him innocent as a way to save Ben is an exercise in futility. Even if you could do it, how long would it take? Time is the one thing Ben doesn't have."

He whirled around and strode off. Devin glanced back at him then pulled a business card out of his pocket and handed it to me. "This whole thing has him understandably upset. Not so much about Kelsey, as in my opinion, their marriage has been a question mark since the beginning. But Ben... He loves that boy more than himself, and that's saying everything because Brett has always been his own biggest fan."

I nodded. "Do you think Lindsay made a mistake on that client's books?"

He shrugged. "She was scary smart. Her mind processed things so quickly that everyone around her struggled to keep up. Even me, and I'm damned good at what I do. But there's no denying the mistake was made. And only Lindsay, Brett, and Brett's parents had access to that account. His parents have been out of the country for years, and why would Brett sabotage his own company?"

"So you believe it was intentional? That she really was working for Spalding to push clients to her father?"

"It's hard to see it any other way. Raymond Beech might have had three kids, but there was only one that he intended to leave in control of his empire—the one who wouldn't lose it all. And that was Lindsay."

"Isn't Jared handling everything now?"

He snorted. "He's losing clients faster than rats on a sinking ship. He was never good at the job, and he's practically a hermit, closed up in that mausoleum they call a house in Magnolia Pass. Clients have to badger him for meetings and potential clients don't like him when they *do* get an audience with him. The spoiled rich kid is too ingrained, and it rubs people wrong. That client that Lindsay lost? He was back with Spalding a month after Raymond Beech died. What does that tell you?"

He tapped his card. "If you have any more questions, call me. I can probably answer anything you need to know, and it will save Brett the stress of it all."

He left the restaurant, and I watched as he got into the driver's seat of a white Mercedes sedan. Brett was already staring out the passenger-side window, looking as if he'd rather be anywhere else but there.

"Well, that was interesting," I said.

Ida Belle nodded. Brett Spalding is a very angry man. I kept expecting him to flip the table over and storm out."

"Kelsey said he wasn't violent," Gertie said. "I don't think she was lying."

"Neither do I," I agreed. "But I think he's definitely got it in him, especially when he's pushed past his 'I'm not in control' limit. I can see why their marriage never really worked."

Ida Belle shook her head. "But he's not wrong about one thing—it would have taken a ridiculous amount of effort for him to have murdered Lindsay over Kelsey's one-nighter with Ryan. Even if he'd had her under surveillance, which is always possible, I think he'd have more likely waited until sometime later and gotten his revenge when he was certain no one could connect them. Like he said—he's not a fool."

"He strikes me as very calculated," I agreed then sighed. "I can't believe I'm saying this, but what if the timing of Lindsay's murder was a legitimate coincidence? We know that neither

Ryan nor Kelsey deliberately targeted each other at that bar. And they didn't even know who the other one was, much less who they were involved with. What if their random hookup just happened to coincide with the night Brett took Lindsay out over the lost account and that's why Brett never mentioned any details about Lindsay's death to Kelsey?"

"That would be some monumental bad luck for Brett," Gertie said.

"Too much?" Ida Belle asked.

I rolled it over in my mind and blew out a breath. "Probably. The clincher is setting up Ryan to take the fall. If Brett was going to frame Ryan for the murder, wouldn't he have made sure Ryan was alone at the motel before he did it?"

"It doesn't look very plausible," Ida Belle agreed. "I don't like Brett at all and wouldn't have tolerated him for five seconds as a boyfriend, but I don't see how he could have managed this."

I nodded. "The murder he could have, but the setup required personal knowledge of Ryan's living situation. And even then, I can't see someone as meticulous and controlling as Brett not verifying Ryan was there before he tried to pin a murder on him. The fact that someone managed to do it doesn't change what his thought process would have been back then."

Gertie put her hands up. "So if we assume it's not about Ryan and Kelsey being together, or Lindsay losing that client, then we're back to the usual suspect—money."

Ida Belle nodded. "Which points directly at Jared Beech. It sounds like Lindsay was the brains of the family. If Jared was never going to be acknowledged and would go from being under his father's thumb to his sister's, it's a great motive."

"Don't forget Holly," Gertie said. "I know people will say she was just a kid, but kids do heinous things all the time.

What if that immaturity she still displays is part of a larger issue? What if it wasn't a schoolgirl crush but a fixation she had for Ryan? I can see where she'd be jealous of Lindsay. Her sister was older, prettier, smarter, and she had the man that Holly wanted."

I sighed. "I really don't want a kid to have caused all of this, but you're right. We can't exclude her."

"So what's next?" Ida Belle asked.

I shook my head. "I really need to talk to Ryan. Someone has to fill in the blanks, and he's probably the only one who can."

"We can still talk to Kenny," Ida Belle said, "and we'll see Father Michael tonight at the Good Friday dinner."

"Then there's only one thing left to do at the moment," I said and waved to get our server's attention.

This situation called for beignets.

CHAPTER THIRTEEN

We found Kenny at the marina, tying up his boat. He gave us a wave and a smile as we approached.

"I ain't pulled no one out of the bayou today," he said, making a reference to his recovery of a girl in the bayou earlier that year.

"Good," I said. "I'm already working a case. I don't need another."

"And I don't need the strain on my heart," he said. "So what can I do for you ladies? Because I know you didn't come to ask me about the fish."

"This is a real long shot, so no pressure, but I need you to think back about ten years."

"Lord have mercy. I can barely remember this morning, but shoot."

I pulled out my phone and showed him the receipt. "You stayed at the Bayou Inn about ten years ago. There was a guy staying there at the same time who was arrested for killing his girlfriend."

Kenny's eyes widened. "Oh yeah! That one I do remember. Hard to forget when you're close to something that awful. I actually talked to that guy. Can you believe it? When I saw a picture of him on the news, I darn near passed out. I'd been chatting at the vending machine with a cold-blooded killer."

He shook his head, and I could tell by his expression just how much the exchange had spooked him.

"I checked out and went straight home when the cops told me what happened," he continued. "Was having my hardwood floors refinished and the floor guys had told me it was best if I cleared out for a couple days. But no way was I staying at that motel another night. I slept in my garage until the smell calmed down."

"Well, Kenny, I'm about to improve your memories—he didn't do it."

Kenny's jaw dropped and he stared at me. "What? He went to prison."

I nodded. "And I have a new witness who swears he was with her all night in a hotel in NOLA. A man can't be two places at once."

"You're shit—fooling me."

"Not even a little."

"And you're sure she's got the right date?"

"Positive. She got pregnant that night but didn't realize the baby belonged to Ryan. Now that kid is deathly ill and needs a kidney. But the person who might be the only viable match is in prison."

Kenny ran a hand over his thinning hair. "Jesus, I think I was happier believing I was talking to a killer. That poor woman and kid. What can I do to help?"

"You said you talked to Ryan, but I know that couldn't have been the night his girlfriend was killed because he was working."

He nodded. "It was the night before. Nice guy... I never could reconcile him being a killer with the guy I talked to. It just never sat right with me. Guess now I know why. Anyway, it was nice weather out and I was feeling a little claustrophobic in my room, so I grabbed a soda and chips and was sitting on that bench next to the vending machine, mostly just staring at the parking lot. And that guy walks up and gets a candy bar and asks if I mind if he sits. I was happy to have the company, so he sat and we got to talking."

"What was his demeanor like?"

"Seemed fine. A little troubled, but he told me he was having woman problems and that's why he was at the motel, so I didn't think nothing of it. Said he was a bartender at the casino in NOLA, and we talked a bit about some of the outrageous things he'd seen. I remember he was from Mudbug, and we talked about fishing in the area. That was about it. I thought he was a nice guy and didn't think about it beyond that. Until the cops showed up at the motel."

"What about the night of the murder? Did you see anything then? Because someone planted the murder weapon in the dumpster and since we know now that it wasn't Ryan, it had to have been the killer."

He paled. "Oh Lord! I woke up around 4:00 a.m. with awful heartburn. Chili dogs, you know? I had some Rolaids in my truck and went outside to grab them. When I was walking back to my room, a guy walked out of the breezeway from the back. He walked right past me and kept going to the parking lot."

My pulse ticked up a notch. "Did you get a good look at his face?"

"No. He was wearing one of those hooded sweatshirts and looking down."

Crap.

"What about size, color? Anything you can remember could help me narrow things down."

"A little taller than me and thin, maybe, but like I said, he was hunched and wearing a big sweatshirt. What I saw of his face, he was white. Didn't see no hair."

"What about his movement? Fast? Slow? Impairment?"

"He moved like a younger man, if that's what you're getting at. Or an older one who didn't let his habits run to chili dogs, like me."

"And he was going to the parking lot? Did you see him get into a vehicle?"

"I'm afraid not. I went into my room, took the Rolaids, and tried to get some sleep. But he was already at the first row of the parking lot when I passed him, and he kept going. I never looked back. Man, if I had..."

"You might not be standing here today," I said. "He'd already killed one person and framed another. You're lucky you don't know more. Did the police question you?"

"No. Which I thought was strange. And I know the motel manager gave them a list of people staying there because he told me as much. He didn't want us surprised if they contacted us. I kept waiting for them to call, but it never happened. I just figured they had all that evidence and didn't need more. But if that poor guy was framed... Well, that's just awful."

I nodded. "I appreciate you talking to me, Kenny. I don't suppose it would do any good to show you some pictures, would it?"

He shook his head. "I'm afraid not. I really didn't see much. You know how the lighting is there and with it being cloudy, I couldn't see much at all."

"Thanks again."

We headed off and all my feelings—frustration, anger, excitement—rolled around as we climbed into the car.

"Well, at least Kenny confirms my theory," I said.

"You think he saw the killer?" Gertie asked.

I nodded. "The timing is right, and the guy was headed from the rear of the motel and into the parking lot, not to a room. If he's not our guy, then I'd be very surprised."

"I'd like to say I can't believe the Magnolia Pass police never talked to Kenny," Ida Belle said, "but I'm not surprised. Angry, but not surprised."

"Me either," I said. "But I find it interesting that the manager told Kenny he'd given the cops a guest list. It's not logged into the police file."

"That idiot Cantrell probably tossed it as soon as he had a good scapegoat," Gertie said. "I mean, why do some actual police work if your case is wrapped up for you?"

"Not to mention the perpetrator was someone Raymond Beech never liked," Ida Belle said. "The whole thing was practically gifted to Cantrell."

I shook my head. "The thing I don't understand is that no one gets to where Raymond Beech was in life without being smart, or at least clever and willing to break the rules. So how is it that he bought all of that when it looks so blatant? I realize he'd lost his daughter, but he doesn't sound like the kind of man who'd let emotion get in the way of logic."

Ida Belle shrugged. "Who knows? Everyone grieves differently, but I agree it seems strange that a man so clearly competent in other ways would accept that explanation without question."

"Unless he knew who the real killer was," I said. "We need to take a hard look at Jared Beech...just as soon as I figure out how."

———

IT WAS GETTING TOWARD EVENING, SO WE HEADED HOME. We were planning to attend Good Friday dinner, and we needed to shower and put on clothes worthy of a man who rose from the dead. Jesus hadn't done it as many times as Dwight Redding, but I figured I could still put on a dress and have some barbecue. Since celebrating Easter was one of the few things the two churches agreed on, they cohosted the event and swapped locations each year, and it was the Catholics' turn to host in their big meeting area.

I figured that meant a night of Celia glaring and complaining, but someone had to make sure Gertie and her purse didn't arrange another crucifixion. I also had some reservations about barbecue and little girls dressed in frilly dresses, but according to Ida Belle—who clearly wouldn't be wearing frilly anything—this was the way it had always been done. Ronald had acquired a nice, plain—his words—dress for me, and I was going to thrill him by not only wearing the dress, but also wearing shoes with a little heel. Nothing I could kill anyone with, but then, I was hoping for a night off.

Carter was on duty, but he'd be there in a sort of official capacity. Since that was where most of Sinful would be, it was the most likely place to have a problem crop up. That and the Swamp Bar, and Andy Blanchet, a retired sheriff from another town, had agreed to be on call that weekend to help with anything Whiskey couldn't handle. I wasn't sure exactly what that might be, but it would be interesting to find out. Deputy Breaux was at the sheriff's department, ready to respond to whoever needed backup.

I blow-dried my hair and left it down, swiped on some of the moisturizer that Ronald wanted me to live in, and dashed on some tinted lip gloss. That was as good as it was getting for me on the girlie end of things, so I pulled on the dress, a sundress in solid turquoise, slipped on the shoes, and headed downstairs. Since Ida Belle and Gertie had to be there early to ensure Celia didn't turn Good Friday into *Friday the 13th*, Ronald had offered to give me a ride over in his new car, a shiny white Bentley with enough gold trim to get it into a rap video.

He had just stepped onto the porch when I got downstairs, and I pulled open the door, ready to see what he was wearing. The only thing he'd been willing to share was it was custom and befitting of the event but with his flair.

He hadn't lied about any of that.

The tuxedo was pink with white pinstripes, and I was pretty sure it was made of silk. His vest, dress shoes, and the band around his white top hat were covered in gold sequins. When he did a model turn, I started laughing so hard I thought I would choke. Right in the appropriate location on the back of the tux coat was a fluffy white rabbit tail.

"Touch it," he said when I finally regained some of my composure. "It's real rabbit fur."

"I'm going to take a hard pass on touching your butt, and I'm going to make a suggestion that you don't extend that offer at the dinner, especially to kids."

He rolled his eyes. "I'm not stupid, but isn't it just the cutest thing? I saw one of those Playboy Bunny bathing suits and thought 'why not for Jesus?' He deserves people wearing cute outfits more than Hugh Hefner."

Since I didn't have a valid argument for that one, I just closed the door and locked it. "You ready? I need to check out this new fabulous car."

"Isn't she though?" He practically danced down the sidewalk. "People thought I was crazy to get the white interior, but I knew what I wanted."

I opened the door and stared. The inside of the car matched Ronald's tuxedo. The carpet was pink. The seats were fluffy white and practically everything had gold trim. There was even a tiny chandelier hanging where the dome light would normally go.

"Sooooooo..." I said as I perched delicately on the fur and prayed my off-the-rack dress didn't stain it, "Bentley offers these options?"

"Of course not," he said as he backed out of my driveway. "I know a guy. He's like those guys on MTV, but without the Harleys and tattoos. You know, class, taste?"

"Flash?"

Ronald grinned. "Maybe just a touch, but not all of us can be happy with clothes from Amazon and driving a Jeep with a title older than our birth certificate."

"Hmmmm, well, it's very nice and perfect for you. I have to admit, it rides like a dream. I don't even feel like I left my couch."

"This car is a lot more comfortable than that couch of yours."

"Maybe, but I can't drink beer and eat spaghetti in here, and you should never let Gertie get a peek. It's right up her alley in looks, but Ida Belle keeps seat covers and tarps in her SUV for a reason. Gertie's the reason."

"I thought you kept tarps in case you had to dispose of a body," he joked.

"That was the original reason, but we use them more because of Gertie."

"You know, it both fascinates and scares me that I'm never really sure when you're joking. Good Lord, look at all the cars. The sinners have really come out for absolution this year."

"Easter and Christmas always draw the big crowds."

He snorted. "I'm pretty sure it's the free barbecue, but I'll withhold saying those things out loud as soon as we get inside. I try to contain myself on church premises."

"So you plan on lying instead?"

"I'm going multiple choice with my commandments tonight. Since Celia's running the show, I have to keep lying and cursing under my breath on the table."

He found a spot at the end of Main Street, and we headed for the church. It was definitely a big turnout, but not surprising. I hadn't attended the previous year—I think I'd faked a cold, which I'd probably go to hell for—but this year, I'd given up the protest and decided that wearing a dress for a bunch of church women's cooking wasn't the worst trade I'd ever made.

The Catholics had a big meeting hall behind the church, so we headed for the sidewalk to the rear. We could hear the noise from the meeting hall before we even got to the door, and I started to feel a fake cold coming on again. That was an awful lot of people in one space. Ronald must have noticed my decrease in pace because he grabbed my arm and tugged me.

"You've put on a dress and you're doing this," he said. "If you go home, that would make Celia happy, and we never want that to happen."

He wasn't fighting fair, but he wasn't wrong, either. I sighed and trudged up to the door and followed him inside. It was as packed as it sounded, but at least there appeared to be a semblance of organization. The church ladies were toting trays of food from the kitchen to a buffet line that stretched across the back of the room and right in front of the kitchen. Tables covered with pink tablecloths ran perpendicular to the buffet and the length of the room with metal chairs spaced along them.

The smell of the barbecue was enough to improve my mood, so I followed Ronald over to the corner where Ida Belle and Gertie were fiddling with gift baskets for the kids. They looked over as we approached and Gertie's expression when she got the twirl from Ronald was priceless.

"Is that real rabbit fur?" she asked and reached for the tail.

"No!" Ida Belle said, and swatted her hand away. "We're in church. You cannot go touching a man's tail."

Gertie rolled her eyes. "As soon as we're out of church, the squeeze is on."

Ronald laughed. "It's absolutely real fur and so incredibly soft."

"I am so jealous," Gertie said. "I've got to get the name of your tailor. I think we could have some fun."

She looked over at me. "And you look lovely as well. I rarely see you with your hair down unless you've been doing spy stuff and it comes out of your ponytail."

Ronald shook his head in dismay. "She's so rough on her hair and skin."

"But still a solid dime." Carter's voice sounded behind me, and I turned around and smiled.

He leaned over and gave me a kiss—on the lips, but light as we were in church. I heard Ronald sigh.

"All that magnificence," he whispered, "and neither of them even try. It makes one homicidal."

Gertie nodded. "But we have flair, and that's not to be discounted."

Carter gave Ronald a once-over. "That outfit *is* something. It appears to match your new Bentley. Nice ride."

"It is nice," I agreed. "I was afraid the seat might eject me for getting into it with off-the-rack clothes."

"Honey, you don't need designer when you're put together like that," Ronald said.

"I agree," Carter said. "In fact, I don't think you need clothes at all."

"Carter LeBlanc!"

Celia's voice sounded behind me, and I turned to see her standing there, hands on hips and glaring at Carter.

"I cannot believe you are carrying on that way in the Lord's house," she said. "And on Easter, no less."

He shrugged. "They let you in here every week and the place hasn't erupted in flames yet. I figure being thankful for what God's blessed me with is okay with Him."

She flushed and stepped closer to him. "Instead of standing here fawning over your disreputable girlfriend, maybe you should get out there and police this lot. Then things like that debacle at the Easter egg hunt wouldn't happen. People are too lax about following the rules, and that's all on you, which is exactly why we need a sheriff with more propriety."

"I could run," Blanchet said as he stepped up to our party.

I choked back a laugh because he was wearing jeans and a T-shirt that read, *On the eighth day, He created beer*, and he was holding a flask, which he'd taken a drink from after issuing his statement.

"I've got more experience and as you can see, way more propriety," he continued. "But I have to wonder why you're over here complaining about propriety when you've got a slab of cow on your buffet table. I thought you weren't supposed to eat meat on Good Friday."

Celia whirled around and stomped off, clearly at a disadvantage. The rest of us started laughing.

"What are you doing here?" Carter asked. "I thought you were staying at Walter's house on Swamp Bar call?"

Andy shrugged. "I can take calls just as well here as I can from Walter's couch. I figured if your lot and Celia were all together in one building, you might need backup. Plus, now I don't have to cook."

"Are you drinking on the job?" Ronald asked.

"Of course not," he said. "This is water. I just brought the flask to aggravate Celia."

I laughed. "So what you really came to do is help stir the pot."

He grinned. "I cannot tell a lie. Not on Good Friday, anyway."

"You just lied about propriety," Ronald pointed out.

"Depends on who you're comparing me to," Blanchet said. "Shall we get some food before the good stuff is gone?"

"No worries there," Ida Belle said. "The Catholics won't eat the beef, pork, or chicken. They have a stack of fish."

"So they have to serve up the food but can't eat it?" Blanchet asked. "That's rough."

"They won't eat it in front of the Baptists," Gertie said. "But they'll sneak it out in their purses and dig into it as soon as the clock strikes midnight. Have you ever seen a bigger collection of cheap, ugly handbags?"

I glanced around the room and realized Gertie was right. Ronald blanched and started waving his hand to fan his face.

"It's the purse apocalypse," he said.

"Better they haul a slab of ribs in a Walmart special than a Louis Vuitton," Gertie said.

"You're not making it any better," he said as they headed for the ribs.

"Where's Walter?" I asked Ida Belle as we headed for the food.

"Home. He knows better."

CHAPTER FOURTEEN

We all stacked up our plates with home cooking and found a table. I noticed the room was mostly divided, Baptists and their ribs on one side and Catholics and their fish on the other side. Their longing stares at our plates was a bit unnerving, but I couldn't blame them. I loved a good fish fry, but it would never beat a plate of ribs. And these were so tender they were falling off the bone.

By the time I plowed through the ribs, potato salad, coleslaw, corn on the cob, and green beans, I was glad my dress was stretchy fabric but worried that my stomach was not. I wasn't sure how I was going to fit in peach cobbler but was still going to try. I'd just settled down with my bowl when Father Michael and Pastor Don stumbled to the front of the room and turned on a microphone. Everyone stopped talking when it let out a loud screech, and all you could hear was the sound of forks hitting plates as everyone clasped their hands over their ears. I saw one of Celia's group run for an electronic board in the corner and finally the screeching stopped.

The two church leaders had never even flinched at the sound and were standing there, arms around each other's shoulders and grinning as though they were at a Swamp Bar party instead of leading a religious event.

"They're drunker than Cooter Brown," Gertie said.

"I thought the Baptists got the ribs but not the drinks," Blanchet said. "You guys are confusing."

"Father Michael and Pastor Don were eating together," Ronald said. "I saw Father Michael go twice to refill their drinks."

"Oh Lord," Ida Belle said. "Pastor Don isn't a drinker. If he's been chugging whatever Father Michael is serving up, he might not even be back from the abyss to preach on Sunday."

Ronald pointed to the other side. "That nun was eating with them as well, and she's face down in her cobbler."

Carter sighed. "Let's just hope they get through this, and everyone clears out without problems. Gertie, I want you to put your purse under the table and don't touch it."

"You gonna ask her to empty her bra as well?" Ida Belle asked. "Because boobs aren't shaped like that at the bottom. I'm just sayin'."

Carter grimaced and then gave us a hard stare. "Pretend it's elementary school. The three of you should put your hands on the table and not move them for anything except your food."

I stuffed another bite of cobbler in my mouth. Father Michael and Pastor Don didn't scare me when they were sober —assuming Father Michael ever was. Based on the way they were swaying, I was pretty sure blowing on them would take them out at the moment.

Pastor Don tapped the microphone, cleared his throat, and started.

"Dearly beloved, we are gathered here today in the presence of God and these witnesses to join—"

"That's a wedding ceremony!" someone yelled.

Pastor Don looked confused, but Father Michael gave him

a pat on the back. "Let me try," he said as though it was a carnival game and one of them was going to 'hit' on the right sermon.

"Dearly beloved, we have gathered here today to get through this thing called life."

"That's a Prince song!" someone yelled.

"I love this town," Blanchet said.

"It's Easter!" someone yelled, hoping to give the two religious leaders a cue.

"Oh!" Paster Don's face cleared. "Jesus died for our sins."

Father Michael looked stricken. "He died? Then we must light a candle."

He turned around and fished a white candle out of a box behind him, then pulled a lighter out of his robes.

I shook my head. "Two drunk men with a lit candle in a hundred-year-old building, with only two exits and half the town inside. What could possibly go wrong?"

"Crap." Carter jumped up and hurried for the back of the room, where he grabbed a fire extinguisher and started trying to convince people to exit.

"You don't look worried about it," Blanchet said.

"Because if this place goes up in flames, I'm diving out that window. But this room full of knee replacements does *not* have that option."

"I'm glad I'm not wearing heels," Ronald said. "They don't do well in a stampede."

"Neither does silk, and half those hands stampeding are going to have barbecue sauce on them."

"Lord help!" Ronald said. "I'll just toss this plate in the wash bin and make my way toward the door."

And he was off.

The two drunk men had abandoned the microphone and were now standing there with the candle, swaying and singing a Taylor Swift song. I think. It was hard to hear over the general grumbling of people. I couldn't figure out if they were upset that their religious celebration had gone pop or that good manners required that they stop eating until the debacle was over.

I saw Ronald creep up to the table in the back and deposit his plate and utensils in the wash bin. As he turned around to slink out, the sequins on his hat caught just right in the light, and they shot out a beam that blinded Father Michael and Pastor Don. The two religious leaders cheered, mistaking the beam of light for a sign from God, and Blanchet started laughing so hard I thought the folding chair he was sitting on would collapse from the vibration.

When the beam of light shifted and they could see again, Father Michael launched into the "Hallelujah" chorus, but Pastor Don looked over, trying to figure out where the light had gone.

And locked in on Ronald's tail.

Pastor Don shot off faster than I thought he'd be able to manage given his obvious intoxication, and I silently willed Ronald to run. But instead, he caught sight of the rapidly approaching preacher and froze.

Wrong move.

Pastor Don let out a squeal of delight and grabbed the rabbit tail.

"It's so soft!" he called out.

The entire room erupted in laughter, and Ronald finally came to his senses and darted away. Unfortunately, the crowd had moved in closer to see the tail and the exit was blocked. Ronald set off running and dodging people and tables as Pastor Don chased him through the room with an outstretched arm.

Blanchet fell onto the floor and Ida Belle and Gertie collapsed on the table. But I stood, my eyes still locked on

Father Michael—the man standing in the middle of what was fast becoming pandemonium—eyes clenched shut, singing at the top of his lungs, and still holding a lit candle.

I inched through the crowd toward the front, but Celia beat me to it. She burst through the last line of people and started chasing Pastor Don.

"Stop trying to touch that man's butt!" she yelled. "It's a sacrilege!"

Ronald made a quick ninety-degree turn and ran right in front of Father Michael, with Pastor Don—only an inch from grabbing the tail—right behind, and Celia on Pastor Don's heels.

And then Celia Gertied.

She tripped over the microphone cord and crashed into the singing priest. Father Michael dropped the candle as he fell, and his robe went up in flames. Carter stepped out with the fire extinguisher, but the thing was probably as old as the building and not a single drop of foam came out.

I sprinted for the fallen priest, yanked off his robe, and tossed it in an ice chest, grateful that he was fully clothed underneath. Celia was back up and flapping around like a chicken, the hem of her dress starting to kindle. I was just about to heave some of the water out of the ice chest when Blanchet stepped up and threw the contents of his flask on her.

The fire extinguished, Celia stopped flapping and glared at Blanchet. "You threw alcohol on me!"

"It's water," Blanchet said. "I filled it from the holy water basin on my way in."

The crowd went silent, and everyone stared. Then Gertie stepped up and asked the question on everyone's lips.

"Does it burn?"

Celia's face turned beet red, and she put her hands on her

hips and stomped off. The entire building erupted in laughter. Father Michael stood there looking completely confused as to what had happened. Pastor Don, halfway to heart attack level between the alcohol and all the running, was collapsed in a chair, and some of the church ladies were fanning him with napkins.

My phone went off and I saw it was a text from Ronald.

Sorry. There's a BBQ spot on my tail and I have to get vinegar on it. Catch a ride with someone.

Celia, who must have partially recovered, stomped up to Carter and pointed her finger at him. "Why didn't you do anything about those men?"

"I did. I had a good quarter of the building emptied before you caused a fire." He shoved the fire extinguisher at her. "And the date on this is older than me. You're in violation with that piece of useless crap. So before you start yelling at me about doing my job, I suggest you do yours. I'll be writing up a citation when I get back to the sheriff's department."

Celia's jaw dropped, and I knew she desperately wanted to let loose a witty defense, but since she lacked both, she couldn't. Carter glared at her before heading my way. He gave me a brief kiss.

"I'm going to get the rest of these people out of here and then head home. I'll give you a call in the morning."

I nodded as he headed off and Blanchet watched him leave, his grin turning to a pensive look.

"He's not okay, is he?" Blanchet asked.

"Not yet. But I think he will be when this is over."

Blanchet nodded and gave me a quick side squeeze. "Let me know if there's anything I can do. You've become like family to me."

I smiled. "Thanks. I feel the same."

He gave me a nod and left.

Gertie stepped up and sighed. "We've got a ton of fish to deal with. The Catholics fled with the rest of the barbecue, of course. I'm going to start packing up to-go containers for the fish. What I can't get rid of, I'll take to Godzilla. He's one of God's creatures, after all."

"I have to agree Godzilla's got more utility than Celia," Ida Belle said after Gertie headed off. "But I'd never tell her that."

I nodded. "I know he's drunk, but I still want to ask Father Michael about his motel stay."

"He's always drunk. Tonight is no different...just a tad bit more entertaining."

We headed over to where the dazed priest was standing, staring around the quickly emptying room as if trying to figure out where he was and for what purpose.

"Father Michael," I interrupted his thoughts. "I wondered if I could ask you about something that happened quite a ways back."

He brightened. "From the Old Testament?"

"Not quite that far. About ten years ago."

"Oh, heavens. Well, we can certainly try. But if it's personal, you might do better if you don't go any further than last week."

Given that he'd clearly been dipping in the communion wine for the past several decades, I was pretty sure going back to ten minutes ago would prove problematic, but I wouldn't be doing my job if I didn't follow all the leads.

"Back about ten years ago, you stayed at the Bayou Inn. See, here's your receipt. Do you remember staying there?"

He frowned as he stared at the image on my phone, his brow scrunched in concentration. Finally, he shook his head. "I don't think so."

"But this is your name, credit card, and signature."

He beamed at me. "If you say so. You're very smart."

"You don't remember staying there? It was the night a young woman was murdered in Magnolia Pass, and the man arrested for it was staying at the motel."

"Oh, that sounds vaguely familiar. I remember the police cars...sirens are so loud. I think I left, but I'm not sure. Wait... Was I there? Yes, I remember now. Proverbs 23:4."

I sighed. This was going nowhere. "Thanks, Father Michael."

"Bless you, my child," he said. Then he beamed at me and practically skipped away.

"Do you think Nora's been spiking the communion wine with her own brand?" I asked.

Ida Belle snorted. "Father Michael's been hitting the Good Friday sauce."

"Is the Good Friday sauce stronger than regular Friday?"

"I heard he skips wine altogether and goes straight for whiskey on religious holidays."

"Of course he does. I mean, who would want a sober man delivering the Easter sermon?"

"Have you ever talked to him when he's sober?"

I thought for a minute, then shook my head. "I don't think so. Have you?"

"Only the one time after that surgery. Sober as a monk and just as boring. Well, I guess I best help Gertie with that fish so I can go home and take off these shoes. Anything but tennis shoes or boots is uncomfortable after about ten minutes in them."

"I'll help," I said. "I need to catch a ride. Ronald had a barbecue-sauce-rabbit-tail emergency and abandoned me."

Ida Belle shook her head. "They say you're known by the company you keep. I worry for both of us."

We made quick work of boxing up the fish, and Celia's group waved off our offer to help with the cleanup, stating that their year meant their mess. We'd get a go at it next year, so we headed out. As soon as Ida Belle dropped me off, I went straight upstairs for a long shower. I'd fed Merlin before I left, but I figured he'd be happy to get a treat, so I gave him a piece of the fish. He almost looked pleased.

I grabbed a bottled water and my laptop and headed for my recliner, anxious to check my email, just in case I'd heard from the prison. My pulse quickened when I saw the email from Angola. I clicked on it and let out a whoop Gertie would have approved of when I saw the notification I'd been waiting for. I was cleared to visit Ryan.

And the next available time was the next day.

CHAPTER FIFTEEN

I WOKE UP THE NEXT MORNING, ANXIOUS TO GET THE SHOW on the road—literally. Even though Ida Belle and Gertie couldn't come inside with me for the visit, she'd still insisted on driving us there. I wasn't about to argue since her SUV was a lot more comfortable than my Jeep for a long haul.

I'd contacted Alexander right after receiving the email and let him know I was going to visit Ryan. He'd been excited that I'd gotten clearance so quickly and told me to report back as soon as I got out. If Ryan was up for the DNA test and the procedure, Alexander was prepared to deal with the warden by whatever means necessary.

I'd already checked the visitor dress code, which was fairly standard—nothing remotely revealing or sexy, nothing that looked like a prisoner, and nothing that looked like a prison guard. In addition to that, opting out of gang colors was always a wise choice, so I chose jeans, a yellow T-shirt, and white tennis shoes. Since vehicles were subject to search as well as visitors, we'd all be leaving our weapons at home, which meant no matter how many clothes I had on, I'd still feel naked.

I'd just swallowed the last bite of my egg sandwich when

Ida Belle and Gertie walked in, looking as excited as I was. I grabbed my notebook and laptop, which I could use on the way if we needed to research stuff, and we headed out. Gertie popped open her handbag and pulled out a protein bar and offered it to me.

"No thanks. I just finished breakfast when you guys pulled up," I said.

"I just finished breakfast before we left to pick you up," Gertie said, "but I'm hungry again. I think all this is burning the calories off me."

Ida Belle snorted. "You just want an excuse to eat chocolate."

"It's a protein bar," Gertie argued.

"Wrapped in chocolate," Ida Belle said.

Gertie took a bite. "It's still better for me than a Snickers."

"How's it taste?" I asked.

She frowned. "Not nearly as good as a Snickers. Why do they all taste like chocolate-wrapped cardboard? Oh well, I also brought a meatball sub, peanut butter and jelly sandwich, two cans of Pringles, and a family-size pack of Oreos."

I turned around and stared. "All of that is in your purse?"

She nodded. "And two bottles of water. Without my weapons, I have extra room. And you know how Ida Belle is about stopping. I have grapes in my bra and a package of licorice under my boobs just in case we run into traffic."

Since I didn't have words, I turned back around and pulled out my notebook. Might as well go over the questions I had for Ryan to see if they could think of anything I'd missed. We had a two-and-a-half-hour drive to Angola, so plenty of time to go over what we knew, especially since what we knew wouldn't get us out of Sinful. Discussing the list of things in Gertie's bra might take longer.

By the time we arrived at Angola, I was no closer to

answers than I was when we left and my excitement had picked up a thread of anxiety. So much was riding on this interview. Usually when I took a case, someone was already dead. This time, someone was going to die if I didn't solve the case, and there was a ticking clock on how long I had to do it.

Ida Belle and Gertie wished me luck, and I could see their stress levels mirrored my own. I pulled out my cell phone and passed it to Ida Belle, grabbed my notepad, and headed inside. The guard dog did his sniff routine and passed on to the next person when he didn't find anything interesting. Then the guard checked my credentials, did the usual pat-down, asked me the questions, checked my approval, and finally twenty minutes later, I was waiting for the bus that would take visitors to the main building where Ryan was held. I was told that I'd be limited to an hour due to the number of visitors expected, so that would have to do.

The visitation area was unlike any I'd been to. It had food counters staffed by and the food prepared by inmates, and the smell of Southern cooking wafted over me. Families sat at tables scattered around the building, and if one could overlook the armed guards every couple feet, then it might resemble a church social. But despite the attempt at a cheerful, normal display, the atmosphere was the same as all of them—sad, depressing, and with an overwhelming feeling of despair that seeped into you and left you cold like slow rain in the winter.

I cased the room and spotted Ryan at a small table in the far corner and headed that way. He looked up as I approached, and I maintained eye contact as he rose.

Early thirties but easily looked forty. Six foot two. A hundred seventy pounds. Good muscle tone showed he'd been working out, but prison food wasn't allowing him to bulk up as he probably would on the outside. He favored his right side as he extended his hands, and I figured he'd either had broken ribs at some point or had been stabbed.

His face showed the wear of ten years inside, but at least his eyes hadn't gone dead. There was still a flicker of hope in them.

"Fortune Redding," I said as we shook, and I motioned for him to sit. "I'm sorry we have to meet under these circumstances."

He held his hands up. "Look around, Ms. Redding. My circumstances were already in the toilet."

I nodded. "Would you like something to eat? It smells good. How is the food?"

"A bunch of Louisiana boys in the kitchen. The food is great. I wouldn't mind gumbo and a po'boy."

"Sounds good." I hopped back up and headed for the counter and ordered two gumbos, a po'boy, and two glasses of sweet tea. They ran better than a lot of restaurants I'd been in, and the food was up within minutes.

I headed back to the table and set the tray down, but Ryan didn't make a move for the food.

"Are you sure he's my kid?" he asked.

"Kelsey said she was only with two men—you and her current husband. Ben is not her husband's biological child, so you're the only other option."

"And you think she's telling the truth?"

"Why wouldn't she be? Did you sleep with her that night?"

He nodded. "I guess she doesn't have a good reason to lie, does she? I'm the last person she'd want as a father for her boy."

I opened my notebook and pulled out some photos from inside. "This is Kelsey. I just want to verify that she's the woman you spent the night with."

He looked at the photo and his expression softened, then he nodded. "That's her. She's a little older but still just as beautiful. How is she?"

"Scared, depressed, and I think she feels an enormous

172

amount of guilt that you're locked in here and she could have alibied you if she'd known."

He shook his head. "Raymond Beech wanted me to go down for this, and I'm not sure she could have done anything about it. I used to be a good judge of character—bartender skills, you know—and I think Kelsey was a good person. It didn't sound like the guy she ended up with valued her as an individual, which was sad. I liked her. I still loved Lindsay, but I really liked Kelsey. Even though it was only one night of my life, she stayed in my mind, and not just because it was *that* night. I always hoped she'd ended up with the life she deserved."

My heart clenched a little for this man, whom ten years of prison hadn't quite broken. I pulled out another photo and slid it across the table. "This is your son."

He hesitated and a sliver of fear crossed his face, then he reached for the photo and picked it up. As he studied the photograph, his lips trembled.

"He looks like me," he said. "When I was a boy, I mean. When Hot Rod told me, I didn't want to believe it, but I knew he wouldn't lie. Then I thought maybe she was lying although I couldn't come up with a good reason why. But this..."

He put the photo down and looked away, as if it hurt him to see it. "This photo clinches it. Hot Rod said he's going to die."

I nodded. "He needs a kidney. The last transplant failed, and it's highly unlikely the transplant board would approve him for another. Even if they were inclined to..."

"It might be too late. But what am I supposed to do? My hands aren't just tied, they're in cuffs."

My heart ached for him. His situation was already heartbreaking but now his incarceration, for a crime that I didn't believe he'd committed, might result in the death of his son.

Unless I could prove him innocent.

"My friend and attorney—your attorney now—is going to start to work on the warden just as soon as I tell him you're willing to do this."

"Of course I am! Why wouldn't I be?"

I held my hands up, and he nodded.

"I get it, but you can tell your—my—attorney to do everything he can. Hot Rod said he'd help cover his fees. I don't know how I'm ever going to repay him."

"I wouldn't worry about that just yet. Your attorney is semiretired and often takes on cases for his own enjoyment. He loves nothing better than taking down the bad guys and championing the good ones. You'll need to notify the prison that you've got new representation. His name is Alexander Framingham III."

Ryan's eyes widened. "The Grim Reaper? You're friends with the Grim Reaper? And he's going to represent me? You're making this up, right?"

"Didn't Hot Rod tell you anything about me?"

"Not really. Just that you were a PI and could figure out everything. We spent more time talking about how I had a kid."

"I'm former CIA. And I collected the evidence that helped Alexander take down a lot of bad people. We understand each other and have common goals. More importantly, we both believe you're innocent. If he says he can get the warden to bend, I have zero doubt that he can. So the first thing we need is a DNA test. You need proof that you're the biological parent. Then he'll be able to proceed with the requests for you to donate a kidney."

"Hot Rod said all that would take too long."

"If it was any other attorney, I would agree, but Alexander has a way of expediting things."

He nodded, then looked down at the table. "And the other thing?"

"I'm working on getting your conviction overturned, but you have to know how hard it is to get evidence on a crime after this much time has passed."

"Yeah. At first, I thought something would shake loose, you know, but then another year passed and nothing happened. Then another year and another. I finally realized it was never going to because no one had an incentive to work on it. Except Hot Rod, but he's a mechanic, not a detective or an attorney. He's had people review it every year or so, but no one came up with a good enough reason for an appeal."

"I'm working on that, but I need information, and you're probably the only person who is willing to level with me on everything except Kelsey. So let's dig into this gumbo and you can fill in some blanks for me. Then when I leave here, I'll have more directions to look."

He studied me silently for a couple seconds, then nodded and picked up his spoon. "CIA, huh? Were you like an agent or something?"

"If I told you that, I'd have to kill you...and I could."

His eyes widened a little and he smiled for the first time. "What do you want to know?"

"Let's start with you and Lindsay. Since we both agree you didn't kill her, the easiest way to get your conviction overturned is to figure out who did. I know you two were separated at the time, but it hadn't been very long. So who had issues with her?"

He took a couple bites of gumbo while he considered. "My problem has always been figuring out who had a big enough beef with Lindsay to kill her, but I guess I need to stop thinking that way. I know what it would take for me to kill someone, but I guess I can't make that call about other people."

"That's exactly right. I need you to tell me everyone who might have had a problem with Lindsay. Any problem. Leave it to me to figure out the depth of the issue and whether or not it was enough to send the person with the problem over the edge."

"Well, clearly her father was a problem, but I don't think he killed her." He sighed. "Sorry. That's for you to decide. Anyway, her father tried to control everything about her life, and he managed right up until the time she graduated and got a job with another firm. That's when their relationship really went south, she said."

"He expected her to work for him?"

"He always said he expected her to take over the firm, but there is no way that man was relinquishing control to anyone, not even Lindsay. He would have had to die first, and she knew that, which is why she stayed away."

"But she wouldn't move out of Magnolia Pass. I know that was a problem between the two of you."

He nodded. "That's the reason I left. I couldn't take living there anymore. The whole place is creepy. I mean, it looks so pretty on the surface, but underneath, it was just a handful of horrible people telling everyone else how to live."

"So why didn't she want to move? You both worked in NOLA. She had no desire to bend to her father's will. Why stay?"

"She said she needed to keep an eye on Holly. Their father was never much of a parent, and Lindsay had basically been raising Holly since their mother died. She didn't trust Jared or her father to see that Holly got the care she needed. Have you met her?"

"Yes. She doesn't seem quite normal."

"She's not, and Lindsay was trying to convince her father to let her take Holly to specialists. Teachers tried for years to do the same thing, but instead of listening, he got the teachers reprimanded. He finally pulled her out of school altogether and hired tutors."

"What did Lindsay think was wrong with her?"

He shook his head. "She wasn't a doctor and wasn't allowed to take her to one, but she guessed maybe some form of autism, or worse—maybe a personality disorder."

"Why a personality disorder?"

"Holly would fixate on things and wouldn't let go, even making up her own stories and 'facts' to back her constantly shifting moods. And she was far more immature than her age. She was fifteen back then but often acted so dramatic, more like a ten-year-old. Except when it came to men, and then she was suggestively inappropriate for her age. It was disturbing to watch."

"You said her father ended up hiring her tutors."

"She was developmentally delayed as far as education went. Read on a third-grade level and couldn't handle even basic math. Until she went off to university, Lindsay said she still read to Holly, then she switched to audiobooks. Raymond told Lindsay that he pulled Holly out of private school to get her more qualified teachers, but Lindsay always figured Holly had been kicked out. She figured Holly was having meltdowns there like she did at home and they were over it."

I nodded. "Did Lindsay ever mention Holly being violent?"

His eyes widened. "You don't think...wow. Lindsay told me from the beginning that when Holly didn't get her way, she could snap. I figured she meant crying and screaming, but then Jared called late one night when I was working, completely frantic. Apparently, Holly had insisted on going to see a new litter of kittens in the barn and their father had refused. My understanding is that he didn't trust her around his prize horses, so the barn was off-limits to her. She responded by locking her bedroom door, setting the room on fire, and climbing out her window, while the rest of them scrambled to put out the fire, panicked that she was still inside. Lindsay found her in the barn, playing with the kittens like she'd done absolutely nothing wrong."

"Good Lord."

He shook his head. "I was dumbfounded when Lindsay told me about it. I've never known anyone like that. General assholes and bitter people, sure, but that's something well beyond a personality flaw."

I nodded and made some notes. Nothing Ryan had said had necessarily surprised me, and more importantly, it had put Holly firmly on the potential suspect list. Everything he'd said pointed to a huge mental instability. And the fact that she appeared to be untreated and living in that environment had certainly made her worse.

"I understand that Holly had a crush on you. Was that a problem?"

"Oh yeah! To be honest, I wanted to leave Magnolia Pass because of Holly probably even more than Raymond."

I shook my head. "So the main reason you wanted to leave was also the main reason Lindsay wanted to stay. I can see why you two were at an impasse. What did Holly do to make you feel that way—aside from setting fires when she didn't get her way?"

"She followed me around like a puppy. Always coming over to visit on my days off when she knew Lindsay wouldn't be there. I got rid of her as quickly as I could, and never allowed her in the house, but she kept coming back."

"Smart not to be alone with her."

"No way was I setting myself up for that kind of trouble.

Holly had a history of telling lies about people who wouldn't cater to her. She got a few people at the estate fired before her father realized how manipulative she was. But Raymond just paid them off, and it all got swept under the giant rug that they hid all Beech discretions under."

"Did Lindsay ever talk to Holly about her fixation on you?"

"Sort of. I mean, she didn't want to come right out and tell her to stop stalking me. Holly had never admitted to the crush, and Lindsay didn't want to embarrass her and risk setting her off. But she did tell her not to bother me on my days off because I needed to catch up on my sleep. And she made it clear that she was only to visit when Lindsay was home."

"Did Holly take that advice?"

"Of course not, so I stopped answering the door. I figured I could just play it off as I was sleeping and didn't hear her ring the bell. I always had the TV running and the blinds drawn so she wouldn't have known I was lying. I even deleted my social media accounts because she stalked me there. If I posted or replied to someone during the day, then she knew I was awake."

He shook his head, frowning.

"What?" I asked.

"I know it sounds stupid coming from a big guy like me, but Holly kind of creeped me out the way she was always lurking, and not just online. If I went to the store, she appeared. Same with the post office, the butcher, the library. I know she was just a kid, but she made me uncomfortable. I don't like admitting it, but you asked me for the truth, and that's it. I know Lindsay wanted to help Holly, but to be honest, I would have loved to have cleared out of Louisiana altogether and never had any dealings with her family again."

I nodded. "She was stalking you. That would creep me out

as well, especially after that curtain-burning incident. Did she know you were living at the motel?"

"No way. Lindsay wouldn't have said anything about our split. She didn't tell her family anything about our relationship, but she definitely avoided talking to Holly about me."

"But they probably suspected. Magnolia Pass is small and gossipy. Your neighbors would have noticed your vehicle hadn't been there in a while, and Holly would have noticed your absence given that she was stalking you."

"You're probably right. But they wouldn't have known for sure. Not from Lindsay, anyway, and my vehicle was still there some. I still had a key and all my stuff was there. Plus, I kept coming back to talk to Lindsay, trying to figure out how to fix things."

"Your neighbor heard arguing a couple nights before Lindsay was killed."

He nodded. "It was me. I was still trying to convince her to move."

He frowned again, and his brow scrunched as though he was trying to remember something.

"What are you thinking?" I prompted.

"Nothing, really. I mean nothing concrete. It's just that a couple times at the motel, I got that same feeling I did when Holly was following me around town."

"If she was truly obsessed and stalking you, changing location wouldn't have altered her fixation. It's possible she followed you to the motel. Did she have a car?"

"She didn't even have a license. But the estate has several vehicles for staff and all the keys are kept in the main house. Once, when Raymond and Jared were out of town for business, Lindsay took off work early to go check on Holly and caught one of the security guards teaching her how to drive. Lindsay figured she'd paid him to do it or threatened him with his job."

I nodded, wondering what else Holly had paid the guards to do for her. Or how much Raymond and Jared had paid them to forget.

"What about Jared? Did Lindsay have problems with him?"

"Issues between Jared and Lindsay were all one-sided, and that side was Jared's. He wanted to be his father's shining light, but all those accolades went to Lindsay. Jared just wasn't smart like Lindsay, and he was never going to have half of her skills. Raymond knew it and he constantly hounded and pushed for Lindsay to come to the firm so she could be groomed for the top spot. The only time Raymond acknowledged Jared existed was when he was berating him for not being as good as his sister."

"That's a great way to create a grudge between siblings."

"Raymond was one of the worst human beings I've ever met, and I've been in prison for ten years. There are guys in here who are hard and dangerous and some that probably weren't born with a conscience, but Raymond seemed to go out of his way to make people miserable. He liked everyone to feel incompetent."

"Because then they'd have no choice but to relinquish control to him."

"Exactly."

"So Jared had a lot of reasons to want Lindsay out of the way."

"I'm sure he played the grieving brother, but I don't think for a minute he's sorry Lindsay is gone. But with that said, I can't imagine him killing her. He's got the backbone of a squid. And Lindsay could have taken him in a fight, hands down."

"According to the medical report, it's likely the first stab was through the back of her neck. I think that would have severely limited her ability to counter."

He swallowed, and I saw his eyes cloud with tears. "I shouldn't have moved out. If I'd been there—"

"You still would have been working that night, so the killer could have just done it earlier or a different night or during the day when you were away. You can't blame yourself for this. When someone wants another person dead, they'll figure out a way to do it, regardless of perceived obstacles."

"But us being separated like that made me look guilty."

"Not in and of itself. Most domestic murders are committed by the partner, so you would have had the spotlight on you anyway, especially with Raymond Beech owning the local cops."

He blew out a breath. "I really never had a chance, did I?"

"No. But I'm going to do everything I can to change that. Let's shift gears for a minute—I talked with Mandy Reynolds. She said that Lindsay was having some trouble at her job."

"That's a polite way of describing it. Her boss was hitting on her—and he'd moved past suggestive and into threatening."

I blinked. That was new and something no one had ever mentioned. "Brett Spalding was harassing Lindsay?"

He nodded. "She didn't want to tell me at first, but I knew something was bothering her. She finally said she was getting unwanted attention from her boss. A couple weeks after that I went to a business party with her—one of those fancy ones with ice sculptures and small food. He was too touchy-feely for my taste. Always pulling her away to 'make introductions,' and always with his hand on her back, like she was a prized possession."

I shook my head. "It seemed that everyone wanted to own Lindsay."

"Not me," he said sadly. "I just wanted to get away from all the bad stuff and for us to live our lives. I never asked her to be anyone other than who she was. And she was a great person—

beautiful, kind, smart. I know a lot of people say they're going to change the world, but I honestly think if she'd been given a chance, Lindsay could have."

"Did she tell you what the harassment involved exactly?"

"Not down to specific words. She probably knew I'd track him down and punch him, but the gist of it was he wanted certain favors and if she wanted to be promoted, she'd get on board."

I blew out a breath. "Mandy didn't say anything about that, and I'm certain she would have if she'd known. I wonder why Lindsay didn't tell her?"

He shrugged. "Lindsay was embarrassed by the whole thing. I know we're always telling women they shouldn't be. That it's not their fault...but you know how it is. She didn't think she'd caused it, but she thought she should be the one to fix it."

"I suppose, but it seems like the kind of thing you'd tell your best friend, especially since they'd known each other all their lives."

"My guess is Lindsay didn't want to pile any more onto Mandy than she already had on her plate. She's not a happy person. Her mother was a housemaid on the Beech estate. Did she tell you that?"

"No."

"That's how she and Lindsay became friends, much to the dismay of Lindsay's parents. They never thought Mandy was good enough, and if they were being honest, I think the Perkinses blamed Lindsay for Mandy hooking up with their son. That's stupid, of course. It's not like Magnolia Pass is New York City. Sebastian knew who Mandy was whether or not she was hanging out with Lindsay."

"It seems the founding families aren't big on personal responsibility."

"Ha! It's practically nonexistent. But Mandy messed up marrying Sebastian. She's a talented artist, but her parents couldn't afford school and there's really nothing else she was good at. Lindsay tried to talk her out of marrying him, but I think she saw a way out of her mother's life."

"It seemed that everyone at the estate is afraid of him, including his wife."

"I think he tunes her up. Sometimes she'd be wearing long sleeves when it was ninety-five degrees out and a hundred percent humidity. Meanwhile, everyone else would be walking around in the least amount of clothes they could get by with legally."

I nodded. That tallied with my thoughts. "The trouble Mandy was referring to was a mistake on a client's account. Mandy said it cost the client a lot of money and he ended up moving his money to Raymond's firm. The suggestion was made that Lindsay had intentionally screwed up the account to get her father the business."

Ryan shook his head. "No way! Lindsay was too ethical to do anything of the sort, and why would she send business to her father when she had no intention of ever working for him?"

"So nothing deliberate—just a mistake?"

"I don't believe that either. Lindsay could have never made a mistake that big. She'd never seen a number she didn't remember, and she was a magician with investing. I'd been giving her my tip money—probably five hundred or so a week —for a couple months. She turned that two thousand into twelve thousand in the same amount of time. I hate to say I don't believe Mandy, but maybe she's confused. Lindsay never told me anything about it, and if she told me her boss was hitting on her, I don't know why she wouldn't tell me that."

"I think it happened right before her death, so you'd probably already moved out. Brett Spalding confirmed the error and that it lost them a client to Raymond. I'm going to verify with the client, of course, but at this point, I have to assume it really happened."

He looked worried and frustrated. "If that's what got her killed... I didn't even know. Because I wasn't there."

"We've been through this already. You couldn't have prevented what happened. The only thing that would have changed was timing."

"Maybe. But if Lindsay had made a mistake and really cost them a big client, then why didn't Brett fire her?"

"He said because you didn't fire your best employees without investigating first. But maybe it was because he was hitting on her. He might have thought keeping her on would gain him favor."

"That sounds about right," he said, his disgust apparent. "All those money-obsessed guys are the same. But I still find it hard to believe Lindsay made a mistake so big she was killed for it."

I nodded. "Who had access to your house?"

"Only me and Lindsay."

"But you rented it, right? So the landlord had keys, and maybe the previous renters if he didn't change the locks. There was no sign of forced entry. If we discount a professional thief breaking in—and given that nothing was stolen, I think that's a safe bet—we're left with two options: someone had a key or Lindsay let them inside."

"She would have let anyone we've discussed inside."

"Even in the middle of the night?"

"If she thought what they wanted was important enough, sure. It would have never occurred to her that someone she knew was going to kill her."

"I get it."

He sighed. "You're not going to be able to solve this, are you? No one believed me back then, and it's been too long. Even if someone knew something, why would they stick their neck out now? They'd just be in trouble for not telling what they knew back then."

"I know it seems hopeless, but I'm not going to give up. I don't want you to, either. The guard is signaling, so I have to go, but keep thinking about everything. If you can think of anything else, call me as soon as you have privileges."

"And Ben?"

"I'll call Alexander as soon as I leave. He'll get everything in motion."

As I headed for the impatient guard, I glanced back. Ryan was staring down at the table, the picture of Ben in his hand. Even from across the room, I could see the tears glistening in his eyes. I prayed that I could come up with something quickly.

There were two lives on the line.

CHAPTER SIXTEEN

AS PROMISED, I CALLED ALEXANDER AND GAVE HIM THE ALL clear for going after the warden, guns blazing. He told me he'd already worked out a plan and would launch it that day. I reminded him that it was a holiday weekend, especially in the Bible Belt, and he laughed and said that just meant God was on our side. I hoped he was right, because we desperately needed something to go our way.

As soon as I disconnected with Alexander, I started filling Ida Belle and Gertie in on what Ryan had told me. Like me, they were confused over the harassment claim.

"I assume the mistake with the client happened after Ryan moved out," I said, giving them my take. "Which would make sense as Brett said she died before they investigated."

"I suppose," Gertie said. "But why didn't she tell Mandy about the harassment? That seems like the sort of thing you'd tell your girlfriend but not your boyfriend, even though I know that's not smart."

"I know," I agreed. "It's all reversed. She told her boyfriend about the harassment and her girlfriend about the mistake. I'm going to leave a message for the client and get the timing of that 'mistake' confirmed. I should have asked Brett, but I'm not sure I would trust his answer at this point or that of his good buddy Devin."

Ida Belle nodded. "Since Brett was ultimately responsible for the choices Lindsay made on accounts, I imagine he got quite the dressing down from his folks over losing a big client, especially to his protégé's father."

"Assuming they even knew about it," I said. "It doesn't sound like they were very present in Brett's life."

Gertie sighed. "Does anyone else feel like this is all one big giant stinking mess, swirling around in a pot?"

"Oh yeah," I said. "I didn't like the case from the beginning, but the weirdness that is Magnolia Pass, and the creepy Holly, combined with the bizarre coincidence of the victim having worked for the client's husband, is all too much for me. Something is clearly rotten—likely more than one something."

Ida Belle nodded. "I just hope we can untangle this mess and save that boy and get Ryan out of prison."

My cell phone signaled an incoming call, and I saw Detective Casey's number come up.

"I swear, we're not in NOLA," I said when I answered.

Casey chuckled. "I know. My radio hasn't issued a single request for backup on a bizarre situation."

"Then you must have it turned off or you've left town," Gertie said.

"Got me," Casey said. "This is supposed to be my day off, but I've been doing some poking around into the Beech murder, and I came up against an interesting and immovable problem."

"What's that?"

"The FBI."

I groaned. "Don't tell me the Beeches are under investigation."

"No. But Spalding Financial is. And before I say another word, this goes no further than the four of us. Well, and the captain."

"Our lips are sealed," Gertie said. "Well, sort of. I'm having some grapes, but you know what I mean."

"I couldn't get much out of them," Casey said. "FBI... You know how it is getting information out of the Feds."

"I have some experience."

"Well, apparently, I set off the alarms when I pulled the old case files and then did a few background checks on the major players. So I got the knock on my front door about an hour ago and two constipated guys in bad suits were standing there, trying to scare me with their reflective sunglass stare."

"Definitely the FBI," I agreed.

"They showed me ID, escorted me into my own living room, and directed me to stand down on my investigation before I compromise years of work. I told them I had an innocent man doing life for a murder he didn't commit, and they said that was unfortunate, but it didn't change the situation. They'd already spoken to my captain, and I was to cease all inquiries into Lindsay Beech's murder until they'd made arrests."

"Did they bother to say how long that would be?" I asked.

"Given that this investigation stretches back over a decade, who the hell knows?"

I sighed. "And I was just about to ask you to run down some information for me."

"What do you need? I have ways around some things."

I told her about my conversation with Ryan and the accusation of harassment. "Lindsay didn't tell her best friend, which Ryan says is probably because of her precarious marital situation and resulting mental state, but I thought since she was being harassed—"

"You figured it wasn't the first time Brett's pulled that crap on a young, attractive, female employee."

"Exactly. There's one woman on the company website who was working for the firm back then, but since she's toughed it out this long, I don't figure she's going to tattle on the boss now. I was hoping you could check employment records and find me someone who worked for the firm back then. Someone who fit the profile for harassment and might be willing to talk turkey now. But I don't want you getting into any trouble. If you start checking employment records for Spalding Financial, that will be a problem."

"True, but my daughter just happens to be doing an internship right now down at the Workforce Commission. They've got her converting old system data over to their new software. She could tell you about every person employed in NOLA for the last thirty years."

"Finally! A coincidence that works for me."

Casey snorted. "Yeah, I feel the same. There's too many moving parts crossing each other here. And they all stink to high heaven."

"The FBI didn't give you any indication of what they're shadowing the firm for? Or who's involved?"

"No. You know how they are, but the two guys I talked to looked like they spent more time with a calculator than in the gym. Given the firm's business, it's definitely financial. My guess, given the wide scope of their holdings, is money laundering."

"Kelsey told me that Brett's parents always wanted him to take over so they could travel. But maybe traveling isn't the only reason. I think they have a handful of clients they still personally handle."

"Staying out of the country is a good way to avoid arrest,

for sure, but it's a dick move to leave their kid holding the bag. You think his wife has any idea?"

"No way. If Kelsey knew, she'd have left already. She'd never expose her son to that. I doubt she would have ended up married to Brett at all if she hadn't gotten pregnant. His money has never seemed to motivate her."

"Good. The less invested she is with him, the better, because at some point, the lid is going to blow on that FBI thing, and the further away from the fallout she is, the better. I'll get with my daughter and see what she can find out on Monday. If you come up with anything else I can do, let me know."

"Isn't your captain going to call you off because of the FBI?"

"Depends on how punchy he's feeling. He hates people telling him what to do. If his wife's been nagging him, he might blow them off and tell me to keep digging but be quiet about it."

"He's more afraid of his wife than the FBI?"

She snorted. "Have you met his wife?"

"What now?" Ida Belle said when I'd disconnected.

"I think we need to talk to Kelsey first. She's going to be waiting to hear about our conversation with Ryan, and we should relay that in person. I'll text her now and see where she wants to meet. But first, head to Sinful so we can load up on weapons again. I feel naked."

"I hear that!" Gertie said.

We were almost to New Orleans when Carter called.

"We've got a problem," he said when I answered. "Holly Beech is here."

"Where?"

"At the sheriff's department in the interview room. Apparently, she came in insisting that she talk to me, claiming she wants to reopen her sister's murder investigation. I went in and explained to her that I have no jurisdiction, but she's not listening. And she's got the whole station uncomfortable. She came in dressed like she's going to a club, and she keeps leaning over the interview table. I swear she's trying to get me to look down her shirt. She also brought me gifts—a ridiculously expensive bottle of whiskey and two crystal tumblers."

"Oh Lord! She must have looked me up after we talked and made her way over to you. She's got a history of somewhat obsessive behavior with men."

"Somewhat? That whiskey cost more than my new hunting rifle. How do I get rid of her?"

"I don't know. The last guy only managed to when he went to prison for a murder he didn't commit."

Carter cursed and I didn't blame him. Holly Beech fixating on him was a problem we definitely did not need.

"Let me call you back," I said and disconnected. Then I called Jared Beech.

I didn't expect him to answer but I suspected either curiosity or a need to know what I was looking into next won out, and he issued a short, clipped greeting.

"We have a problem," I said, "and by that I mean *you* have a problem that better not become a problem for me and mine."

"What on earth are you talking about, and how dare you speak to me like you have authority?"

"Holly has apparently done her research on me, and she's in Sinful right now, chatting up my boyfriend—the sheriff— wearing a dress suited for clubbing, and attempting to ply him with expensive alcohol that I can only assume came from your personal collection. Your family tries hard to hide Holly's oddness, but other people know and have no trouble talking about it. I want you to get her out of Sinful and make it your full-time job to ensure that she doesn't fixate on another woman's man again. Trust me, if your sister comes after me like I suspect she has others, it won't end well for her."

There was stunned silence on the other end of the phone, then he simply disconnected.

"Do you think he'll do it?" Ida Belle asked.

"He better."

I sent Carter a text.

I'm going to call in an emergency to dispatch. Sorry about this.

As soon as I sent the message, I called Gavin, the young man who worked day dispatch. "This is Whiskey. I done pulled a body out of the bayou and need the sheriff over at the Swamp Bar. No one but the sheriff will do. Do you understand?"

"Fortune?" His voice was low and confused.

"No one but the sheriff. Got it?"

"Oh!" he whispered. "This is a rescue call. Got it!"

He disconnected and we all sat in silence, waiting for my phone to ring. It took less than a minute.

"What the hell?" Carter said when I answered, and I could hear the agitation in his voice.

"Trust me, I'm not any happier about it than you are."

"Am I understanding you correctly? You think that girl killed her sister because she wanted her boyfriend?"

"I don't know, but if she did, and she attempts that method of obtaining what she wants again, it won't end the same. I've contacted her brother and suggested exactly that to him."

"And he said?"

"Not a single word. But what he chooses to do will prove very interesting either way."

"This is a dangerous game you're playing."

"Would you prefer to be fending off the advances of a woman-child-potential-murderess instead?"

"Hard pass on that one. I'm headed out in the boat. At least she won't be able to track me down."

"You're going to have to pay Myrtle some overtime hours. I'm going to call her in to see what happens with Holly if Jared shows up."

"Whatever. I don't care. Where are you?"

"On my way to see Kelsey and tell her about my visit with Ryan. I'll fill you in tonight. But he's a go for the surgery."

"That's good. Okay, I'm pushing off the dock. Tell Myrtle if she needs to look legit, there's a stack of old files in a box in the interview room that need cataloging."

As soon as I disconnected with Carter, I called Myrtle and gave her a brief set of instructions with zero explanation. As expected, she simply said, "On it," and hung up. It was really nice to have people on your team who didn't need reasons before launching into action.

"I'm exhausted just listening to all of that," Gertie said when I dropped my phone in my lap. "No wonder you ran complicated missions at the CIA. You thought up all those angles in a matter of minutes and not only came up with a plan but got everyone moving on it with a couple phone calls and texts."

Ida Belle nodded. "It is rather impressive to watch—like when we had that showdown with Herpes at Nora's Mardi Gras party. But I wish the situation wasn't so close to home."

"Me too," I said. "The last thing Carter needs right now is something else to worry about."

"And the last thing you need is another reason to worry about Carter," Gertie said. "We know you're trying to hide it, but the strain shows. At least to the two of us."

I sighed. I thought I'd been doing a better job, but I should have known that Ida Belle and Gertie would see right through my attempts. I might have been a master at undercover work at the CIA, but pretending to feel differently with people who really knew you was a lot harder than faking with strangers.

"It's fine, guys," I said.

They both gave me hard looks.

"What do you want me to say?" I asked. "That I'm worried? I am. Carter is better than he was a few weeks ago, but he's still lost inside his mind a lot of the time. And I don't think it's about the case because we all know Alexander will raise heaven and earth to take down Kitts, although it sounds like Kitts has already done a pretty good job of taking down himself."

"You think Carter's dwelling on his service?" Ida Belle asked.

I nodded. "I've tried to suggest that once a mission is complete, you have to lock it away in a box and never open it again. You do your job, and our jobs were action based on orders, not fact-gathering and decision-making."

"He hates that he was nothing more than a weapon at one man's disposal, and now that man's entire character is under question," Ida Belle said.

I shrugged. "But that's what we were. You can tell yourself that you're an instrument for good and that what you're doing protects this country and saves the lives of citizens, and all of that is true, but at the end of the day, you're still the one who pulled the trigger."

"But *you* pulled the trigger," Gertie said. "I've never seen you struggle like this."

"But I was absolutely certain that the people I targeted were bad guys. Everyone knew it. And I was a specialist. It was only me or me and Harrison, and our target was one man. The only collateral damage were guards, and they were aligned with the criminals and had made that choice. Wives, sisters, children, servants—those in their proximity that might not have the right information or choices—weren't injured or killed during our missions because we were ghosts. Hit the target and disappear. We were never even there. There was no unit to command, no tanks or airplanes announcing our arrival. Assassinations are not war. My and Carter's jobs had as many differences as they did similarities."

They were both silent for a while, but I knew they got it. They'd both been military spies during Vietnam, and I was certain had seen their share of bad situations erupting from otherwise good intentions. The amount of chaos that deliberately poor decisions could make was astronomical, especially during war.

"Is there anything we can do?" Gertie finally asked.

I shook my head. "I don't know what I can do, except be there if he ever wants to talk. I've made it clear that I can discuss anything. I've also given him contact information for the best therapists at the CIA. Both of them would talk to him for free for as long as he needs as a favor to me. These are people I've trusted with my own life, so Carter is assured of their propriety."

"If he's not talking to you," Ida Belle said, "then I don't know who else he'd confide in. You're uniquely positioned to understand his situation, and you love him. We can only pray that he eventually comes to terms with all of this and is able to lock it away, like you do, and move on with the rest of his life."

CHAPTER SEVENTEEN

MYRTLE CALLED AS WE WERE EXITING THE INTERSTATE TO enter NOLA, and I quickly put her on speaker.

"Good Lord, girl!" she said as soon as I answered. "Next time warn me before you send me into the mouth of madness."

"I take it you met our problem."

"Met her, got roped into a long conversation with her, and now I need a bottle of whiskey and therapy to clear everything out. I'm not sure what's going on, so I don't know where to start."

"Just start at the beginning. Anything might be important at this point. We're in gathering stage."

"Okay, so I arrived at the sheriff's department and Gavin looked like someone had wound him up tighter than Celia's panties when she catches sight of Gertie's bird. I told him Carter had asked me to come in and handle some old files if I had the time and I was going to use the extra cash for a new fishing rod."

"Good call." No one questioned working overtime when things like a new fishing rod were at the end of the rainbow.

"Then he tells me that Deputy Breaux has locked himself

in the bathroom and the lock broke, so I won't be able to use the facilities."

"It's a sliding dead bolt—on the inside of the door."

"Apparently, Gavin doesn't remember that. Or he doesn't lock the door when he's using the facilities. I thought it was strange, but I kept going. When I stepped into the interview room, I saw this young lady lounging in one of his visitor chairs. One look at her told me she was the reason you'd asked me to head down there and get a handle on things.

"So I do the polite greeting and ask if I can help her with anything," Myrtle continued. "She says she's waiting on Carter to return, and I ask if there's anyone else who can help her because he's on a call and will be a while. That cheeky thing says, and I quote, 'No one else is as cute as him.'"

I groaned. It was worse than I'd even imagined.

"That was exactly my reaction," Myrtle said, "and then I understood why Deputy Breaux had suddenly forgotten how to use a dead bolt. So I agreed that Carter was an attractive man but he was also a very attached one. So she says, she didn't see a wedding band and until he Beyoncé'd somebody, he was available."

"Oh, Lord!" Gertie said. "Don't tell Carter that or he'll be ring shopping this afternoon."

"I'm not one to rush people and their romantic entanglements," Myrtle said, "but if it got rid of that girl, I might consider it. Maybe you could fake a wedding."

"In Sinful?" I asked. "I could more easily fake my death. Did you at least manage to get her out of the sheriff's department?"

"Yes and no. I kept trying to convince her that Carter would be at a crime scene most of the day and that unless she had information about that crime, he wouldn't have time to speak to her, so she should just go home. She said she took an

Uber here and she'd wait for Carter so he could give her a ride home. That way, they could get to know each other better."

"Good God," Ida Belle said.

"I also suggested that she rethink her pursuit as I had known Carter all my life and was absolutely certain he cared for no one but his current girlfriend and never would. She just said 'we'll see.' I was just about to march her out of there like the petulant child she was when her brother showed up. I assumed you wanted me to see what I could overhear, so I excused myself and left them in the interview room and went next door and turned on the speakers."

"I owe you a fifth of Crown," I said.

"And a box of Ally's cookies. That girl was a *lot* of work. Anyway, her brother asked her what the heck she was doing, and she tried to sound all 'I'm just seeing about the investigation' but he wasn't buying it. He said what everyone else has said which is the sheriff has no jurisdiction over that case. Then he started talking low and I couldn't make out exactly what he said but it was something like 'if you do this again' and then I definitely heard 'lock you up.'"

"Interesting. Did she leave after that threat?"

"Oh yeah. She must have bolted from the room because by the time I peeked out, she was barreling out the front door, her brother hot on her heels. I saw him drive off in a white BMW, and she was sitting in the passenger seat, pouting like a grade-schooler. What the heck is wrong with her?"

"I'm not sure exactly, but I appreciate you getting that information."

"Mark my words, this is not the first time she's caused trouble. Her brother didn't look remotely surprised when he stomped in there. Just angry and a tiny bit frightened. Does she stalk men? Is that what's up?"

"She definitely has a history of stalking a man she was

attracted to. I'm trying to figure out if she killed the man's girlfriend."

"Heaven help! You're kidding me?"

"I wish I was, especially since the girlfriend was her sister."

"Fortune, you have *got* to keep her away from Carter."

"That's why I called her brother and told him what she was doing. I wanted to see if he'd ignore it or bolt over there to get her out of sight. Thanks again, Myrtle."

Ida Belle shook her head as I disconnected. "This is much worse than we thought, but now I understand your play."

I nodded. "And Jared confirmed what I suspected—that he was well aware of Holly's obsessions with men and he's afraid of what she might do."

"You think Jared was threatening to put her in a mental institution?"

"Sure sounded like it," I said. "And the fact that she bolted right after he mentioned it makes me think she's probably been there before."

"Wouldn't people know?" Gertie asked. "You can't just disappear from a prominent family without people wondering where you've gotten off to."

"She had private tutors, remember? And I imagine the staff all know better than to talk, except among themselves."

Ida Belle nodded. "And they're wealthy. They could have told the staff she was studying abroad or visiting family or feeding pigeons in Paris. They would have known better but they wouldn't have proof, and even if they did, what would it get them?"

Gertie frowned. "It's looking more and more like she did it, isn't it?"

I shook my head. "I don't know. But it *would* explain why her father didn't push for an investigation."

"And why Jared isn't perturbed by your declaration of

Ryan's innocence. He either firmly believes you're wrong and Kelsey is lying, or he already knows who the real killer is."

I nodded. I agreed with everything she'd said. I just wished I knew which one it was.

———

KELSEY MUST HAVE BEEN STARING OUT THE WINDOW OF HER house when we pulled up because she had the front door open before we ever exited the SUV. The house was in the Garden District, but instead of the mansion I expected, the house was small and neat. She stepped out as we walked up, and her anxiety was so apparent I could almost feel it rolling off her.

"Beautiful house," Gertie said. "Your roses are coming in nicely."

She nodded. "Thanks. Brett picked it out, of course."

"That surprises me," I said. "I figured he'd go for a penthouse or one of the huge mansions in the neighborhood."

Kelsey shook her head. "That's one of the few things we agreed on. Neither of us is flashy—I always joke that Devin has enough flash for all three of us, but it's true. One of the reasons I didn't catch on to Brett being from a wealthy family is that he didn't look the part. He dressed like any other normal college student and drove a late-model Toyota. Neither one of us has ever owned a luxury vehicle. Even Devin was basic back then, but the older he gets, the more he indulges. Whatever makes you happy, right?"

I nodded as we walked inside. "Is Brett still living here now?"

The home was beautiful but like most older homes, had small rooms with lots of division.

"It seems like a small amount of square footage given the two of you aren't getting along," I explained.

She sighed. "Brett moved into an apartment in the French Quarter yesterday. Things were just too weird between us. I'm trying to figure out a way to explain it to Ben."

"Is he home?"

"No. Brett took him to a baseball game—Ben's team—or the team Ben used to play on when he could. He still likes to go to the games and cheer them on."

We followed her inside and back to the kitchen. "I just made tea and I can put on a pot of coffee."

"I'll find everything to serve the tea," Gertie said. "You sit before you fall over. When is the last time you slept?"

She plopped into a chair at the breakfast table and ran a hand through her hair. "I'm not sure. This is Saturday, right?"

I sat down in front of the exhausted woman and looked her straight in the eye. "Let me start with saying that Ryan is absolutely in for everything—the DNA test, the kidney—all of it."

Her entire body slumped with relief, and she started to cry. "I've been so afraid. All this time I knew it was possible that Ryan was Ben's biological father, but I deliberately closed my mind to it. If I had faced my own issues sooner and tried to find Ryan, then maybe he would never have gone to prison, much less had ten years of his life wasted there."

"You can't think like that," Gertie said as she placed the glasses of iced tea on the table. "This is not your fault. Someone deliberately framed that poor boy, and it couldn't have had anything to do with you because you didn't even know him before that night."

She sniffed and nodded. "I know, but I can't stop wondering how differently things might have turned out if I'd just gone looking sooner."

"I think any of us would think that way," I said. "But as soon as you knew, you moved to do something about it. When you ran into issues with the cops, you hired me. You're doing everything you can."

"But I have an ulterior motive."

"So you're saying that if Ben wasn't sick, and you'd decided for other reasons to do a DNA test and attempt to hunt Ryan down, you wouldn't have pushed the issue of his innocence?"

"Of course I would have!" She gave me a small smile. "I guess that makes your point, doesn't it?"

"Ryan told me that he thought you were a good person. That even though he was still in love with Lindsay when the two of you spent the night together, that he'd always remembered you, and not just because of Lindsay's murder. He said he liked you. I like you too. And I'm a pretty good judge of character. From where I'm sitting, the only mistake I can see that you've made was marrying Brett. But we don't all make the best decisions when we're young, and you were pregnant and hadn't established a career yet. All those things weigh in."

"I knew it was a mistake...marrying him. I knew it when I said yes to his proposal. And on my wedding day, I remember standing at the back of the church, harnessing every ounce of resolve that I had to keep from running. I keep asking myself why I didn't. Or why I stayed."

"And what did you decide?" Gertie asked.

She shrugged. "The easy answer is Ben, of course, but that's not all of it. There's a part of me that loved Brett, probably left over from before I really knew him. And he *is* a great father. I worried about that, given that his parents seem so uninvolved and distant—not just in physical form but emotionally—but I've never once questioned his love for Ben."

"I could see the toll this is taking on him when we spoke," I said. "But you don't have to be his wife in order for Ben to be his son."

"Yeah. I wish I'd come to that conclusion sooner. But here

we are, and my marriage is the least of my worries. What happens next?"

"I've already spoken to my attorney friend, and he's going to represent Ryan. He's got a plan in place for dealing with the warden. The first thing we've got to do is establish that Ryan is the father. He sent me the information for a testing center that he'll use. I'll send that to you, and you just need to get Ben in for a quick mouth swab. Nothing invasive. That way, he's already on file when we get Ryan's sample."

"What about Ryan? Is there anything I can do for him?"

"You've already done it—you hired me. But I have some questions for you. There's a lot of overlap between your life and Ryan's. I don't like coincidences, especially when they're all revolving around a murder."

"I'll tell you anything I know. Anything to help Ryan."

"Did Brett ever mention one of his employees making a mistake that cost him a client?"

"No. But he almost never talked about work with me. He knew I wasn't interested, and I assumed there was confidentiality stuff as well."

"And you never attended work functions—parties and the like?"

"I did way back in the beginning of our relationship but after we married and had Ben, I had the perfect excuse to get out of them. That wasn't me—the pretty, complacent wife of the boss. And I'm an introvert. I know kitchens have employees and they're loud, but those are my people, you know? The place I fit. The whole nail, hair, expensive dress you only wear once thing wasn't me."

I nodded. I'd figured that was what she'd say.

"Is this about Lindsay? Was she the one who cost the firm a client?"

"Yes. At least that's the story I've gotten, but I'm going to speak to the client and make sure I've been given the correct information."

Kelsey sucked in a breath. "You don't think—no, Brett is a lot of things, but he's not a killer. Besides, it's just one client. I'm sure others have made mistakes before."

"Yes, but I've been told this one client transferred over a hundred million to Lindsay's father's firm. Millions of lost fees for Brett, plus the damage to Spalding's reputation. That's a pretty big motive, especially if he believed she'd done it intentionally."

Kelsey's eyes widened. "You think she was using her job to poach clients for her father?"

"I don't think so, but that doesn't mean Brett didn't feel that way. Did you ever talk to any of the other employees back when you used to attend the events?"

"Briefly, probably, but I couldn't tell you a single name or conversation. Well, except Devin, of course, but he and Brett were friends since high school, so I've known him for years."

"I didn't realize they'd known each other that long."

She nodded. "They both went to St. Marks. Devin's parents moved to Sicily after he graduated. They owned wineries over there. Devin attended Oxford, but he and Brett always stayed in touch. After graduation, Devin moved back here and went to work for the Spaldings."

"But his parents are still in Sicily?" I asked.

"Yes. He's got an aunt who lives here—a hospital nurse. I think she's the only family that Devin has here anymore."

"Why wouldn't he stay over there with his family?"

"It's complicated, I think. They're not close. According to Brett, Devin's parents were even worse than his own. I think Devin was mostly raised by the household staff—I don't think Brett's ever even met them. They were never at home. And since Brett and Devin were both only children, I think their childhoods were pretty lonely."

"So they bonded over similar childhoods and lousy parents. That's unfortunate, but it makes sense."

She nodded. "Ever since I've known him, Devin has been Brett's beck-and-call boy. I think they consider each other family more than they do their own blood."

"So aside from Devin, you never spoke to any of the other employees, beyond pleasantries, I mean?"

"No." She narrowed her eyes at me. "What aren't you telling me?"

"I'll explain, but you can't repeat this. It could cause major problems with the investigation, and if things he's told me are exposed to certain parties, Ryan might renege on his agreement to help Ben."

"Of course! I won't say a word."

"Ryan said Brett was harassing Lindsay—suggesting she exchange 'favors' for promotions."

Kelsey's eyes widened. "Seriously? Good God. Do you think it's true?"

"Unless I can figure out a reason why she or Ryan made it up, then I have to assume it is. But it's something I'm looking into. I just thought you might have heard whispers of similar issues with other female employees, given that you've been around so long."

She blew out a breath. "Now I wish I would have gone to those damned parties. If Brett had anything to do with her death, it would kill Ben. Jesus! That's a poor choice of words."

"I don't know anything for certain," I said. "It's always possible that she made it up to cover for costing them the client. Maybe she was afraid she'd be fired and needed an excuse because she didn't want to admit to Ryan that she'd made a mistake and lost a big client."

"Ryan didn't know about it?"

"No. But it's also possible the mistake happened after they were separated."

Kelsey shook her head. "I don't understand any of this. It's all such a tangled ball. I don't want to believe Brett is capable of killing someone or harassing employees, but I can't see any reason for her to lie about it either."

"What about Brett's parents? I know you said they were uninvolved parents, but what were they like?"

She pursed her lips, thinking about my question for a moment. "His parents are hard people to read. They wear poker faces 24/7, even the handful of times they were around Ben. Who's guarded around a child? I mean, I know they hear everything and can repeat it because they don't know any better, but they were that way when he was a baby. Like they couldn't let the mask slip, ever, or they might not be able to get it back in place. I never liked them. And not because they didn't like me."

"You thought they were fake?" Gertie asked.

"I'm certain they were," Kelsey said. "Not fake as in pretending to be rich or successful. That much was obviously true, but fake as in caring about anything other than themselves. They were cold to everyone, even Brett. I got the impression he was an accident. They certainly never seemed to care that they had a son or a grandson."

She sighed. "I think part of the reason I've stayed with him is because I felt sorry for him. With me and Ben, he had something he'd never had with his own parents. He was pretty much raised by nannies. And as soon as his parents were able, they dumped the business on him and left. They haven't been back here in years and they never ask Brett to visit."

"They didn't come back when they heard about Ben's condition?" I asked.

"No. Brett tried to cover for them and say they were having problems getting out of some obscure country they'd gone to, under the pretense of making economic investments into the local population, but I don't buy it. They were probably sitting in their villa sipping expensive wine. I'm pretty sure they avoid coming back to the States because then they'd be forced to visit us."

I nodded, but I wasn't quite sure I agreed with her completely. I had no doubt she was right about the Spaldings' blood running ice cold, but I didn't think they were avoiding the US *only* because they didn't care about anyone else. They were also avoiding the US because of the FBI.

CHAPTER EIGHTEEN

THERE WERE NO EASTER EVENTS SCHEDULED FOR SATURDAY night—thank goodness—so I told Carter I'd throw one of Gertie's casseroles in the oven and pull some of my stash of Ally's cookies out of the freezer. We intended to sit on the couch, eat, watch TV, and do absolutely, positively nothing. The last couple days had been a lot, and both of us were ready to chill.

We polished off half a casserole and way too many cookies and made it through a couple episodes of *Shetland* before my phone rang.

Carter sighed. "I really hoped neither of us would get a call. Then I prayed that if one of us did, it was me. Your late-night calls are always worse than mine."

It was only eleven, but I knew what he meant, and as I glanced at the display, I prepared myself for the worst. It was Gertie. And it was date night with Jeb.

"Fortune," Jeb said when I answered, sounding a bit breathless. "We have a situation here and need your help. Is Carter with you? I'm not sure you have the height and the muscle we need. Might take two of you."

"Is everyone dressed?" I asked.

"Of course. We're in the backyard."

"Okay. We'll be right over."

Carter sighed again. "Date night?"

I nodded. "At least they're dressed."

"But is it real clothes?"

"Hmmmm."

We put on shoes and headed over to Gertie's house, both of us silent and probably worried about what we might encounter. Carter was right that I'd missed the mark clarifying the whole clothes thing. Gertie's opinion of suitable was a bit different from mine and the law's. I just prayed that whatever they'd gotten themselves into in the backyard, they'd turned the porch light off first.

We headed for the gate when we got there, shining our flashlights to light the way. The porch light was indeed turned off and with the moon dipping behind storm clouds, there wasn't much natural light.

"Hello," I called out as we entered the backyard.

"Over here," I heard Jeb reply somewhere behind the house and off to the right.

We headed around, shining our lights around as we went, trying to pin down the emergency. When we reached the porch, the moon popped out from behind the clouds and the situation became completely clear.

Gertie dangled by one leg from what looked like a swing that was attached to the limb of a big oak tree. But the swing appeared to have shredded, and her foot was trapped in the fabric a good six feet off the ground. She was wearing a pink bikini with a fluffy rabbit's tail on the back, and I spotted pink bunny ears in the grass below her. Jeb stood in front of her, wearing a helpless look and not much else.

Good. God.

His thong appeared to be black leather but no way I was looking long enough to be certain. Carter made a noise that sounded a bit like a strangled cry and a frightened porpoise, and I knew he was one second away from leaving and calling the fire department to deal with whatever this was.

"Thank God," Jeb said when he saw us. "I tried climbing up on a chair, but I can't lift her enough to get her down."

"Why didn't you climb the tree and cut that strap to the swing?" Carter asked.

"I didn't want her to fall on her head," Jeb said. "She did her hair up special for me."

"Listen to the man," Gertie said, her voice weak, probably from all the dangling. "It took me two hours to get my hair this way."

"Why is the swing up so high?" I asked, still trying to figure out what the heck was going on.

"That's the longest cord it came with," Jeb said.

I threw my arms in the air. "What the heck are you doing on a swing in the middle of the night?"

"We were testing it out," Gertie said. "It's a sexy time swing. I heard someone mention one when we were in NOLA the other day, so I bought one online and paid for a rush delivery. But it didn't come with instructions. I think we got something wrong."

Carter and I froze, and I think he stopped breathing altogether as I realized that the chair hadn't broken when she sat in it. It was supposed to be in pieces, and that strap around her ankle was intentional if not utilized correctly.

"Good Lord Almighty," I said, breaking the silence. "This belongs in your bedroom."

Carter shook his head. "*This* belongs in a different parish. With other people. People I don't know."

"We know it belongs in the bedroom," Gertie said, "but we

figured we best test it outside before we hung it around break-ables. It's not like we're out here naked. And we weren't going to *use* it out here. Just figure out how to get *in* the darn thing."

Carter closed his eyes and looked skyward, probably asking why he'd been abandoned on a religious weekend.

I elbowed him and pointed to the chair, ready to get the entire thing over with. "Get up there and prepare to catch her when I cut this thing down. And not a word from either of you about me ruining your swing."

"Whatever you need to do," Jeb said. "Just get her down before she passes out again."

I shinnied up the tree and made my way out onto the limb, wondering how they'd managed to get the swing up here in the first place, but not about to ask any more questions.

"Ready?" I asked, and Carter wrapped his arms around Gertie's waist.

"As ready as I'm getting," he said.

"Here goes," I said and cut the cord.

Carter was strong enough to hold Gertie, even standing on a chair, but he wasn't a wizard. So when Gertie's weight hit him and the chair leg snapped, they both went flying back-ward. Right into Jeb.

I swung out of the tree and landed, surveying the damage, which was considerable.

Jeb was laid flat out underneath Carter, and Gertie was splayed out on top of him. It was probably Carter's worst nightmare.

"So help me God, if you take a picture of this, I will shoot you," he said.

It had crossed my mind, but since I would have been just as upset to be in his position, I figured I better leave it to a verbal rendition with no visual aids. I extended my arm and pulled Gertie up and Carter sprang off Jeb like Merlin when he was startled. Jeb lay on the grass groaning, and I wondered if we should call 911, but since Carter was already halfway across the yard, I figured I'd leave Gertie to make that call.

"Thanks!" Gertie said as I took off after Carter. "I'll let you know how it goes once we get it in the bedroom. You might want to get one yourself. You two are entirely too tense."

———

EASTER SUNDAY WAS SO MILD IN COMPARISON TO THE OTHER holiday events that I almost slept through church service. Unfortunately, it looked as though Pastor Don was sleeping through it too. His sermon was applicable, at least, but he seemed to doze off from time to time. I wondered exactly how much he'd drunk with Father Michael Friday night—and what —because he was still struggling for normal over thirty-six hours later.

There were no other Easter events after service. The afternoon was time for families to gather for meals and kids to hunt eggs. Then everyone turned on whatever sports were on that day and the adults took naps while the kids fought over candy. I didn't have the kids thing to contend with, but I had a great meal with Carter and Emmaline at Carter's house before he flipped on the television and promptly went to sleep. Emmaline intended to spend the afternoon painting, so I headed home to handle a couple of domestic chores and get in some exercise. I'd been eating like a pig all week and needed to work off some of the calories.

I tossed in a load of laundry, changed into running clothes, and set out. It was a beautiful, sunny day with a nice breeze, so I did a full circuit around Sinful, logging in five miles before heading for home. I slowed to a cooldown walk a block from my house and checked my phone. Ronald had sent me a text while I was running and asked if I could come over. I'd let him know I was out but would swing by on my way home. So here I was, headed up the walkway to his house. He'd also said the front door was unlocked and to come right in. Usually, Ronald came over to my house, so the cryptic request with no details already had me wondering what I was walking into.

I inched open the door and called out, not wanting to risk scaring the man. Like Gertie's purse, I was never quite certain what he might have up his sleeve. Or his dress, or in his kitchen, or wherever the heck he was.

"Help."

The feeble reply came from the hallway behind the living room. I hurried into the hallway and jolted to a stop. The stairwell to the second floor of Ronald's house was one of those tucked away so that it couldn't be seen from the main rooms. But I was pretty sure it did not come decorated the way it looked now.

A huge ball of lacy pink ruffles appeared to be stuck on the stairs between the wall and the spindles a couple feet before the first-floor landing. I would have assumed someone had shoved a giant pink tumbleweed down the stairwell, but it was moving. Since Ronald didn't have any pets and wouldn't tolerate vermin for half a second given his shoe collection, I decided he was probably wrapped up in the pink disaster.

"Ronald? Are you in there?"

"Of course I'm in here. Talking dresses aren't a thing yet. Get me out."

I stared at the wadded mess, unable to spot so much as a finger or toe or even a strand of hair. "Let me get a knife from the kitchen."

"You can't cut this! It's couture. This lace is collectible."

"It's either cut it or hold your funeral right here. I would think dying in it would ruin the value of the lace more than cutting it."

"There's a zipper up the back. I just can't reach it. If you could unzip me, I could get out."

I shook my head as I climbed up the side of the stairs and over the banister. When I started poking at the dress, I finally realized what had happened. There were giant stiff hoops on the bottom. At some point, Ronald had tripped, pitched down the stairs, and now the hoops were wedged between the wall and the spindles, leaving him dangling.

"Why would you try to go down stairs this steep in something like this?" I asked.

"Because the party I'm attending is in one of those old hotels with no elevator, and you have to walk down steps into the ballroom. I had to test my entrance."

"I think you failed. Maybe you should go for sweats and tennis shoes. You never see me face-first on a stairwell."

He grunted and said something, but I couldn't make out the words. It was probably better that way. I flipped the lace around, searching for a zipper, but I couldn't even figure out whether I was looking at the front or the back. There were so many layers, and it's not as if Ronald had boobs to tip me off.

"I can't see a zipper," I said. "Tell me where your head and feet are at least."

"I'm not sure. I did a complete somersault and a bit of a tuck-and-roll. It all happened so quickly. I think my head is lower than my feet because it's pounding from all the blood rushing to it. And I'm sure I'm facing down because I caught a mouthful of carpet runner before the hoops took over, so my backside should be up."

I went to the top of the mass and started flipping ruffles. If I could just find a leg, then I had something to work with. I wasn't even going to consider what undergarments I might be exposing. Given his outlandish choices in outerwear, I was afraid his unseens might be things Gertie would want to duplicate. And to be honest, I didn't like anyone but Carter enough to be okay getting exclusive views of the underwear.

My hand hit something hard and I flicked another piece of lace back and saw a pink platform shoe. But it was a letdown—not because the heel was broken off it but because it was no longer attached to a foot. I grabbed the shoe and tossed it into the hallway.

"What was that?" Ronald asked.

"I'm going to guess it's the reason you fell. The heel is broken off one of your shoes."

"And you're just tossing them any which way?"

"You want me to nail the heel back on and duct tape it? Because that's the only way you're walking in them again."

He let out a strangled sigh, and I wasn't sure if he was crying or if the dress was so constricting it had prevented a bigger dramatic moment. I kept flipping and finally, my hand brushed against metal. Jackpot! It was a zipper.

"Found it! I'm going to unzip you so you can crawl out of there."

Except...gravity.

Ronald didn't inform me that the dress was strapless, and in the pile of ruffles, I couldn't tell what I was looking at. And since I wasn't a dress connoisseur and had less than zero chance of becoming one, I didn't realize the precariousness of the situation until it was too late.

Ronald had already Gertied. Now, he Celiaed.

I gripped the dress at the top seam and pulled the fabric tight as I worked the zipper down. It was hard to start but then I must have gotten past the breastplate and it slid all the way to the end with a single hard tug.

Ronald shot out of the dress as if he'd been launched—a

bright purple missile. His body launched straight down the remainder of the stairs and into the hall, where he finally slid to a stop and remained there, a silent lump. I jumped up in horror, still clutching the dress, wondering what in the name of all that is holy I was looking at.

The best I could figure, it was a bright purple unitard with short legs and arms.

Ronald groaned and rolled over. I let out a strangled cry and clutched the dress even harder, as if the ruffles might protect me from the horror.

In the middle of the front of the unitard was a superhero-type medallion with a single shiny gold stiletto in the middle. The lettering above the medallion read "The Fashionista."

I tossed the dress down on top of Ronald and he let out a shriek as though he'd just been attacked by moths. He jumped up, flailing around in the dress, and hit a table, sending the table, the dress, and himself tumbling farther down the hallway.

I felt a little guilty about causing a second round of terror, but not guilty enough to go help a man parading around in his underwear. I eased down the stairs as Ronald struggled with the dress, wondering if I could make it past his elbows and out the front door before he caught sight of me, but as I inched into the living room, I saw the front door was open a crack and I froze.

I was absolutely positive I'd closed it.

CHAPTER NINETEEN

I RAN TO THE DOOR AND SAW A FIGURE SLIP INTO THE bushes at the side of the house. I yelled, "Intruder," before bolting outside. They must have heard my battle cry because their footsteps turned into a frantic run. Not that it mattered. Most criminals were not going to best me in a footrace. I burst through the bushes and tackled the fleeing woman, realizing exactly who it was as I connected with her.

Holly Beech.

The girl flailed around as I sat on her back, the ice pick she had been holding a few feet away.

"Stop moving or I twist your neck and break it," I said. I wouldn't, of course, but she didn't know that.

She brought her hands in to cover her face and all movement ceased, except for soft sobbing.

"What in the world?" Ronald's voice sounded behind me, and I turned to see him stroll through the damaged bushes, and unfortunately, he had not paused to put on pants or a trench coat before following me outside.

"You're out here in your underwear and you're wondering about me tackling an intruder?" I asked.

He put his hands on his hips and glared. "*This* is a super-hero costume. I am The Fashionista!"

"You are seconds away from being arrested," I said as I heard sirens in the distance. "Because I'm pretty sure that is illegal in Sinful, especially on Easter Sunday."

Ronald's eyes widened and he whirled around, ready to stalk back to his house, but he was too late. Carter's truck pulled up to the curb and he jumped out and hurried our way. Instead of blending back into the bush for cover, Ronald froze and stood there, in all his purple-clad underwear glory.

Carter had his gaze fixed on mine as he rushed up, but when he was a couple steps away, he caught sight of Ronald, and I swear some of the blood rushed from his face.

"What the heck is going on here?" he asked.

"There was a problem with my dress," Ronald explained. "And then an intruder."

"Good God!" Carter said. "It's Easter. The least you can do is pull an Adam and Eve and hide behind a bush or something. That's not a dress, and whatever it is, I'm pretty sure it's illegal."

"Told you," I said.

Ronald opened his mouth to protest, then must have thought better of it, because he turned and stalked back through the bushes. I hoped he was on his way to find more clothes because no way Carter was taking his statement dressed that way. Heck, I was considering putting my house up for sale just knowing he was currently inside his own house dressed that way.

"They don't pay me enough," Carter said as he studied my situation. "Please tell me you grabbed that ice pick on the way out the front door."

"I don't even own an ice pick, I just use my pistol," I said.

He held his hands up. "I should have known better. Do you know the intruder? And why was she breaking into your house?"

"Not my house, Ronald's—and yeah, I know her. So do you." I reached down and pulled Holly's hand away from her face.

Carter gave me a stricken look and closed his eyes for a moment. I was pretty sure he was contemplating resigning his position and fleeing the state. I didn't exactly blame him.

"I refuse to get off her until you break out the handcuffs," I said. "And you might want to bag that ice pick."

Twenty minutes later, Myrtle was processing the ice pick and giving Holly the side-eye. She wasn't the only one. Deputy Breaux had just returned from breaking up a brawl over the last biscuit at Bomber Bruce's house, and when he stepped inside and got a look at Holly wearing cuffs, I wondered for a moment if he was going to lock himself in the bathroom again. But since Carter stepped out of his office at that moment and caught sight of him, he'd missed his opportunity.

His shoulders slumped. "Do you need help, boss?" he asked.

Carter nodded. "Call her brother and let him know I'm arresting his sister for breaking and entering and threatening Fortune with a deadly weapon."

Deputy Breaux stared, clearly confused.

"The threat doesn't have to be viable for it to be illegal," Carter said.

"Right, of course," Deputy Breaux said and headed for his desk.

Carter turned and pointed to Holly. "You are going to a cell, unless you'd like to tell me why you broke into Mr. Franklin's home?"

It must have finally registered with the girl that she was in trouble but apparently, she refused to understand just how much.

"I don't even know him," she said. "I was after her."

Then she glared at me as if somehow I was the problem.

"She must have been watching and saw me go into Ronald's house after my jog," I said. "The door wasn't locked, and I didn't knock because he'd told me to come right in."

"So she assumed it was your house," Carter finished. "Which doesn't make it any better. Why are you stalking Ms. Redding?"

Holly pursed her lips like a petulant child.

"My guess is she was hoping to kill me like she did her sister," I said.

The blood rushed from her face. "I did *not* kill Lindsay."

"So you say, but you were in love with Ryan. You probably figured if Lindsay was gone, you'd have him all to yourself."

"I was—I didn't—" she stammered, but it was clear I'd called it correctly. "I couldn't have killed her. She was my sister."

"But you don't think Ryan killed her either."

"I'm certain he didn't."

"Why? Because he loved her so much?"

She clamped her mouth shut and shook her head, but I could tell she was done talking.

Deputy Breaux walked back over. "Jared Beech is on his way with their attorney. He said you are not to question her until he's present, and that if you do, he'll sue you for harassing someone with diminished mental capacity."

He delivered that last sentence with a nervous glance at Holly, but she looked completely unfazed. I imagine, given her lack of control, that she'd heard that line of defense before.

"Then please take her to a cell," Carter directed.

Deputy Breaux looked less than thrilled, but he wasn't about to suggest to his boss that he handle the woman who'd just come to town to kill his girlfriend. Even if there was less than zero chance it would have happened.

"What are you going to do?" I asked.

Carter blew out a breath. "Given the situation, I don't think I have any choice but to ask questions about Lindsay's death. But I'm also going to assume they have an excellent attorney who will convince her to say nothing."

"How long can you hold her?"

"Not long. Maybe not at all. Did you see her in Ronald's house?"

"No, but the door was open, and I'm certain I'd closed it."

"But it's still your word against hers."

"I see. So she showed up here just to walk through Ronald's bushes holding an ice pick?"

"Of course not, but you know a good defense attorney would tear that apart in minutes citing speculation and that with her diminished mental capacity, we can't know intent."

I snorted. "I swear, I understand vigilante justice more every day. Basically, someone has to die before our system takes things seriously, and even then, they still get it wrong. Look at Ryan."

"Do you think Holly killed her sister?"

"I was already leaning that way. At this point, she's top of my list."

———

CARTER TOOK MY STATEMENT, THEN TOLD ME TO HEAD HOME and if I was feeling generous, check in on Ronald. I wasn't certain how much generosity I had left, but since most people weren't used to having randos break into their homes with ice picks, I figured I could at least stop by and make sure he hadn't rung up Gertie to borrow one of her handbags.

I just hoped he was dressed. For real dressed.

He cracked the door a tiny bit after I rang the bell, and I heard his sigh of relief as he removed the chain and swung the door back. Thankfully, he was decked out in a three-piece suit and pink fuzzy slippers.

"You're a little overdressed for TV and after-dinner drinks," I said as he waved me inside.

"I thought I'd have to give a police statement."

"They don't require you to wear a suit for it. At least, I don't think they do. You know what—they might. It's Sinful, after all."

Ronald sank onto the couch, and I perched on his coffee table. I wasn't planning on staying long. I just wanted to make sure he wasn't freaking out and then I was going to head home for a much-needed shower and a stiff drink.

"Are you all right?" I asked.

"You're going to have to be more specific. My shoe is ruined and I'm going to have to find a new dress for the event because that one is clearly not suited for stairs. A crazy woman came into my home with an ice pick for God only knows what intent, and half the block has seen my undergarments. Today has been a lot."

I nodded. I felt the same way.

"What happened with that woman?" he asked. "Please tell me she's chained inside a cell somewhere with no access to anything pointed or metal."

"She was in a cell when I left, but her brother is on the way with their attorney. They're already claiming diminished mental capacity."

"Like that wasn't apparent. But if she wasn't aware that she was in the wrong, she wouldn't have run."

"Also true. I gave my statement to Carter. He said he'd contact you tomorrow to get yours."

"But what did she want?"

"I'm pretty sure she was coming after me."

He sucked in a breath. "She has a death wish? Good Lord, get her out of town."

"I think she's decided that Carter is going to be her boyfriend and she thought she'd eliminate the competition."

"We all know how that would have turned out, so why are you frowning?"

"Because I'm pretty sure I'm not the first person she's gone after over a man. I think she killed her sister."

Ronald's eyes widened and he gulped. "You're serious? Of course you're serious. Good Lord, I just thought she was crazy like Nora, maybe even smoking the same weed, but you're saying she's actually clinically disturbed."

"It's a very real possibility. Unfortunately, there's another man in prison, serving a life sentence for her sister's murder, and I'm certain he didn't do it. I've got a couple potential suspects but I'm currently leaning hard toward her."

"Sounds right to me, and I barely know anything. So what's the problem?"

"Extremely rich family. Insulated from most everything. And since this isn't the first time she's exhibited less-than-desirable behavior, I have a feeling her attorney and the health system are going to wrap her up like a prize vase."

"And you're afraid the poor sod in prison won't get out." He sighed. "That sucks. You know, I really appreciate what you do to help people, but I can see how it would be a total drag on your own mental health."

I nodded. "If you're all right, I'm going to head home and hit the shower."

"Of course. Let me know if there's anything I can do. And I know I didn't get to say it earlier but thank you for helping me with the dress situation."

I managed a smile. "You know, you're giving Gertie a run for her money."

"Hush your mouth! I am so much better dressed when I have a fluke."

I was still laughing as I walked into my house.

————

Gertie and Ida Belle insisted on coming by to check on me after I called and told them the basics of what had happened with Holly. Gertie brought slices of roast beef and potato salad, and we all dug in while I went through everything, including Ronald and his dress escapade. Both of them were howling when I described Ronald's Fashionista outfit, but immediately sobered when I got to the part about Holly and the ice pick.

We discussed the situation from every angle possible, but no matter which direction we started, we always ended up back at the same place. We all believed Holly had killed her sister. They took off a couple hours later, and after an extremely long shower and a couple shots of the whiskey Ida Belle had brought over, I settled into my recliner to wait for Carter.

He finally showed around 11:00 p.m. and I couldn't help but feel agitated at how exhausted he looked. He didn't need this hassle from the Beech family. Not with everything else he was already dealing with. And I felt guilty for introducing them into his existence. Not that it was really my fault, but it was only because of me that Holly Beech had discovered him.

He sank onto the couch, and I retrieved him a beer, which he opened silently and took a big swig from. Then he shook his head and slowly let out a breath.

"That bad, huh?" I said, desperate to break the tension.

"It went exactly like I thought it would. Jared Beech showed up with his attorney—and he's a doozy. Not Alexander, but right up there in his line of work."

"Which is?"

"Criminal defense and strictly on grounds of mental incompetence. The guy was a psychiatrist. Who the hell is going to argue against a defense attorney who's an actual doctor? Anyway, he showed up with paperwork to have Holly committed on a psych hold and that was that. And what would be the point in protesting? The girl is clearly troubled, and there is no way this is the first time she's done something like this. He produced that paperwork like he had it ready to go. I got a glimpse of her file in his briefcase, and it was thick."

"Did you even get to question her?"

"Why bother? Her attorney and her brother had already told her not to say a word, and I think the seriousness of the situation had finally sunk in. When the attorney handed me the paperwork for the psych hold, she lost it. Tried to bolt out of the room, but her brother caught her. She clawed him up pretty good before I managed to get her restrained again. I should have left the cuffs on her, but they raised hell about it first thing. The last thing I need is a complaint about the treatment of women in my custody, so I removed them."

"Good God. I guess they changed their minds on that one after her explosion."

"Nope. When I got her arms behind her back, the attorney

walked up, slick as oil, and jabbed her with a needle. Five minutes later, she was a lump in the chair."

"He had sedative with him?"

Carter nodded. "It's clear they both know what they're dealing with, but I think she took them by surprise on that one. I think they believed she'd behave until they got her out of there and then they figured they'd sedate her in the car."

"But Holly didn't like their plans."

"I'm going to hazard a guess that she's been institutionalized before."

"I'd say definitely. And she's not interested in going back. Did she take another Uber to kill me? I'm thinking the driver would have seen the ice pick and kept going."

"Ha! No, apparently she lifted the keys to a truck the groundskeeper uses. Deputy Breaux found it parked around the corner from your house. We kept it for processing."

"Did Jared or the attorney offer up anything at all? She came into what she thought was my home with an ice pick. Surely they're not suggesting we pass that off as childish pranks, especially after how her sister died."

"I said exactly that. The attorney has a poker face like a corpse, but Jared looked nervous. I think he's scared of what Holly might do or say."

"Of course he's scared—for himself. He's been covering it all up, which I'm guessing is what her father did before he died. Holly ticks all the boxes for my case. She's violent, Lindsay would have let her in the house and turned her back to her, she was obsessed with Ryan, and you can bet she knew Ryan was living in the motel because she stalked him."

Carter nodded. "And given that the local cops—who basically worked for Raymond Beech—barely gave the whole investigation a glance before putting it to bed, and Raymond never pushed for more, I'm going to guess that he knew exactly what happened."

"Everyone I've talked to said Raymond Beech was a cold bastard, but how do you send an innocent man to prison for life for murder, and then let the killer live in your home every night without worrying you'll be next?"

"Maybe that's why Jared Beech looks so strung out. That guy is hanging on by a thread."

I nodded. Maybe if I broke that thread, Jared Beech would be my trump card.

CHAPTER TWENTY

I AWOKE SUDDENLY AND IN PITCH-BLACK, MY HEART pounding in my chest. Merlin stood on the end of the bed, his back arched, and I could see the ridge of fur on his spine standing straight up. The house was quiet except for the occasional sounds of the tree outside brushing against the window. But I hadn't been dreaming and even if I had, it wasn't a nightmare that had Merlin on alert.

I grabbed my cell phone and checked the alarm. The app showed an error, which meant someone had a jamming app—and one that worked on military-grade equipment. The cameras were all black, and when I replayed motion footage, I could see two figures—in all black clothes and masks—approach them and spray the lenses with paint.

I threw the covers back and grabbed my gun as I slid out of bed. I slid my phone into my shorts pocket and slipped silently into the hallway and listened. Their movement approaching the cameras was with military precision, and I had no doubt this was a hit and knew exactly where it had originated.

The house was eerily quiet, but I heard a faint sliding sound at the back of the house and realized they were entering through a window in my office. I motioned to Merlin and crept into the master bedroom closet, which contained the secret panel and ladder into the attic. Merlin, for once, took instructions like a soldier and padded silently beside me into the closet and didn't make a sound when I carried him up the ladder.

As soon as we were secure, I pulled out my phone and sent a text to Carter.

Intruders. Military. Protect yourself.

Merlin had gone to perch on top of some boxes, and all I could see were his eyes glowing in the dark room, but I didn't need to see anything else. I knew my way in the dark—had specifically designed a way out of the house, complete with a padded walkway and reinforced structure so there was no sound at all as I passed. All the people in my house would find was an empty bedroom, and as they started searching for me, I'd flank them.

Because no way in hell I was going to flee.

Breaking into an assassin's house to kill her was like signing your own death warrant.

I eased up the window at the end of the attic and crept onto the roof. I made my way across and into the tree that took me onto Ronald's roof, then I scaled down another tree and dropped down into his bushes. I crept around to my backyard to see if I could spot movement in the windows and saw a shadow pass across the upstairs window in the guest room.

I headed for the office, planning on entering the house the same way the intruders had. I eased myself through the open window without a hint of a sound and crept to the doorway. I could hear them moving upstairs—one set of footsteps in the master bedroom, the other in the guest room. It wouldn't be long before they decided I was no longer in the house and retreated.

I edged into the living room and set my cell phone on a bookshelf, recording. Then I crouched behind the recliner, in position to strike as soon as they stepped off the stairs. I heard footsteps in the hallway and then low voices, and slowly drew in a breath, preparing to make my move.

Their footsteps sounded on the stairwell, and I counted down the steps as they drew closer...five, four, three, two, one, STRIKE!

I leaped like a jaguar, grabbing the arm of the first man. I ducked and twisted, breaking his shoulder and wrist as I aimed the pistol in his hand at the man behind him and shot him right between the eyes. The first man reached for his backup weapon with his good arm, and I twisted his broken arm again and fired a round into his other shoulder.

He let go of the gun, screaming in pain, then stumbled backward. I spun around and kicked him into the living room, where he fell over the coffee table and crashed onto the floor. But this was no ordinary intruder. Even with two broken limbs, he still reached for his backup weapon.

I fired another round into his thigh, just an inch from the thing that mattered most to men. "The next shot will be one inch up and over," I said, and he finally went still.

I gave the guy on the stairs a glance, but he was no longer a threat, then I stepped toward the other man and pointed my nine right at his crotch.

"Who sent you?"

His jaw was clenched, and he shook, trying to control the pain, but didn't say a word.

"You've got one more chance to answer me and save your-self. Otherwise, I'm going to put a round through you and have a beer while you bleed out on my living room rug. Your choice."

"You know I can't say," he managed to sputter, waves of pain flashing across his face.

"Why would you protect the man who sent you here to die? He knew you couldn't take me. He just gambled with your life that I might make a mistake. Well, here's a tip—I don't make mistakes."

I fired a round into the floor, right between his legs, so close to his crotch that the round split the seam of his jeans. He flinched and then groaned as the movement sent waves of pain through his shattered shoulders.

"You had to know what I was. Did Kitts tell you I had let my training go? If so, he lied. I just cleaned up his mess in Iran. He knew that when he sent you here to be executed. You don't matter any more than the soldiers he's sent to the slaughter. He was gambling, and your life was a cheap ante."

I leaned over and looked him straight in the eyes. "The house always wins."

He cursed and spat blood onto the floor. "Kitts! But you'll never take him down. He's got too many behind him."

"We'll see about that. Thanks for your confession," I said and pointed to my phone. "I don't figure you'll last too long in lockup. Kitts will see to it that you don't. But this might put that final nail in his coffin if you're not around to tell it to the DOD."

"He's untouchable."

"Maybe by the justice system. But if I can't get him through proper channels, he'll find himself looking down the same barrel you are."

As I reached for my phone, Carter burst through my front door, weapon drawn and clearly panicked. He took in the guy writhing in pain on my floor and the body slumped on my stairs and relief flooded his face.

"Are you all right?" he asked.

"I'm going to need a new rug. What about you?"

"Ha!" He ran one hand over his head. "There's no one at my house. Only one team, maybe, and they decided to start here."

I nodded. It made sense. With Carter's recent injuries, I was more of a threat. A smart assassin always eliminated the biggest threat first.

A dumb one underestimated his prey.

———

IT ONLY TOOK TWENTY MINUTES FOR THE STATE POLICE TO get someone out to accompany Intruder Number 1 to the hospital. They'd taken one look at the situation and at me, calmly eating cookies on the couch while my rug slowly turned rust brown, and had clamped his broken arms to the gurney. Carter had given them a brief explanation of the situation and of my background, so they understood the danger the man presented.

Because the real threat wasn't diminished by his broken shoulders. The real threat was his mouth, and we both knew Kitts would do everything he could to ensure he didn't open it again. I had my video, but live witnesses were always a much better sell. Still, I hoped this would be enough to get Kitts brought up on charges and eliminate or at least reduce the number of people willing to stick their neck out on his behalf. Money spoke volumes, but how much you had didn't matter if you were dead. Intruder Number 2 had learned that the hard way.

I'd sent a text to Ida Belle, Gertie, and Ronald—who had called the cops when he heard the gunfire—and let them know that the situation was in hand and to stay put because the state police would need to process my house. I assured them that everyone who mattered was safe and promised to give them all the details in the morning. Then I'd excused myself to check on Merlin and had freed him from the attic. As soon as I put him down on the closet floor, he'd shot right under the bed, and I figured he might be there until sometime next June.

The first police unit left with the paramedics and a second one arrived shortly after. I'd called Alexander while the paramedics were doing their thing, and he'd advised me to mostly tell the truth about the night's events but to make sure the video was saved to the cloud and forwarded to him before I turned over my phone.

The second state police duo walked in slowly, studying me, and I knew they'd already been brought up to speed about who I was and how I'd dispatched two men with relative ease. They asked me to explain what happened, so I did. Sort of. Obviously, I left out my secret closet space and my attic escape hatch. Instead, I played it off as I heard them coming through my office window as I was asleep on the couch, so I hid behind the recliner.

I went on to say I'd checked my cameras and alarm on my phone and knew they'd been disabled, so I'd set my phone to record and upload to the cloud so that if I didn't make it out, Carter would know what happened.

"But you didn't call 911?" the first cop asked.

"Even if I could have gotten word to dispatch without signaling where I was, the deputy on duty is a young man with no military training and has rarely had to discharge his weapon. Why would I invite him to a duel with professionals that he would have lost before he got in the front door? I don't need or want that on my conscience."

The first cop glanced at the second one when I was done, cleared his throat, and then asked, "So when they went upstairs, why didn't you run out the front door?"

"Because I can't outrun bullets and they would have had clean shots from the upstairs windows."

"So you were hoping they'd decide you weren't here when they didn't find you upstairs and leave?"

"Sure, let's go with that."

They glanced at each other again and the second one said, "Can we see that video?"

I clicked on my television, so we could watch it on the big screen, and queued it up from the cloud. Carter's jaw clenched as he watched me dispatch the first man on the stairs and I know he was seething that Kitts had made a move like this against me. The two cops stood there, jaws dropped, and watched the entire thing play out. For several seconds after the footage ended, neither of them moved or spoke. I have to admit, it was kinda impressive on playback.

Finally, the first cop swallowed. "Are you standing by your statement concerning not fleeing when you had the opportunity?"

I cocked my head to the side. "Those men are mercenaries, not Mormons. Do you think when they didn't find me, they'd just move on to the next house?"

Carter gave them both a hard stare. "Need I remind you gentlemen that Ms. Redding is well within her rights to defend herself in her own home. I'm sure the men were debriefed on who their target was before they took the job. Maybe they should have taken their intel more seriously."

Both their eyes widened, and the first cop nodded. "We'll need to take your phone into evidence."

I looked over at Carter. "Now you see why I have two phones."

The first cop frowned, and I knew he was wondering how often people tried to kill me. "Who is this Kitts you referred to?" he asked.

I smiled. "A four-star general in the Marine Corps."

"Good God," the second one said. "Are those men..."

"Soldiers? I'm sure they were at one time, but it's offensive to all the good men and women who served and are serving to acknowledge them as such now."

He nodded and looked slightly panicked. "I'm afraid we're going to have to process the house as a crime scene as well before we move that body. Is there somewhere else you can stay until we finish?"

"No problem," I said, trying to sound calm and reasonable, but I'm pretty sure that just unnerved them even more. "I have a cat hiding upstairs that I need to collect, though, and my spare phone in my office, and I'll need a change of clothes. I have blood on these, and it stinks after it sits in fabric a while."

Carter covered his mouth with his hand to cover the smile threatening to break through. I gave him a wink as I headed upstairs to wrangle Merlin into a pet taxi. I was pretty sure that was going to be the most dangerous thing I'd attempted all night.

———

SINCE TINY WAS IN RESIDENCE AT CARTER'S PLACE, AND I had no desire to play referee between the two of them, I dropped Merlin off at Ally's. A very alert and not quite fully clad Mannie let us inside and it was funny to see the enormous tower of a man giving Merlin the side-eye. It was also cute to see Ally blushing over the man standing in her living room in the middle of the night and showing more skin than I'd ever seen. I was absolutely in love with Carter, but I'm not blind and had to admit, Mannie was as nicely built as he was scary.

I gave them a brief rundown of what happened, and Ally

gave me a terrified look and grabbed my hand to squeeze it. Mannie just shook his head.

"Kitts either has rocks the size of Texas or he's desperate," he said. "Either way, I don't like it. I'll put out some feelers tomorrow and see what I can find out. Let me know if you get an ID on the men."

"I'll send you the video on the off chance you recognize them."

He nodded. "And in the future, call me if you need backup. And I don't mean catsitting."

Carter snorted. "She didn't call *me* for backup. She sent me a warning to protect myself."

Mannie grinned and clapped his hand on Carter's shoulder. "Good luck with all of that, my brother."

We headed out and I looked over at Carter. "Maybe you should have dated a baker."

He shook his head. "So I could worry even more? At least I know you can handle the trouble you attract. You're certain the guys were mercenaries?"

"Yeah. I checked the video footage history from before they took out the cameras. Classic military movement."

"What the hell is Kitts thinking?"

I shrugged. "That maybe he'd get lucky? That those two guys didn't matter so it was no loss if they failed? I'm guessing the one thing he didn't consider was that I'd leave one in good enough shape to talk."

"Yeah, we just have to make sure he stays that way. Kitts will immediately move to cover his tracks."

"Denial is his fallback. He can claim that it was well-known in our realm that he and I had a beef, and one of my enemies used that as a cover for their own retaliation. You won't find a paper trail linking that guy to Kitts."

"I can't believe I'm going to ask this but if you knew his story wouldn't stick, why leave him alive?"

"Because it should be enough potential for a huge stinky media mess to get the Marines to back off their support. And it will just make the DOD even more stringent in their evaluation and pursuit of Kitts."

"So you're throwing jet fuel on the fire."

"It's what I do best."

———

I GOT A PHONE CALL FROM KELSEY EARLY THE NEXT morning just as I'd joined Carter on the back porch for coffee. She was wound up so tight that if she let go she might have sprung into the stratosphere.

"What's going on?" I asked as she blurted out her breathless, obligatory greeting.

"Your attorney—he's a miracle worker. The DNA test has been done already and Ryan is the father. I know we already knew that, but I can't help feeling this is huge."

"It *is* huge. And a relief that he got it accomplished so quickly."

"I don't know what your attorney has on the warden, but I need something similar on everyone who's ever wronged me."

"For the right amount of money and time, he could probably get it."

"Ha. Anyway, the next step is the medical testing for the transplant. The prison doctor told me that they'll be transporting Ryan to the hospital sometime today. If he's a match and he's in good enough shape to warrant the surgery himself, the transplant could happen within a week or two."

"That's incredible news!"

"But there's a problem. Brett has to sign off on the transplant, and I can tell he's hesitant."

"Is the man so proud and vain that he'd risk his son's life over his hurt feelings?"

"I don't know, but I'm afraid that when the documents are presented, he'll refuse to sign, or just hesitate long enough for them to call it off. The warden still has the last say. If Brett doesn't look completely invested, he could use his behavior as an excuse to delay the surgery or cancel it altogether."

"Has Brett said anything outright?"

"No. He barely speaks to me, and even then, it's only when he absolutely has to. I get why he's angry, but it's not helping things."

"Do you think it would help if I talked to him?"

"I don't know. Maybe. I suppose it couldn't hurt. You're an unbiased third party, per se. I know I hired you, but this isn't personal for you."

On paper, her statement was accurate. But in reality, every case I took was personal.

"I'll run him down today," I said. "Maybe if I can blindside him somewhere, I can get him to be real with me, instead of wielding that brick wall in front of him like last time."

"Monday is always chicken breast and boiled eggs for lunch. He hasn't deviated since I've known him. There's a small park around the corner from his building. If the weather is good, he likes to eat outside. I just have no idea when that might be."

"I can figure that out. Try not to worry. I really don't think Brett is foolish enough to ruin this chance to save Ben. But I'll make sure he understands the stakes."

I shook my head as I dropped my phone on the table and Carter frowned.

"He's playing a dangerous game. Trying to punish his wife might cost him his son."

"I know. And the ridiculous part is that he doesn't have any right to be mad about Kelsey sleeping with Ryan. They'd broken up and according to Kelsey, he was off with other women before she'd changed her status on social media."

"I don't think that's what he's mad about. At least, it's not all that he's mad about. He sounds like a controlling person, so I'm sure he hates that he couldn't control what she did then and still can't today. But ultimately, what he's angry about is that he's not Ben's father, and because of that, he can't do anything to save him."

"But he *can* do something. He can stop with the attitude and roadblocks and put up the money so that Ben gets the absolute best care available."

Carter nodded. "Then maybe you should tell him just that."

"I plan to."

"You didn't tell her about Holly Beech?"

"No. She's got enough on her plate. I know she wants Ryan cleared, but she needs to focus on Ben and let me handle Ryan's case."

He nodded his agreement.

I stared out across the lawn and huffed. "I guess I have to get someone to clean my house. I am not big on domestics and no way am I trying to get blood out of the hardwood. I'm just going to toss the rug."

"I have a couple services I can call. Let me see who has availability and I'll get someone over there. Don't worry about timing. If you're not available, I'll stay myself or get someone you trust who can."

I shook my head. "What exactly does it say about the two of us that I'm put out over the dead guy stinking up my house and ruining my rug and you know more than one person who can handle it?"

"That we've got the right contacts for our jobs? That we have the proper perspective when it comes to the bad guys? Although, I'm guessing Ronald will accuse you of having a poor attitude concerning your rug."

"It was ugly and drab. If anything, the bloodstains dressed it up a bit, but the smell is intolerable, especially in wool. I just left it there when I bought the place because I hate shopping and had no desire to spend a lot of money on a rug. Have you ever priced them?"

He nodded. "And that is why I have bare bachelor floors. Well, that and Tiny. He still chews up my bath mats. If I spent thousands on a living room rug and came home to find he'd eaten half of it, then I'd have to make decisions I don't want to make."

I heard the side gate creak, and then Ida Belle and Gertie walked through.

"We rang the doorbell," Ida Belle said, "but when no one answered, we figured you were back here having your coffee."

Gertie cut a glance at Ida Belle. "Figured it because it's too early to be doing anything else," she grumbled.

"Stop your grousing," Ida Belle said. "You know you wanted to get the details on everything that happened last night as much as I did."

"True, but I could have waited long enough to shower."

Carter wrinkled his nose. "We could have waited long enough for you to shower as well. What's that smell?"

"If you must know, I was too wound up to sleep after I got Fortune's text, so I canned pickles. And yes, I took a shower—two as a matter of fact—but it takes forever for that smell to get off your skin."

I grimaced, getting a whiff of the pickle smell myself.

"Carter's going to call someone about a forensic clean for my house. Maybe we could include Gertie in the deal."

"When none of you get fresh pickles this year, you'll know why," Gertie said.

Since I didn't particularly like pickles, it didn't seem like much of a threat. But then, in the past twenty-four hours, I'd been stalked by a woman with an ice pick, and two mercenaries had entered my home to assassinate me, so the whole pickle thing wasn't likely to gain much ground.

"So what happened?" Ida Belle asked.

I filled them in on everything that had happened, and when I was done, I asked if they'd like to see video of the takedown.

"Good God, woman!" Gertie said, jumping out of her chair. "You have video and you've been wasting time with words."

We all headed inside, and I queued up the video on Carter's big screen. They watched in silence until I sprang, and then Gertie sent up a big cheer and an arm pump. When it was over, she turned to me, shaking her head.

"You know, every time I see you in action, it's incredible, but this one was magical. You dispatched them like they were vacuum cleaner salesmen. I know you took them by surprise, but you eliminated the threat so quickly and you weren't remotely winded."

Carter studied me for a second and I knew what he was thinking.

Or fazed.

He wasn't wrong. The mission to save him had sent me a step or two back into my dark past. I'd hoped that my reemergence from the other side would be as swift as my return to it, but so many years of training and a single-minded focus were hard to undo. We all had our baggage, I guessed. At least mine kept me and the people I loved from harm. I knew Carter was worried that everything that I'd been forced to do would return me to the person I was when I first arrived in Sinful.

But that was my past, and this was my future.

"If you'd take up running with me," I said to Gertie, "you wouldn't be as winded after one of your flukes."

"Ha!" Ida Belle laughed. "You'd be just as successful telling her to stop having them altogether. Since Carter's generously offered to handle the house, what's on our agenda for today? Getting the security system back up and running?"

"Nope. Mannie is going to get his people on it right away. And Merlin is hanging out at Ally's until I can bring him home and not have to worry about him attacking me in my sleep. He was pretty shook up over the whole thing but didn't make so much as a sound or extend a claw when I carried him up into the attic."

"Animals know," Ida Belle said. "Merlin might be a typical disgruntled, self-centered cat, but he also knows when he and the person who feeds him are in danger."

I nodded. "Since everything in Sinful is covered, we're going to head into NOLA for a chat with Brett Spalding."

I told them about my conversation with Kelsey, and they both cheered when I got to the part about the DNA match.

"I think Brett will do the right thing," Ida Belle said, "but I agree that a bit of urging from your end might help him remember exactly why he needs to be 100 percent committed in voice and action. What about Alexander? Have you heard anything from him yet about the video?"

"Just a lot of exclamation points and compliments. He'll try to run down identities. The state police will balk at giving him information, but I'm sure he knows which arms to twist. I figure I'll text him on the way and let him know we'll be in town in case he wants to meet up and cover anything he doesn't want to say over the phone."

"Road trip!" Gertie clapped her hands, and Carter cringed.

"Can you three please try not to get into any trouble? I'm running on two hours of sleep."

"For the record, I didn't ask Holly to come stalking me with an ice pick, nor did I invite mercenaries into my house. I will admit that I brought that one on myself by going toe to toe with Kitts, but it was unavoidable."

He sighed. "Do you realize how many situations you get in that fit that 'unavoidable' description?"

I grinned. "All of them—well, except for anything Gertie does. I'm not taking responsibility for any of that."

"Me either," Ida Belle agreed.

"Anyway," I continued. "I'll need to swing by my house and change clothes, and then we can grab some breakfast at Francine's and head out after."

"It's 7:00 a.m.," Carter said. "Even if you take your time changing and eating, you'll be in NOLA midmorning. What do you plan on doing until Brett heads out for his sad lunch in the park?"

"Rug shopping."

CHAPTER TWENTY-ONE

DETECTIVE CASEY CALLED ON OUR DRIVE TO NOLA. NOT only had her daughter already come up with a former Spalding employee to question about Brett's alleged hitting on Lindsay, she'd gotten her phone number and the woman still lived in New Orleans. I called and left a message, stating that I needed information about her former employment at Spalding Financial and asked her to call me back. I wasn't sure what the information would mean at that point, but it was something I'd prefer to nail down. I hated loose ends.

By noon, I'd purchased a thick, fluffy navy rug and had set up delivery for the next week. I'd splurged and bought some matching pillows and lamps as well, and Gertie had declared me 'so domestic she might faint from the shock of it all.' Ida Belle had pointed out that my choice of darker colors was just plain smart, that the pillows had zipper covers, which were handy to stash weapons in, and the lamps had solid iron bases and could kill three people with one good swing.

It was nice when someone really understood you.

A fake call to Spalding about a delivery that needed his personal signature had netted me the lunch hour that he'd be out of the office, so all that was left was to head over to the park, find Brett, and get up in his butt with both feet. The sun was shining bright, and it was a pleasant seventy degrees out. The park was tiny but pretty, with blooming bushes and flowers placed along a brick walkway that traveled around the entire area, giving people a small walking path. Park benches dotted the path under shade trees, and I could see why Brett chose to leave the office in favor of eating here.

I spotted him at a bench in the back of the park but unfortunately, he wasn't alone. Devin Roberts sat next to him, and I could tell the two of them were in a heated conversation.

"Looks like the two best friends aren't feeling very friendly," Ida Belle said. "I wonder what that's about?"

"Could be work," I said.

"Could be personal, too," Ida Belle said. "As long as they've been friends, Devin probably knows more about his life than anyone else, even Kelsey."

"That's true," I agreed. "Still, I was hoping to get Brett alone."

"So ask Devin to leave," Gertie said. "He's not a puppet master."

I nodded. "Do me a favor and hang back. Feels fair to be one on one. And just out of curiosity, see if Devin goes back to the office."

They gave me a nod and crossed the street to find a stakeout spot. I headed into the park. Brett was staring ahead, probably trying to ignore Devin, so he caught sight of me first. His eyes widened and he glanced at Devin and said something that had the other man ceasing all conversation and whipping his head in my direction.

"Brett," I said as I approached. "I'd like a few minutes. Alone."

I gave Devin a pointed look and he bristled at the

dismissal, but Brett gave him a nod and he left, cutting his eyes at me as he walked by.

"I couldn't help but notice you two were arguing," I said as I sat.

Brett shrugged. "It takes two to argue."

"True enough. But it only takes one to listen, so here goes —Kelsey is worried you're going to ruin Ben's chance at the transplant. And I have to say, I agree with her. The warden has a reputation for being difficult at best, sadistic at worst. Whatever pressure he's under to give approval might be short-lived, so you have to strike while the opportunity is available. And you have to do it with no hesitation. Otherwise, he might use it against you."

He sighed. "I have no intention of harming Ben's chances. But asking me to be happy with the option is too much."

"No one's asking you to be happy about anything. But all that anger you're lugging around is only going to weigh you down, which is going to hinder your ability to be the father Ben needs if he's going to get through this."

He turned to face me, his eyes flashing with anger. "What the hell do you know about being a parent to a dying child? About finding out that the only good thing in your life isn't even really yours? That your spouse has been lying by omission your entire marriage?"

Something flickered in his expression as he delivered that last sentence. He contained it quickly, but that split second was all it took for me to know the truth.

"You knew about that night Kelsey spent with Ryan, didn't you?" I asked. "You knew and never told her. Were you following her?"

"No! What would have been the point?"

"To get information you could use to manipulate her back into a relationship."

"Why would I want to be with her if she didn't want to be with me?" he asked.

"Because Kelsey is probably the only person who ever told you no. The challenge can be very appealing to a certain type of person."

He shook his head. "I had plenty of other options, and my job is all the challenge I need. I *loved* Kelsey and she chose to return to our relationship—*before* she knew she was pregnant, not because of it."

"And maybe all of that is true, but you never answered my original question—did you know about her night with Ryan?"

He stared at me, a range of emotions flashing through his eyes, and I knew he was trying to decide how to respond even though his hesitation had already provided me with the answer.

"I didn't know the extent of it," he said finally. "I didn't know that she'd slept with him and never asked. When he was arrested for killing Lindsay, I assumed they'd parted ways at the bar and both gone home."

"How did you know they were together at all?"

"A picture. Someone sent me a picture of the two of them kissing."

"Who sent it?"

He shook his head. "I don't know. The number was blocked, and trust me when I say that I used every available option I had to try to track that person down."

"It had to have been someone you knew if they had your number."

"It was my work cell. It's listed on the company website. And even if it wasn't, there are plenty of people in my social circle who not only had that number but would have been happy to see Kelsey and me part ways."

"Other options who were trying to get rid of the competition?"

"Something like that."

"And you never once questioned Kelsey about that night?"

"No. Not until..."

"Until you knew for certain that Ben wasn't your biological son. You realize the man who fathered him is going to sit in prison the rest of his life if I can't find suitable evidence to prove otherwise. And the best evidence I have right now is Kelsey's statement. Do you think she's lying about spending the entire night with him?"

"No. The photo was date-stamped, and I received it that night. And since the DNA test was positive, there's no denying the extent of their involvement. I have no reason to believe she's lying about anything that happened that night."

"Even if it meant getting Ryan out of prison to save Ben?"

"Even if she lied to get access, there's no reason to continue to lie. At least not to me. Ryan's agreed to the transplant if he's a match."

I nodded, then played devil's advocate. "Maybe he agreed because he thought Kelsey would help get him exonerated if he saved Ben."

"If Kelsey said she was with Ryan that night, then I believe her. I know it probably seems foolish from where you're sitting since you could make the argument she's been lying by omission this entire time, but you don't know Kelsey like I do."

"Then why didn't you tell her about Ryan being arrested for killing Lindsay? You'd received the photo and knew she was with him that night. Why didn't you tell her when he was arrested?"

"Because the police had an open-and-shut case and said so from the beginning. As her employer, they questioned me right after it happened, but it was cursory, at best. They made it clear they already had their guy and the evidence to convict. I figured it was just a kiss at a bar and there was no point in throwing who he actually was and what he did in Kelsey's face."

Brett was trying to come across as magnanimous, but he didn't fool me for a minute. He hadn't *wanted* to know if Kelsey's relationship with Ryan had gone any further than that kiss and was probably happy to believe the man had committed murder because it meant he'd be permanently out of the picture.

"But since you believe Kelsey, then you know Ryan didn't kill Lindsay."

He blew out a breath. "I do now."

"Do you still have that photo?"

He gave me a single nod.

"Good. I'm going to need it. It corroborates Kelsey's statement that she was with Ryan that night. Even though it doesn't account for the range of time when Lindsay was killed, it lends credibility to Kelsey's entire claim."

He nodded but remained silent, and I could practically feel the emotional turmoil rolling off him in giant waves.

"Look," I said, "I know none of this is what you wanted. But what has happened isn't justice. Not for you, Kelsey, Ben, or Ryan. And most of all, not for Lindsay."

"I'll send you the picture. I've kept it all this time... I don't even know why."

"Maybe it was the universe protecting Ben. He's really the only person you need to consider right now—what's best for him? If the surgery is a go and it gives him a chance at a full life, will it be good for him to find out his biological father is in prison for murder?"

"Of course not."

I raised one eyebrow at him.

He blew out a breath. "You're right. I need to push my personal feelings aside. Devin was saying the same thing—just sign whatever is necessary, write checks, and save Ben. Everything else can be addressed once we're sure he's okay."

"Sounds right."

He pinned his gaze on me. "I know you probably won't believe me, but Ben means everything to me. Being his father is the best and most important thing I've ever done. And I don't want him in pain—physically or emotionally—for one second longer than he has to be. I'll do *anything* to lessen his burden. Kelsey has nothing to worry about where I'm concerned."

"You're a great father, Brett. It might not mean much to you right now, but Kelsey said the same thing to me the first time we met. She wasn't wrong."

He drew in a breath, and I saw tears glistening in the corner of his eyes. Finally, he rose and walked away.

————

IDA BELLE AND GERTIE WERE ALREADY IN THE SUV WHEN I got back, and I filled them in on my conversation with Brett on our way to Alexander's office. Like me, they were initially surprised about the photo someone had sent Brett and were anxious to see it. I wished ten years hadn't lapsed because technology was always improving, and I might have been able to track the sender. Although Brett's assumption that it was one of his social circle was probably accurate.

I sent Kelsey a text letting her know that Brett wouldn't be a problem and that I'd call her later to fill her in. Then Ida Belle and Gertie gave me a rundown on Devin's movements after he left the park.

"We thought he was going back to the office," Gertie said,

"but then he turned the opposite direction at the end of the block. We followed him about halfway down, where he went into a building."

"We couldn't tell what it was at first," Ida Belle continued. "And we didn't want to walk right by it in case he had a view out the window, so we crossed the street."

"I wanted to buy Mardi Gras masks, but *someone* wouldn't go for it," Gertie said.

"Because it's not even noon, we're not on Bourbon Street, and Mardi Gras was weeks ago," Ida Belle said. "We needed to blend, not draw attention."

"So anyway?" I interrupted. "Did you figure out what the building was?"

"A boutique hotel," Gertie said. "Looked ritzy. And no restaurant. You know what that means—someone is getting before noon delight."

Ida Belle shrugged. "No restaurant but they might have a meeting room. Or maybe a client is staying there."

Gertie rolled her eyes, and I laughed.

"The way he kept looking around while he was walking," Gertie said, "he was definitely having a nooner and was making sure no one saw him going in."

"Did you see anyone else enter the hotel?"

"No," Ida Belle said. "We hung around until you texted us that you were headed back to the car, but no one entered or exited in that time. Do you want to go back and stake it out?"

I shook my head. "I don't know how it would be useful, and I want to see if Alexander found out anything on the mercenaries."

Alexander was practically bouncing when we arrived, and I couldn't wait to hear what had him so excited. He waved us into his office and we all took seats. He perched on the edge of his desk, his legs swinging slightly like a schoolboy, and he grinned at us as though he knew something awesome and was savoring the moment before telling us.

"Did you find out who the mercenaries were?" I asked, unable to wait a second longer.

"Ex-Marines," he said. "And I use 'ex' rather than 'former' because they were both dishonorably discharged for war crimes two years ago."

I nodded, not a bit surprised. "And let me guess, they served under Kitts."

"Not directly, of course, as those two failures would have never achieved enough rank to be a direct report, but yes. Even more interesting, they were under investigation for other crimes by the DOD but mysteriously disappeared just when they were going to be arrested."

"Someone tipped them off," Ida Belle said.

I nodded. "I'll bet any amount of money it was Kitts. Preparing his own private group of soldiers to handle his dirty work.

"Probably," Alexander agreed. "The DOD was never able to locate them, and finally someone suggested they'd been eliminated to keep them from talking."

"So the DOD assumed they were dead until they turned up in my living room."

He nodded. "They were very happy to hear you'd left one alive. I don't have to tell you how much of a boost that was in your favor."

"I'm sure the DOD knows I did it for my own reasons and not to help them out."

"Absolutely, but this is one of those times when one action serves two purposes."

"And the video where he named Kitts?"

"Enraged the Marine Corps and delighted the DOD." Alexander beamed. "The Marines have completely withdrawn their support. They won't even allow him military counsel, claiming that the attack on you, on American soil, is a civilian issue rather than military."

Gertie gave a loud hoot, and Alexander laughed.

"They hung him out to dry," Ida Belle said, looking equally happy.

"Oh, it gets even better." He leaned forward and grinned. "I heard through my contacts that Kitts is going to be arrested for crimes against the United States. It's supposed to happen sometime today. And with all the knowledge and connections he has to make fleeing and hiding a stroll in the park, there's no way he's getting bail."

I sat back in my chair, completely stunned. I knew the video and the attempt on my life had been a fatal decision in Kitts's plans, but I had no idea it was going to be the wind running with the loose thread.

Kitts's entire sordid life was about to unravel.

CHAPTER TWENTY-TWO

WE WERE ALL STILL SMILING SO HARD IT HURT WHEN WE climbed back into the SUV. Alexander was leaving in a few minutes to go to Sinful and relay the news to Carter. He'd offered to let me do it, but he was the one who'd played all the right angles to position the evidence for takedown, so I told him to take his glory and let Carter know we'd have a pre-celebration tonight. He looked beyond pleased, and while I knew he was ecstatic that things had swung so hard in our favor, I also figured he was happy about another opportunity to talk to Emmaline. I hadn't missed the energy between them and if I was being honest, I was pulling a bit of a Gertie, putting them in the same space.

"Where to now?" Ida Belle asked.

"Magnolia Pass. I want to have another chat with Jared."

"He's never going to let us in," Gertie said. "Not when Holly's been locked up for coming after you with an ice pick."

I looked back at her. "You know what I noticed when we were on the Beech estate? No cameras. They have guards and poles where cameras used to be but there's nothing on the mounts anymore. Why do you think that is?"

Ida Belle shook her head. "Because then they don't have evidence of Holly's shenanigans lying around. I wonder if they had them before Lindsay was killed."

"It's an interesting question, right? They're not mentioned in the police reports, but that doesn't necessarily mean anything given the farce of an investigation."

We were just exiting the interstate headed to Magnolia Pass when my phone rang. It was the investor whose account Lindsay had made a mistake on.

"Fortune Redding," I answered.

"Ms. Redding, I got your message. But I'm confused as to why you're inquiring about a personal issue that happened over ten years ago."

"I'm attempting to find enough evidence to reopen Ryan Comeaux's case. A new witness has come forward that puts him far away from Magnolia Pass the night Lindsay Beech was murdered."

"Really?" He sounded surprised. "I thought they had an open-and-shut case. The whole thing was very sad."

"Even though she'd lost a big sum of your money?"

"The amount that I lost was barely a blip on my investment charts."

"But you still switched firms. To be more specific, you switched to her father's firm."

"Yes. That's true enough, but it wasn't because of the mistake—it was because Raymond Beech had access to an opportunity that Spalding didn't. I wanted to make a large investment, and Beech was the only one who could make that investment for me. It was simply a business decision based on an opportunity I wanted to take advantage of. It had nothing to do with Lindsay's mistake. That's just how the timing worked out."

"But you left Beech and are back at Spalding now."

"Spalding is one of a few firms I use, and yes, I left Beech after Raymond died. His son simply doesn't have the mind for the business like his father and his sister did."

"But if Lindsay was so smart, how did she make such a big mistake?"

"To be honest, I've never quite believed she did. Lindsay had a mind for numbers that rivaled my own, and I was twenty years her senior and no slouch at what I do."

"I was told it was her password used to make the ill-fated trade."

"That's true. I suppose I should accept that everyone, no matter how extraordinary at something, can still make a bad decision. Maybe I don't like to consider that because then I'm subject to the same flaws."

"I can appreciate that. Do you happen to remember when this mistake occurred?"

"Of course. Hard to forget when it was the week before she was killed, but I'm not sure of the specific day. I'm about to go into a meeting. Is there anything else you wanted to ask?"

"Not at this time. I appreciate you returning my call."

He was silent for a couple seconds, then said, "In addition to respecting her business acumen, I liked Lindsay. Her death was a tragedy both as a professional and a human. She was excellent at both. If her boyfriend didn't kill her, I hope you find who did. Because the guilty party needs to pay for cutting short what I'm certain would have been a life filled with accomplishment."

"He doesn't sound like a good candidate for the perp," Gertie said when I disconnected.

"No, he doesn't," I agreed. "But then, criminals are usually good at playing a role. Still, I did some general poking around and he appears to be as rich as Caesar. Maybe it was just a case of the timing being suspect."

Ida Belle nodded. "It wouldn't make much sense for someone with that kind of money to risk the rest of their life in prison for killing someone over what amounts to pocket change to them."

"But it doesn't let Brett off the hook," Gertie said. "That million in fees probably wasn't pocket change to him. And even though he got the business back, he didn't know for sure he would. And there's still the part where he was harassing Lindsay. I know you couldn't ask him about it today because of Ben's situation, but I still wonder."

I nodded. "Me too. And I'm not letting him off, but for the moment, my chief suspect is Holly."

"Mine too," Ida Belle agreed.

Gertie sighed. "I just don't want it to be her. That poor girl —if she'd just gotten the help she needed a long time ago, maybe Lindsay would still be alive."

"It's quite possible," I said. "I doubt her environment did anything but make her worse. All that covering for her instead of addressing the problems just seems to have given her permission to escalate. But if she keeps stalking men and going after their significant others, she's going to wind up in a grave next to her sister."

"I wonder how many other men she's done this to," Ida Belle said. "How many the Beeches have paid for their silence."

"Good questions and ones I'll be putting to Jared Beech. I get the impression he's not as keen to spend the rest of his life cleaning up after Holly as his father was."

"I can't blame him," Gertie said. "If people find out the extent of the things she's done that they've hidden, they could be held responsible for anything she did after. Well, Jared could anyway, as he's the only one left."

My original plan was to have Ida Belle drive by the gates to the Beech estate and let me out as the road curved behind a group of trees. I planned on making my way across the estate and cornering Jared Beech. But as we rounded a bend and the guard shack came into view, I saw someone jump out of a car and hurry through the open gates as the car sped off. They were wearing sweatpants and a hoodie, but I knew that gait. I'd seen it from the same angle just the day before.

"That's Holly Beech," I said. "Pull up to the gate."

Ida Belle and Gertie, who'd locked their gazes on the fleeing figure at the same time I had, both stared.

"Holy crap!" Gertie said. "Why the hell did that guard let her in? She's supposed to be on a psych hold."

"I plan on asking him exactly that," I said and climbed out of the SUV.

The same surly guard that had been there before cut his eyes toward Holly, then back at me. "You're not welcome here," he said. "I suggest you turn around and leave or I'll call the sheriff."

"Please do. I'll be glad to explain to them that you just opened the gate for someone who is currently being detained by the Sinful police on a psych hold. Did you even call Jared to warn him? Is he at home?"

His expression flickered with just a tiny bit of fear, so I pressed on.

"If she tries to burn the house down again, I'm going to be absolutely certain that I tell the state police that you not only let her in but didn't report her turning up here to the authorities. Anything that happens to Jared Beech will be your fault for letting a known disturbed person have access when they should be locked away for everyone's safety."

Now he looked downright panicked, which meant Jared *was* home and the guard knew exactly what Holly was capable of.

"Call Jared and warn him and let us in."

"No way," he said. "I'll be fired."

"We're trained in hand-to-hand combat. We can apprehend her without killing her. Can you say the same for Jared? Is he capable of handling a psychotic break? Is the rest of the staff?"

The guard paled. "It's their day off," he said, and ran into the guard shack. I saw him grab his phone with one hand and slam his hand down on the gate control with the other. I jumped back into the SUV, and Ida Belle floored it.

I scanned the grounds as we went, but there was no sign of the elusive Holly. I knew from chasing her before that she was a fast runner, and our delay convincing the guard to let us in had given her enough time to get to the house. I prayed she wasn't still in the red zone about the psych hold and coming home to punish Jared for it. The fact that he hadn't had an option probably wouldn't matter with her.

Ida Belle slammed on the brakes, and we all jumped out and ran for the front door. It was locked, of course, and since it was the staff's day off, no snooty butler to look inconvenienced. I'd hoped the guard would get hold of Jared and he would unlock the door himself to let in the cavalry when we arrived. The fact that nothing stirred inside made me extremely anxious.

"You want me to break a window?" Ida Belle asked. "Because you're not picking the lock on that door."

"No. There's no way to hide the sound of breaking glass. If she's got Jared cornered somewhere inside, we'll need the element of surprise."

I climbed on top of the SUV and took a running leap for the balcony above the entry. I just managed to grab the rails, then pulled myself up and over the rails and onto the tiny ledge. I pulled out my pocketknife and made quick work of the simple lock on the door, then cracked it open and peered inside.

It looked to be an office and it was empty. The door to it was closed. Fortunately, it had thick carpet to mask my passage, so I hurried to cross the room, but as I passed the desk, I brushed against a set of papers and the top one flew onto the floor. I saw the word *Trust* at the top of the document and a section underlined. I knew I needed to hurry, but Holly's name caught my attention and I quickly read a handful of sentences. Suddenly everything Jared had done made sense.

When I reached the office door, I attempted to open it but realized it was locked, which fit given what I'd just read. I twisted the lock and eased the door open and peered down a long hallway. No one was in sight, and I couldn't make out any noise except for a grandfather clock ticking downstairs. I exited into the hallway, and when I reached the end of the wall in front of the giant staircase, I paused again.

This time I heard voices drifting up from downstairs. I couldn't make out the words, but it was definitely a woman's voice, and she sounded angry. I hurried silently down the stairs, grateful it had a thick runner, and stepped into the downstairs entry. For a split second, I thought about unlocking the front door to let Ida Belle and Gertie in, but I remembered the noise it had made when we'd first visited and knew I couldn't risk it.

The voice was louder now and seemed to be coming from the drawing room we'd been placed in when we'd visited before. The main doors were paned glass, so that way wasn't an option, but I remembered Holly had entered through a solid rear door. I edged along the far wall, praying that no one was close enough to the entry doors to spot me, then hurried down the hallway, scanning for that way in. There were two sets of doors along the long hallway, but I knew it couldn't be either of them. One was a large double door, and both faced the wrong direction.

At the end of the hallway, I found myself in the kitchen and immediately turned right. I found the butler's pantry and moved through it, exiting in a large dining room. There was a door on the other end, and it all clicked—this was the staff's passage to take care of guests. That door on the other side of the dining room was the one that opened into the drawing room, and I was certain that was where Holly and Jared were.

I crept over to the door and pressed my ear against it. Holly's voice was louder now, and I could hear Jared pleading with her not to 'do it.' I had no idea what 'it' was, but I knew it wasn't pleasant. I prayed she didn't have a gun because I really didn't want to have to shoot her. The door hadn't made any noise when Holly had entered and exited through it the other day, so I eased it open a crack to get the lay of the land.

I spotted Jared sitting in a chair in the middle of the room, his knuckles white from clenching the wooden arms. His face matched his knuckles. When I looked toward the window, I saw why. Holly stood there with a can of lighter fluid in one hand and a burning candle in the other. I could see squiggly lines on the dark curtains and knew they'd already gotten a dose of the fluid.

Not another candle. I was so over fire.

"You said you'd never put me back in that place," Holly ranted.

"I didn't," Jared said, clearly pleading. "It was either the hospital or jail."

"I would rather go to jail. At least they wouldn't try to pump me full of drugs and make me a zombie. I want to live. Not be in some walking coma. Why won't anyone listen to me?"

"You *can* live, Holly, but you can't continue to do some of the things you're doing. They're illegal. Don't you get that?"

"It's not illegal to like a boy."

"It's illegal to stalk men and to trespass into their girl-friends' homes to attack them."

"It's not wrong to claim what's yours. I don't care what the law says. Father always said you had to take what was due to you. The means don't matter."

I shook my head. That was the overwhelming crux of the problem. Holly couldn't comprehend that her behavior was wrong. In her screwed-up mind, she was completely justified to take what she wanted through whatever means necessary. And the constant yo-yoing of overindulging then completely denying by her father had made her worse.

When I looked back at Jared, I saw a drop of water fall from the seat of his chair and hit the carpet, where a small round stain was forming. At first I thought he'd peed himself, but then I saw a second can of lighter fluid discarded on the floor behind the chair, and my heart sank. One flick of that lighter from Holly and she would send Jared up in flames.

CHAPTER TWENTY-THREE

THE LIGHTER FLUID EXPLAINED WHY JARED HADN'T TRIED to flee. He couldn't outrun an accurate lob of the candle, and his pants were soaked with the stuff.

I could shoot her without killing her, but that wouldn't ensure she couldn't still toss the candle. I'd seen people do some pretty remarkable things when shot, and Holly had a broken mental state to help spur her on. Then I had an idea, so I ran back to the kitchen and drew up short when I saw Ida Belle and Gertie coming in through the back door.

"Unlocked," Gertie whispered.

I nodded and hurried to explain the situation. "Gertie, you come with me and cover the butler's door after I go in. Ida Belle, you cover the main door of the drawing room. If Holly tries to escape, tackle her."

Ida Belle hurried off, and I dashed over to the sink and grabbed a large pitcher sitting beside it and filled it with water. Gertie grinned and gave me a thumbs-up. I crept back through the butler's pantry, Gertie right behind, and stopped at the door, positioning the pitcher in my right hand. I twisted the doorknob with my left hand and inched the door open to make sure everyone was still in the same position, then I threw the door open and launched.

Holly let out a shriek as the door slammed against the wall, but I was already halfway across the room. She lifted the candle to throw it, and I chunked the entire pitcher of water on her.

Bull's-eye!

The candle went out and Holly took off running for the front exit. I yelled for Ida Belle and set off after her, Gertie hot on my tail. Holly ran right through the doors without even opening them and I heard the wood splinter. I made it to the opening just in time to see Ida Belle dive-tackle her onto the entry floor.

I saw a flash of metal and yelled, "She's got a knife!"

I grabbed a pillow from a chair and sprinted for Ida Belle just as Holly swung the knife around, right at her chest. I launched, my arms extended, and stuck the pillow out like I was reaching for the end zone. I slammed into Ida Belle, knocking her over just as Holly embedded the knife into the pillow.

I sprang up in time to see Gertie flying toward us with the drapes from the other room. She tossed them over Holly, who was halfway up, and I tackled her to the ground again. She thrashed beneath me, and I swore.

"If you don't stop moving, I'm going to relight that candle and drop them on these drapes."

All movement ceased and her body went slack. A couple seconds later, she started wailing like a child. Jared stumbled out of the room, his expression so dazed I knew he was in shock. Gertie pulled fuzzy handcuffs out of her bra—something I never wanted to discuss—and I fished around in the drapes until I got Holly's hands secured behind her back.

Ida Belle had guided Jared into a chair, and he was now

sitting, his whole body shaking. The disgruntled guard finally showed up, and when he saw Jared sitting there, his shoulders slumped with relief.

"*Now* you show up," Gertie said, shaking her head.

"Call the paramedics," I said. "He's in shock. Jared, I'm going to call the state police. I'm not interested in getting the runaround from the locals over this. And I need your attorney's number. Let him handle Holly. Do you understand?"

"Don't call the paramedics," Jared said. "I don't want people to know..."

The guard, who already had his cell phone out, glanced at me.

"Not an option anymore, Jared," I said and motioned for the guard to leave. "I've got this under control. Call the paramedics and get back to the gate to let the state police in."

As the guard left, Jared pointed to the drawing room, his hand still shaking. "My phone. She made me throw it into the corner by the big plant."

Gertie hurried off to retrieve the phone, and I hoisted Holly up from the ground and plopped her into a chair before using the ruined drapes to tie her there. She had stopped wailing, but it looked as if the reality of the situation was finally beginning to sink in and she turned to softly sobbing.

I called the state police and gave them a brief explanation and told them I needed assistance well beyond what the local force was capable of as Holly would need a police escort to a locked-down facility. Then I stepped in between Jared and Holly and glared at both of them.

"This nonsense ends now," I said to Jared. "Because I won't be here the next time she tries to kill you."

Some of the color had returned to his face, but he still shot a nervous look at Holly and gulped.

"I know why you're covering for her. I saw the documents

on your desk. But you can't keep doing this. She's dangerous and she's escalating."

"I am not!" Holly yelled.

"And she's back," I said and sighed. "You can't reason with her, Jared. Surely you understand that. How many more people are you going to put at risk? This entire nightmare could easily be taken off your hands."

"I don't see how. I've been trying to figure out a loophole."

"Have you talked to your attorney about it?"

"No, because I didn't want to—couldn't tell him…"

"That Holly killed Lindsay?"

I glanced over at Holly, but she'd gone silent again, staring at me with wide eyes and—finally—a heavy dose of fear.

"There's a man doing life in prison who doesn't deserve to be there," I said. "He's already lost ten years. How many more people are you going to sacrifice before you tell the truth?"

He stared down at the floor. "I don't know the truth."

"Then tell me what you *do* know."

"I can't, or I lose everything."

I stepped close to him and bent over, then whispered, "If Holly committed a crime, the *courts* will put her away, not you. So technically, you won't be in default of the requirements of your trust."

His eyes widened and he shook his head. "It can't be that simple. Besides, I promised my father, and I've been hiding stuff all this time. They'll throw me in jail too."

"I doubt it. Don't get me wrong, you're in serious trouble, but you can either fess up and hope for a lenient judge who takes into account the circumstances, or you can keep covering for Holly and roll the dice for the rest of your life, which might be shorter than it should be. Your choice."

His shoulders slumped. "I'm so tired. I don't even think I care anymore. I just want it all to end."

"That power rests solely with you."

"Don't tell her," Holly pleaded, sounding more like a child than an adult.

He looked at her for several long, silent seconds, and I could see the love and sadness in his expression, but exhaustion and fear had finally trumped duty.

"She's off her meds," he said quietly. "I stand there and watch her take them. Watch her swallow, but I saw them in the bottom of the toilet yesterday morning. I don't know how long she's been doing it."

"Please, Jared," Holly begged. "Don't send me to the bad place. I'll be good."

He broke his gaze with her, as if looking at her any longer was painful, and let out a defeated sigh.

"Father and I were in his office most of the night," he said. "He was mad over some business decisions I'd made and yelling at me made him happy. Holly had retreated to her room —so we thought—right after dinner, which is when the yelling started. When he was done, I was all worked up, so I went downstairs to grab a beer and ended up falling asleep on the couch watching TV."

He looked at his sister, tears in his eyes. "I'm sorry, Holly, but I can't live with this anymore. These secrets are destroying not just me but other people. Holly came in about 3:00 a.m. She was frantic and had blood all over her clothes...and she was carrying a knife."

"Did she say anything?"

"Not right away. It was like she was in a walking coma. I sat her down in the kitchen and went to get our father. He made everything worse by thundering about, of course, demanding answers. Finally, Holly said she saw Ryan and Lindsay fighting and he'd struck her."

"I did *not* say that!" Holly yelled. "I always said it couldn't have been Ryan."

"You *did* say it." Jared looked up at me. "She swore she had no idea where the blood or the knife came from. That she remembered looking in Lindsay's kitchen window and then everything was a blank until she was sitting in our kitchen."

"That's true," Holly said, her voice barely a whisper. "I still don't remember everything, but without the poison the doctors gave me, I see flashes of that night...of the part I don't remember. I saw him hit Lindsay, and she screamed because it hurt her. But it couldn't have been Ryan."

"Why couldn't it have been him?" I asked, watching her closely.

She seemed as lucid as I'd ever seen her when she shook her head and looked back down at the floor, and I knew she was hiding something.

My phone signaled an incoming text and I frowned. Surely the lawyer or the state police would call rather than text, but I checked just to be certain. It was the photo from Brett Spalding. I opened it and saw Ryan kissing Kelsey outside the hotel bar. But something in the background also caught my eye—a person looking at them from behind a plant in the lobby.

I enlarged the image and looked at Holly.

"You knew it couldn't have been Ryan because you were spying on him at the hotel bar that night."

"No way," Jared said.

"So she managed to get to Lindsay's house and downtown all the time to stalk Ryan; she got to the sheriff's department and my house in Sinful; and she got back here despite being in police custody, but she couldn't have gotten to the casino that night? Your logic is seriously flawed, and you know it. You said yourself that you and your father were in an argument most of the night. No one looked for Holly. You *assumed* she'd gone to bed, but no one checked."

I turned my phone to show him. "Here. This photo was taken the night Lindsay was killed. That's Ryan kissing Kelsey outside the casino bar, and that's Holly hiding behind the plant, stalking him, just like she always did."

"That doesn't mean anything," Jared argued. "Ryan could have left right after that."

I looked over at Holly. "But he didn't, did he?"

She shook her head. "He got into the elevator with the girl. I saw him get a room key."

"And then you left and went to your sister's house."

"Yes! But not to hurt her. Well, not that way. I wanted to tell her that Ryan was cheating on her. Except a man was already there."

"Did you see his face?"

"No... I don't know. Sometimes I think I remember, but then it's gone. Or maybe it's all wrong." She started to sob. "I did it, didn't I? I killed my sister. That's why I was covered in blood and had the knife."

The pitch of her voice kept getting higher and more frantic, and I was relieved to see Ida Belle open the door and let the paramedics in. They took one look at the girl tied to the chair with drapes and I hurried to explain.

"She's supposed to be on a twenty-four-hour psych hold, but she escaped somehow and tried to set her brother on fire. The state police are on their way, so if you can just get her under control for transport..."

As soon as Holly had spotted the paramedics, she'd started thrashing and wailing again, trying to free herself from the chair.

"She's handcuffed, of sorts," I told the paramedics. "But I don't know how well they'll hold."

The first paramedic pushed the drapes down and exposed the fuzzy handcuffs. The second one grabbed a needle and vial out of his bag and jammed it into Holly's arm. She screamed as though she was being slaughtered and the paramedic took a step back and we all watched as the sedative began to take effect. Holly's screaming tapered down to a sigh, and she slumped over in the chair.

"Let's get her into the ambulance," the first paramedic said, then looked back at me. "That sedative won't last long. It's just enough to get her to the hospital."

I nodded. "The state police shouldn't be much longer. Just be ready to leave when they get here. Oh, and she's probably got lighter fluid on her, so be careful with anything that might ignite a spark."

They unwrapped the drapes and removed the handcuffs and within minutes, she was secured on the ambulance, her arms and legs restrained to the gurney. The paramedics were waiting in the ambulance, so I returned to Jared, wanting to get the entire story out of him before the state police showed up. Just in case he lost his nerve.

"You and your father assumed Holly killed Lindsay, didn't you?"

"No! At least I didn't. Not at first. My father told me to take her upstairs and get her cleaned up and make sure she wasn't injured, and he rushed out to check on Lindsay."

"And the knife?"

"She'd dropped it on the kitchen floor, and it was still there when I took her upstairs to her bathroom."

"So your father took it."

"I didn't know that at the time. I just thought he was going to make sure Lindsay was all right. Holly kept repeating that she saw Ryan hit Lindsay but no matter how hard we pushed, she wouldn't say anything else."

"So your father went to Lindsay's house and found her dead."

Jared nodded, his expression one of someone who'd lived through a horrific situation. "He said Ryan wasn't going to get away with it."

"So he put the knife in the dumpster at the motel."

"He was overwrought and angry," Jared tried to explain. "I think he went to the motel to kill Ryan, but he wasn't there. There was no way my father was going to let Ryan get away with killing Lindsay, so he did what he had to do...to make sure Ryan went to prison."

"And to protect Holly."

"He made her swear never to tell that she left the house that night. He told her he'd lock her up if she did. She had a really bad experience in one of those places. She's terrified to be in them."

"So you let an innocent man go to prison."

Jared shook his head. "I didn't know. I always thought Ryan did it. Holly saw him. I know you have the picture from the casino, but maybe he left afterward."

"So he went to the motel room, had sex with Kelsey, then left the hotel and went straight to Lindsay's house and killed her before Holly turned up, even though she'd left the hotel before him? I need you to think very hard about this, Jared—when Holly told you what she saw through that window, did she name Ryan specifically? Or did she just say 'he'?"

Jared scrunched his brow and stared at the floor for several seconds, then he looked back up at me, the blood draining from his face.

"She said 'he.'"

CHAPTER TWENTY-FOUR

WE WERE AT THE BEECH ESTATE FOR SEVERAL HOURS. THE first set of state police left almost immediately to escort the ambulance before the sedative started to wear off. They called for a second unit to come take our statements and process the scene. I was worried that Jared would backtrack on his statement, but when Holly's attorney showed up and he told him everything, the man said he'd have no problem defending Jared's right to his inheritance if anyone managing the trust decided to challenge his status.

He also agreed to represent Jared because charges were certainly going to be levied against both of them, although coercion was certainly a factor in Jared's case. I suspected given Jared's age at the time and the fact that his father and sister were the ones who'd actually committed the crimes, he might get away with probation or a short jail stint. At the time, he'd believed that Ryan had killed Lindsay and Holly had seen it happen, which was why her memory was blank. It wasn't until I showed up and told him about Kelsey that he started to worry that they'd gotten it all wrong.

I'd texted Carter earlier giving him the bullet points and

letting him know we'd be a while, but he was waiting for me on his front porch when Ida Belle dropped me off. I knew Alexander had been there that afternoon to tell him about Kitts, and I'd really hoped this night would be for celebrating, but there was nothing but worry and concern on his face when he rose.

"Long day, huh?" he said after he pulled me in for a long, hard hug before we went inside. "I grabbed dinner from the café. I figured you'd be starving."

"Definitely. I knew it was going to take a while, but Jesus, what a convoluted mess over there. I know the lawyer needed to be there, but why do they make things so much more difficult?"

"I'm pretty sure that's to fluff up their billable hours. Come on, and I'll heat up your dinner."

We headed back to the kitchen, and I flopped into a chair. Carter popped the top on a beer and passed it to me and got to work on the food while I gave him the blow-by-blow of the events.

"Just getting the state police up to speed took forever because the case never had any publicity," I said. "And one of them transferred in from out of state only a year ago, so they were starting from ground zero on everything."

"Have you talked to Alexander yet?"

I nodded. "I called him on the way back to Sinful and filled him in. He told me Kitts was arrested and is sitting in a cell in DC. Looks like everything is finally going to catch up to him."

Carter frowned and nodded. "What did Alexander say about Ryan?"

I knew he was changing the subject because he hadn't processed the situation with Kitts well enough to talk about it yet, so I let it go. We'd have the rest of our lives to work out the damage Kitts had done, although I'll admit I was hoping it didn't take quite that long for Carter to come to grips with it. I missed the mostly happy Carter. The one whose biggest frustration was the trouble Celia and Gertie's purse caused. Selfishly, I wanted him back, and the sooner the better.

"Alexander is going to the ADA with everything tomorrow. He thinks it's more than enough to get Ryan a retrial, at minimum, but he's going in full throttle for an exoneration. He's also going to float the words *civil suit* and *damages*, given that there was never a real investigation."

Carter shook his head. "The whole thing is a really bad look for law enforcement and the judicial system. The public outcry is going to be enormous."

"Exactly. I'm hoping the ADA is smart enough to realize that and make a deal."

"Do you think Jared's testimony will hold up after all these years of lying?"

I laughed. "Yeah, actually I do. He never destroyed Holly's clothes. When the cops asked him why he'd kept them, he kept shaking his head and saying he didn't know."

"Do you believe him?"

I shrugged. "It could be that something told him to cover his butt in case the whole thing fell apart. Or maybe he was going to use them as leverage against his father if he ever developed the backbone to do so."

"I have my doubts on the second one, because if that was the case, why not ditch them after his father died? It's far more likely he was afraid if anyone really investigated Lindsay's murder, he would come up as a solid suspect."

"True. But either way, the clothes are in a safe-deposit box and will be retrieved by the cops and tested. As soon as the lab determines they're Holly's clothes with Lindsay's blood on them, the case is pretty much a wrap."

"Then why are you frowning?"

"Because I still don't know who the guy was that Holly saw hit Lindsay."

Carter shook his head. "You don't know for certain that she ever saw anyone, and even if she did, she probably didn't have the night correct. She doesn't remember what happened because her mind has shut off her horrific actions. It's protecting her from having to face what she did because she probably couldn't handle it."

"I'm sure you're right. But man, I was really hoping for a different answer."

"Would it be any better if Brett Spalding had done it?"

"Of course not. It would be worse, given the situation with Ben. Regardless, Lindsay's still dead, Ryan has spent ten years in prison for a crime he didn't commit, and families will suffer."

He put his hand on my shoulder and squeezed. "It's the part of the job none of us like. But our duty is to the victims and their loved ones, even if the answers hurt them even more."

I nodded, but I was still conflicted. Holly killing Lindsay was an answer for all of the pertinent questions, but something about it all still didn't sit right with me. What if Jared was lying? He'd looked horrified while recounting the entire situation, which I'd taken as reliving the moment when he thought his younger sister had murdered his older one. And he definitely seemed to treat Holly with kid gloves, almost as if he was afraid of her.

But what if Jared was the one Holly had seen through the window? What if she'd blocked it out because she'd seen her brother kill her sister? What if the drugs she'd been flushing down the toilet were the only thing keeping her memory from bursting through, and my visit had prompted her to stop taking them to see if her memory would return? What if Jared kept the clothes all this time in case Holly's memory ever came back? With her documented history of violence, no one would believe her word over his.

Or what if Brett had received the picture and gone to see Lindsay to use it as leverage? To convince her to get involved with him?

Everyone said Lindsay was brilliant with numbers, and no one wanted to believe she'd made a mistake of that magnitude. But what if she'd caught on to the same thing the FBI was hunting? Brett pushing her for a relationship might have been an attempt to get her on his side...to keep her from telling what she knew. Maybe seeing Ryan with another woman hadn't been enough. Maybe Brett was out of options.

When I lay in bed that night, all I could think was, what if the wrong person was in custody again?

———

TUESDAY STARTED UNEVENTFULLY—THANK GOD. I FORCED myself to stay in bed until 7:00 a.m. even though sleeping had been crap, then headed to the kitchen for coffee. Carter was already gone but had left me a note saying that the state police had finished with my house and he'd called in a favor. The forensic cleaners had finished up last night.

I perked up a bit, happy that I'd be able to return home. Not that I hated staying with Carter or being in his house, but there was something about my own place that helped center me. Sanctuary. That's what Gertie would call it. The place you were supposed to be happy and peaceful, and that was mostly true for me. Unless men broke in and tried to kill me.

I downed a cup of coffee, threw on clothes, and headed for home. The house smelled like lemons, and I was astounded that I couldn't spot a single drop of blood on the hardwood. I owed Carter big for this. I put on another pot of coffee and sent a text to Ida Belle and Gertie, letting them know I was back at home.

Five minutes later, they walked into my kitchen carrying a box of pastries from Ally's bakery.

"We were just picking up pastries when we got your text," Ida Belle said. "We figured we could all do with a treat."

"Yesterday was a doozy," Gertie said as she plopped into a chair.

Ida Belle nodded and started putting coffee cups on the table as I poured.

"I suppose everything that happened yesterday put a damper on yours and Carter's celebration over Kitts," Gertie said. "But was Carter happy?"

"I don't know that I'd call it happy," I said. "I'd go with moderately relieved."

"He's still processing everything and trying to figure out where he stands in all of Kitts's treachery," Ida Belle said.

"As a pawn," Gertie said. "I know that answer won't sit well with him, but it's a far better cry than being a willing participant, like those men who came after Fortune."

I shrugged. "They were paid to come after me. Mercenaries don't have a cause or any loyalty. But until Kitts is convicted and we're all officially cleared, I don't think Carter will be able to completely relax or address how he feels about everything. Right now, he's still worried that the four of us might be on the hook for something."

Ida Belle shook her head. "I can't say I'm not worried at all, because I am worried about you and Harrison, but overall, I think they'd be making a mistake to come down on you two when it's become clear where all the problems lie."

Gertie nodded. "Going after a woman who Kitts sent mercenaries to kill because she saved a decorated Marine won't fly with the DOD. They have no loyalty to Kitts and no need to protect his reputation."

"I agree," I said. "I don't think the DOD or the military wants the storm I would unleash if they push things. We'll have to wait for all the red tape to unravel, but I think it will all be fine. Kitts sending those mercenaries put the nail in his coffin."

"Then why do you have that look?" Ida Belle asked.

"What look?"

"The one where you're not finished with something."

I sighed, then unloaded everything that had left me tossing and turning all night—my suspicions about Jared and Brett, my questions about Holly's issues, and what might be the real reason she couldn't remember that night. And my theory on why she was starting to remember.

Ida Belle and Gertie gave each other worried looks.

"I wish I could find fault with your logic," Ida Belle said. "If for no other reason than our own peace of mind, but the way you've spelled it out has me as concerned as you."

Gertie nodded. "I definitely want Holly in a locked-down facility, at least until they can figure out how to manage her behavior, but I don't want her going to prison if she didn't commit a crime."

"She was going to set her brother on fire," Ida Belle reminded her. "That's not exactly a good look for her defense."

Gertie sighed. "True. But what if she was going to kill Jared because somewhere in the recesses of her mind, she knows he's the one who killed Lindsay?"

"Still a crime," Ida Belle pointed out. "So was showing up here with an ice pick to use on Fortune."

I shook my head. "This whole thing is so convoluted. I don't think we've ever had a case with so many strong possibilities for the perp, and all with solid motive and opportunity."

"So what's our next move?" Ida Belle asked.

"I wish I knew."

"We never asked Brett where he was that night," Gertie said. "Maybe we try to run down his whereabouts. We already know where Jared claimed he was, although he could have dashed home and showered and ditched his bloody clothes before Holly made it back."

"But how do we check Brett's alibi?" I asked. "If we ask him, he'll either have one and a friend, like his good buddy Devin, who will lie for him to back him up, or he'll simply say he was at home alone and we have no way to prove otherwise."

Ida Belle shook her head, clearly as lacking in suggestions as I was. "Have you talked to Kelsey yet?

"I sent her a text yesterday saying that we'd gotten tied up with something and I would get in touch as soon as possible. She texted me last night asking me to call when I had a chance, but I was too spent to do it. I figured I'd wait until a reasonable hour and call her this morning."

"I'll bet now is reasonable," Gertie said. "She probably hasn't slept a wink since Ryan went for those tests. And probably won't until she gets the results."

"That's true," I said and reached for my phone.

Kelsey verified Gertie's prediction by answering on the first ring. I immediately launched into an apology.

"I'm sorry I didn't get back with you yesterday," I said. "We had a situation—a huge situation—but I think it's the big break we needed for Ryan."

She sucked in a breath. "You know who killed Lindsay?"

"Her sister Holly has been taken into custody by the state police."

I told her what had happened at the Beech estate.

"Oh my God!" she said when I was finished. "That night when Ryan and I talked, he said his girlfriend's family was what had ultimately caused them to separate, but I never imagined anything like that. How long can they hold her?"

"As long as she's deemed to be a threat to herself or others. But to be honest, I don't think she'll ever see the inside of a courtroom."

"I know she says she doesn't remember, but do you believe her?" she asked.

"Yeah. She's got a history of issues that have been overlooked, glossed over, and outright hidden. She said she's starting to see flashes of memory about that night, so maybe one day she'll remember everything. Who knows?"

"Poor Ryan and poor Lindsay. It sounds like she was the only person trying to get Holly help."

"Unfortunately, that might have been the nail in Lindsay's coffin," I said. "Holly is terrified of mental health facilities. If she even thought, incorrectly as far as we know, that Lindsay's arguments with their father for help were about trying to get her back into one..."

"The whole thing is such an awful tragedy," Kelsey said. "If only their father had listened. Maybe Lindsay would still be alive."

"I know. But the only thing we can do about it now is push for Ryan's release. My attorney is going to see the ADA this morning. I'm hoping they move for an exoneration to try to avoid an even worse thrashing by the public, because you know it's coming."

"As well it should," she agreed. "I've always heard people complain about how the system is broken, but I never realized just how bad it can be until now. I don't think I've ever been angrier than I have been this past week."

"We can't get back the ten years he lost, or in any way erase everything that happened to him while he was incarcerated, but hopefully, we can give him back the rest of his life."

Kelsey sniffed. "I hope so too. I can't tell you how lucky I was that Jenny caught me crying that day. She was so right about you. Thank you, Fortune. This week alone, you might have saved three lives—Jared, Ryan, and Ben."

I felt my chest constrict as I thought about her words. I'd become a PI because I needed something to do and wanted to use my natural ability and some of the skills I already had, but mostly because, since being in Sinful, I'd discovered that I loved solving puzzles. But something else I'd discovered was that I also loved helping people. And the people who deserved the most help were often the very ones who were overlooked.

"So what did you call about yesterday?" I asked. "Did you talk to Brett after our conversation?"

"Yes, and we laid everything out. He said he was always going to support whatever it took to save Ben, but after talking with you, he realized he'd left me with a lot of uncertainty because of our relationship issues. He didn't want me to worry. There is no more 'us,' except when it comes to saving and parenting Ben, but where Ben is concerned, we're on the same page."

"I'm glad to hear it. You've always said he was a great father. You never said he was a great husband, so I figured you weren't lying about the father part."

"Ha. That's true. But that's not all I called you about—the tests came back..."

I sucked in a breath. "And?"

"And Ryan is a match."

Ida Belle and Gertie started cheering, and I couldn't stop grinning. I could hear Kelsey laughing at our obvious celebration.

"I can't tell you how thrilled I am to hear that," I said.

"Us too!" Gertie yelled and whooped again.

"So what's the next step?" I asked.

"The surgeon will coordinate with the hospital and the prison, and Brett and I, of course, and get the surgery scheduled. Ryan will need aftercare for a while, and they have to arrange for guards because the prison doesn't have the facilities or knowledge needed to care for him after the surgery."

"Maybe by the time he's healthy enough to return to prison, Alexander will have worked his magic on the ADA."

"I'm going to be praying so hard for that."

I heard a signal on Kelsey's phone, and she said, "Can you hold on a second? It's Devin texting me and he says it's an emergency."

As she clicked off, I looked at Ida Belle and Gertie and they both stared back at me, all of us clearly thinking the same thing. Our worst fears were confirmed when Kelsey clicked back over, all of the joy in her voice replaced by fear.

"Devin said the FBI came into Spalding and arrested Brett. They hauled him out in handcuffs and made everyone turn over their keys to the office and leave. They wouldn't tell anyone why—just that the office had been seized and they couldn't access the building or the records. They made Devin lock down the server so that no one could access it remotely. What the hell is going on?"

"I'm not sure, but let me see if I can find out. Meantime, you call the FBI and tell them your husband has been taken into custody and you need to arrange his attorney. I'm sure Brett knows not to say anything until he has representation. Does he have an attorney?"

"Yes. The firm has one on retainer. But he does real estate deals and contracts and stuff."

"Until we know why they've taken him into custody, we don't know what kind of support Brett will need, but any attorney can instruct him to keep quiet and advise him on who to hire once they know what the charges are."

"Charges? Oh my God! Fortune, this can't be happening. Brett couldn't have done anything wrong. He's absolutely rigid about certain things, and the law is one of them."

"Don't start panicking until we know more. I'll make some calls and see if I can find out anything, but my guess is you're going to have to wait until his attorney talks to the FBI, and that's going to be when they're good and ready. They are incredibly tight-lipped about their cases, and it's almost impossible to get them to talk outside of their own circles."

"Okay, I'm going to take a deep breath and calm down. Devin is on his way over now. I'll have him contact the firm's attorney since he knows him personally and was there when all this happened and can explain it better than I can."

"Good idea. Call me back as soon as you hear something."

CHAPTER TWENTY-FIVE

As soon as I hung up, all three of us started talking at once. Then we all stopped and stared at one another.

"This couldn't have happened at a worse time," Gertie said. "The last thing Kelsey needs is to be worried about Brett, and the last thing Ben needs is to be heading into a major surgery without his father there."

I nodded. "I wonder if Detective Casey knows anything."

I picked up my cell phone to call her and it rang as I lifted it.

Detective Casey!

"Kelsey told me the FBI seized Spalding's offices and took Brett into custody," I said as I answered.

"That's not all," she said. "Brett's parents have been taken into custody as well."

"What? Where were they?"

"New Orleans, of all places. In a small hotel in the French Quarter."

"Why would they risk coming back here now?"

"I have no idea, but I'm with you—it's stupid. I've spent a lot of years watching criminals and their behavior, and I have to say, this one doesn't sit right with me. Something changed. Something big enough for them to risk coming back into the United States."

"They didn't even come back for Ben's first transplant. What could be so important that they'd come back now? When the FBI is lurking around?"

"I wish to hell I knew, because I don't like it. And all of this on the heels of that mess with Holly Beech yesterday."

"You know about that?"

"One of the cops who took your statements is the captain's nephew. The captain has been pacing and fuming all morning because the state police got the case."

"Who else was I supposed to call? Certainly not Cantrell, and NOLA doesn't have jurisdiction."

"Oh, you absolutely did the right thing. The captain even said as much, but he's still hacked that we've been shut out. He'd love to be part of taking Cantrell out for the botched investigation. But the state isn't going to let him in on that any more than the FBI is going to let him in on the Spalding situation."

"So how mad is he that I'm the one who turned the spotlight on Cantrell?"

She laughed. "At the moment, he's just relishing Cantrell's lack of actual police work and praying it gets him out of a profession he never should have been part of. And he'd never admit it, but I think he appreciates what you've accomplished. He's just disgruntled because we have to play by a different set of rules."

"We've all got our cross to bear. Let me know if you get anything out of the FBI. I told Kelsey I'd call her back with information when I had it."

"Will do."

I disconnected and blew out a breath. Ida Belle and Gertie

were both staring at me, and I was sure we all looked a little shell-shocked.

"What in the world is going on?" Ida Belle said. "Why would the Spaldings come back into the country now? And not just the country—back to New Orleans?"

I shook my head. "I wish I knew."

"I feel like we should be doing something," Ida Belle said. "But I have no idea what."

"I feel the same," I said. "Let's head to NOLA."

"To do what?" Gertie asked.

"I have no idea," I said. "But I have a feeling that if something pops up that we can help with, it's going to be there."

———

WE WERE HALFWAY TO NOLA WHEN I GOT ANOTHER CALL from Kelsey. I'd rung her after I'd talked to Detective Casey, but she hadn't answered. I'd left a message, figuring she was probably dealing with the attorney and would get back with me as soon as she could.

"Oh Fortune, it's so bad!" she wailed as soon as I answered. "The FBI came here after we got off the phone. They told me they've seized everything—not just the business, but all of my and Brett's personal accounts and assets. I called the hotel and asked them to stop direct deposit of my checks, but what am I supposed to do? How long can they keep my accounts tied up?"

"As long as they want to. And I'm afraid I have more bad news—the FBI has Brett's parents in custody as well."

"What? How? They can't just pick people up in Italy, can they?"

"The Spaldings were in NOLA. Unfortunately, my source doesn't know any more than that, but all of this looks really bad. Is Devin there? Did you get in touch with the attorney?"

"Yes. He got here right after the FBI left, after telling me I'm basically a pauper and treating me like a criminal. You're on speaker. What the hell is going on, Fortune? I can't believe Brett did anything wrong. Not something the FBI would be interested in. What happens when the surgeon asks for his money? I have to prepay for the surgery."

"I already told you I'd lend you the money." I heard Devin's voice in the background.

"It sounds like you have a solution," I said. "Take his offer. You'll be able to repay him at some point, and even if you never get your assets back, your son's life is worth years on a payment plan, right? I need you to focus on Ben and try not to even think about the rest of this. You can't help Brett. But you can help Ben."

She blew out a breath. "You're right. I know you're right. I'm just so spaced out. I feel like I'm wound so tight I'm going to explode. And my head is killing me. Thank God I sent Ben to a friend's house right after I talked to you, or he would have heard everything the FBI said. I don't even know what to tell him."

"Nothing. If Brett is still being held when Ben's surgery comes up, you tell him that Brett has the flu and he's not allowed in the hospital or around Ben because it's too dangerous. Ben has been through enough that he'll be disappointed, but he'll understand."

"Yes. That's good. That would work. Thank you, Fortune. Your clear thinking is really helping me."

"We're headed to NOLA now. I want to check in with my source and see if they've gotten any more news, and then we'll come by to check on you, assuming you're up to it."

"Definitely! I can't tell you how much I appreciate everything you've done."

We clicked off and I stared out the windshield, shaking my head.

"This has gone from bad to worse," Ida Belle said.

"I'm just glad Devin is going to lend Kelsey the money for Ben's surgery," Gertie said. "We all know if the FBI has gotten something in their craw, they're not going to give those assets up. Not without a fight."

Ida Belle nodded. "And the Spaldings have been stuck in their craw for over a decade. That's a lot of festering anger and disappointment they're going to want to balance out. They're not going to care at whose expense."

"Maybe we should talk to Alexander," Gertie suggested. "He knows everyone. He might be able to get some inside scoop. Or give some advice."

"Alexander hates the FBI," I said. "He says of all the government agencies, they're the worst to ask for favors, but you're right. He will probably have some advice about how to handle it all."

Gertie nodded. "And he's sort of involved already by way of the fact that he's Ryan's attorney, who is Ben's bio father, who is Brett's son, who needs the money for surgery."

"That was incredibly convoluted, but accurate," Ida Belle said. "And I think a conversation on all your thoughts on Holly Beech is in order as well. I know Alexander has nothing to do with the ADA charging her, but he wouldn't want to be part of railroading another innocent person any more than you."

"I was the first person to defend her," Gertie said, and sighed. "But after seeing Jared sitting in lighter fluid and her holding that candle, my doubts kind of flew out the window."

I nodded. "I get it. And trust me, there's no doubt in my mind that she *could* have done it. And maybe it's like Carter said and she never saw anyone at Lindsay's house that night. She absolutely could have confused her nights, or it's entirely possible it never happened at all."

"But assuming she did see someone hit Lindsay, regardless of the actual day, what are your thoughts on that?" Ida Belle asked.

"I don't know," I said. "But at this point, a second investigation will be up to the ADA. Jared's testimony and Holly's clothes are damning, and her trying to kill him isn't going to help her case. Regardless, it's never going to trial. It's clear that Holly isn't of sound mind, and I don't know that she ever will be."

"I get that," Gertie said. "But what about that small chance that they can fix her? If everyone assumes Holly is the killer, then there's no good reason to make her better when that just means she'll stand trial for murder. She's clever enough to know that and keep ditching her meds."

"Staff at those facilities are trained to handle people like Holly," Ida Belle said. "She won't be able to play them like she did Jared."

I nodded. "Jared should have never been tasked with being Holly's keeper, but then, everyone we've talked to has said Raymond Beech was a butthole. I just wish I knew if he never pushed for outside help because of the terms of the trust or because he wanted to keep Holly close in case she remembered who the guy was in Lindsay's house that night. Assuming there was a guy, of course."

Ida Belle shook her head. "Seeing her brother kill her sister would be a good enough reason for Holly to slip off the edge and into the deep end. The problem is, we don't know for certain what happened—did Holly witness her sister's murder, or did she kill her? Either one would have sent an already troubled mind into lockdown."

I frowned. "How long does it take before those meds start to wear off?"

"No way of knowing for sure," Ida Belle said. "Depends on the med, the person, how long they've been taking them, the dosage. Someone could start to act differently in a matter of a day or two, or it might take weeks or months. Why? What are you thinking?"

"That when they put Holly back on meds, she'll stop remembering that night again."

Gertie nodded. "The meds have probably been keeping it repressed and foggy."

Ida Belle frowned. "If it was Jared she saw, he was in the perfect position to know when she remembered, keeping her closed up with him and with minimal staff in the house."

"Exactly," I agreed.

"Well, if he's sticking close to monitor Holly," Gertie said, "he's doing a crap job of it. That girl has managed to be a lot of places she wasn't supposed to be. And someone needed to cancel her Uber account and lock up those household vehicle keys where she couldn't find them. The woman shouldn't have even been allowed a bicycle."

"It only takes minutes of distraction with a work issue or things like that charity meeting he had after we talked to him that first time to give her the opportunity to slip away," Ida Belle said.

"She managed to leave the hospital without anyone noticing," I agreed. "My guess is Holly is a master of sneaky. And I'm going to guess she doesn't have an Uber account but is using someone else's."

"Probably that disgruntled security guard," Gertie said.

Ida Belle nodded. "Or another of the household staff who won't dare tell Jared about it."

Gertie sighed. "But if Jared killed Lindsay, why didn't he

just kill Holly, too? Surely he could have made it look like an accident given the trouble she got up to."

"Three siblings, two deaths, and one left to inherit?" Ida Belle asked. "I think it might have raised some eyebrows, especially with the trustees. And given Raymond's poor parenting choices, it wouldn't have surprised me if he'd chosen to cut Jared out altogether if Holly was no longer around. It sounds like the sort of thing he'd do."

"True," I agreed. "And to be honest, if Jared killed Lindsay, I think it was a crime of passion. He's just too soft to plan out a cold-blooded murder. When he realized Holly's memory was gone, she was no longer a threat, so he was never faced with that choice."

Ida Belle shook her head. "I almost wish Raymond Beech was still alive so he could witness all the damage he's done. If either Holly *or* Jared killed Lindsay, I contend the blame begins with their father. And Ryan's incarceration lies firmly on him."

"I agree," I said and lifted my phone to make a call to Alexander. But before I could, my phone rang. It wasn't a number I recognized, but it was a NOLA exchange.

"Hi, Ms. Redding?" a woman said when I answered. "This is Trish Maxwell. You left me a message saying you had some questions about my employment at Spalding?"

"Yes, Ms. Maxwell, thank you for calling me back."

"No problem. I'm sorry I didn't get back with you sooner. I just got back from vacation, and I lost my cell phone two days ago. Oh my God, I don't know how people made it before they existed."

"Everything was harder or simpler. Depends on how you look at it, I suppose."

She laughed. "True. So what did you want to know? It's

been a minute since I worked at Spalding, but I'll try to help. Are you interviewing someone who worked there?"

"No. I'm a private investigator. I've been retained to look into Lindsay Beech's murder."

"Oh my God! I haven't thought about Lindsay in forever. I know that sounds horrible, but the whole situation was something I'd never dealt with before and never want to again. Someone you see practically every day and that happening... I had nightmares for months. You just don't ever think about things like that happening to people like Lindsay."

"Why is that? What was she like?"

"Good family, well educated, incredibly smart, and super nice. She was also introverted, like a lot of finance people are, but beyond that, she also seemed very shy and somewhat socially awkward. She always blushed when Brett complimented her on a big score, even though she definitely deserved the praise. I've never known anyone with a mind like hers."

"Did you ever meet her boyfriend, Ryan?"

"Once, at a company thing. He seemed nice. Out of place, but that makes sense. I felt a little sorry for him because he didn't fit with the investor crowd and didn't come from money, so he was well outside the ring. Lindsay didn't appear bothered by it, mind you, but he seemed really uncomfortable. I couldn't believe it when he was arrested. I talked to him for a bit that night, and there was absolutely nothing about him that suggested he was going to kill her. I think that's why I had nightmares for so long. That you just can't tell, you know?"

"I definitely know. I have seen all kinds of things in my line of work."

"You said you're looking into Lindsay's murder... Does that mean you don't think Ryan did it?"

"We've had a witness come forward who was never aware of his arrest and had a one-night stand with him. *That* night.

And she swears he never left the hotel room in NOLA. I have other evidence besides her word, so I'm convinced that Ryan has been convicted for a crime he didn't commit."

"Oh wow! That's horrible. And that means whoever really killed her is still out there, right? Who do you think did it? And what did you want to ask me about?"

"The police brought someone in for questioning, but I'm not allowed to talk about it at this time. And my original questions are probably a moot point now, but I might as well ask them since you returned my call. Ryan told me Lindsay was being harassed by her boss, and I wanted more information. I knew an existing employee was unlikely to talk, but I figured a woman—a young woman no longer employed there—might be willing to speak freely."

"Gotcha. I don't know anything for certain, but me and Suzanne, another coworker, saw her come out of his office a couple times and she had that look, you know?"

I had no idea personally as everyone I worked with feared death if they hit on me, but I understood what she was saying.

"She was looking down and hurrying," Trish continued. "I mean, she was always rushing around and wasn't big on eye contact, but the couple times we saw it happen, she didn't even lift her head and acknowledge us when she passed. In fact, if anything, she dropped her head even lower. She looked embarrassed."

"Maybe she'd gotten chewed out over a mistake on an account."

"Ha. Lindsay didn't make mistakes. She was God's gift to numbers. If I had a quarter of her talent, I'd be retired already."

"Why do you think he picked Lindsay? If Ryan attended a party, I have to assume everyone knew they lived together."

"Sure, but they'd recently broken up. I found Lindsay

crying one day in the break room and she told me about it. I told the other girls, so they'd prop her up if we saw her struggling—female solidarity, you know? But I imagine word of their breakup got around the office fairly quickly."

"And did you or any of the other girls ever have similar problems?"

"No way! Which is why it surprised me and Suzanne. It was out of character, you know? Every year, some of the new interns made their play, but they were always ignored. The office gossip was that he was gay but so far in the closet he was dwelling in Narnia. But I don't think anyone ever had proof. I just figured it was sour grapes started by the rejected."

I frowned at the 'gay' comment. That one seemed totally out of left field given that Brett was married and by all appearances dedicated to Kelsey. And Kelsey had certainly never mentioned anything of the sort, but then, maybe the Narnia comment was accurate.

"Anyway," Trish continued, "after seeing his gaze linger a little too long on hot women at restaurant meetings, I dismissed the gay thing and just figured he didn't want to get involved with an employee. It's the smart move, mind you, especially the interns, because boy would that have been a legal minefield if someone reported him. Which is why Suzanne and I were shocked over the thing with Lindsay. It was sudden and completely out of left field. I mean, she'd been working there for years and nothing. It was like he walked into the office one day and suddenly realized she was attractive."

"And there were never other incidences or even rumors about Brett hitting on other employees?"

"Brett? No way. That man cares about three things—his son, his wife, and money—probably in that order. I thought you were asking about Devin. He was Lindsay's supervisor."

And suddenly, it all started to make sense.

Devin, who had rich parents but was never flashy until recently. Who pushed Brett to shut up and write checks for Ben's surgery. Who had offered to pay for the procedure after Brett's arrest. Devin, who'd had a meeting at a boutique hotel, right around the corner from Spalding offices the day before the Spaldings were arrested. The man the FBI had asked to secure Spalding's server. The man whose parents Brett had never met. The man Kelsey had probably just told all about Jared and Holly Beech.

Lindsay didn't make mistakes.

He's not a puppet master.

But he was. If I was right, Devin had played everyone he'd ever known, and I'd be willing to bet he'd been doing it for a long, long time.

"Thanks, Trish," I said quickly. "I've got an emergency and have to run, but I appreciate it."

I hung up before she could even reply and dialed Kelsey. "Is Devin still there?"

"No. He left right after we talked. He said he was going to see about getting the money for me."

"Did you tell him about Holly Beech being taken into custody?"

"Yes. I hope that was okay. He asked about the investigation."

His aunt is a hospital nurse.

"No problem at all. I'm about to meet with Alexander. I'll call you later."

"Okay—"

I dropped the call on another startled woman and called Alexander, praying he answered.

"Where is Holly Beech?" I asked when he picked up.

Without hesitation, he gave me the name of the hospital.

I repeated the name to Ida Belle and told her to hurry. "We've been wrong. Horribly wrong."

CHAPTER TWENTY-SIX

I EXPLAINED MY SUSPICIONS, AS BEST I COULD, ON THE WAY to the hospital, but I don't think Ida Belle and Gertie were as convinced as I was. I just knew. Knew without a doubt that Devin had played everyone, and he thought he was going to get away with it. The only loose thread he had left to destroy was Holly Beech, whose sketchy memory was threatening to return after a decade of remaining locked away.

But even though they didn't have my confidence, they trusted me. Ida Belle drove the SUV like a NASCAR driver at Daytona. By the time we arrived at the hospital, she'd already sent five pedestrians sprawling for the sidewalk, terrified a group of pigeons so much they'd probably fled the state, and acquired more middle fingers than Gertie had given her in a lifetime. But none of it mattered.

The only thing that mattered was getting to the hospital before Devin eliminated the last shred of evidence against him.

Ida Belle pulled into the valet lane at the main entrance of the hospital and tossed the keys to the guy at the valet stand as we ran inside.

"Scratch it and I'll kill you," she yelled as the startled young man caught the keys.

I slowed only long enough to pin down the path to the psychiatric ward and ran for the stairs that led to it. If the elevator even let us off on that floor, I knew it would be in a locked-down lobby, with nurses behind a solid sheet of bullet-proof glass. But the law required them to have another exit.

When I got to the third floor, I stopped in front of the entry.

"You need an employee pass," Gertie wheezed from the landing below.

"I've got a pass," I said and pulled out my gun. "Cover your ears."

I fired a single round into the card slider and the door popped open. We rushed inside, and a man pushing a laundry cart stared in shock.

"What was that noise?" he asked.

"Something ruptured in the wall," I said. "Maybe old pipes blowing."

"It sounded like a gunshot," he said.

"It did. I'm looking for Holly Beech," I said and described her.

He shook his head. "She's not on my wing."

I spotted the sign indicating the second wing and sprinted off.

"Hey, you can't be up here—"

I was already around the corner before he finished his statement. I heard hospital employees yelling and scrambling behind me and I knew they would sound the alarm, but I didn't care. The more people I had in a frenzy, the better.

I dashed down the hallway, slowing only long enough to look in the windows to the locked rooms. Ida Belle and Gertie checked the other side, but when we made it to the end of the hallway, there was no sign of Holly. Had Alexander gotten the wrong hospital? No way. He didn't make mistakes, either.

"Ma'am, I've called security," a nurse said as I spun around at the end of the hallway. Two nurses and an orderly hovered behind her.

"Where is Holly Beech?" I demanded.

"Only employees are allowed in this area of the hospital," she said.

I pulled out my ID and shoved it in her face. "I'm a private investigator and Holly Beech's life is in danger. She's supposed to be in one of these rooms and she's not."

A nurse standing behind her glanced into the room next to her and gasped. "She's not there."

The head nurse whipped around and rushed to the door. "That's not possible."

"Someone let her out," I said.

"She's heavily sedated," the head nurse said. "She can't have gotten far."

The nurses in the hallway started peering inside all of the rooms, which was a complete waste of time, but then one of them pulled open a storage closet, and a man fell out into the hallway.

The head nurse's eyes widened. "The laundry worker."

"He got her out in the laundry cart," I said. "Where is the laundry room?"

"In the basement."

"Does it have an exit outside of the hospital?"

"Yes. There's a loading dock," she said, her panic building. "The service elevator next to the stairs. It goes all the way down."

"Send security to the basement and tell them to cover

every possible exit. Call the police and tell them to send Detective Casey to assist Fortune Redding. There's a kidnapping in progress."

I pulled out my pistol as I sprinted for the service elevator and motioned to Ida Belle and Gertie to get in before yanking open the door to the stairs. "Get the SUV and block the exit to the loading dock. I'll be faster on the stairs."

I burst into the stairwell and took a flying leap onto the landing below, not wasting a second before sprinting forward and leaping again. I hit the basement level and pushed open the door, not bothering to listen or attempt a peek. There was no time. Devin had a jump on us, and if he got away from the hospital with Holly, I knew we'd never find the body.

The laundry room was completely empty, but I spotted the exit to the loading dock on the far end of the room and ran for it. I burst out of the door and onto the dock, just in time to see Devin's white Mercedes squealing backward out of a parking space. The rear exit was clear, and I cursed. Ida Belle wasn't going to make it in time. I couldn't shoot inside the car. He was driving too erratically, and I had no idea where Holly was.

But by the time I got the rear wheel sighted, he rounded the corner and a delivery van blocked my line of sight. I bolted for the end of the loading dock, leaping over a delivery cart of pastries and startling the driver, who fell backward and lost his grip on the cart at the top of the ramp. The cart shot forward, but I was faster. And I had a clear view of the Mercedes.

As I leveled my nine at the rear tire, I saw movement ahead and then locked in on Gertie, standing on top of a van and pointing a huge gun at the front of the escaping vehicle.

Good God, she had the Desert Eagle out.

I yelled for her to hold fire, but it was too late. Sound boomed from the gun, and Gertie let out a whoop, then promptly fell off the van and rolled right into the path of the speeding Mercedes.

The round hit the windshield of the car and I heard a scream as it exploded and pink paint splashed across the windshield. But my relief was short-lived because there was no way the car would stop before it hit Gertie. I aimed at the right tire and fired. The car veered away from Gertie, missing her by inches, and crashed into a barrier. Ida Belle slammed her SUV to a stop across the end of the loading dock drive, and I sprinted for the car.

Praying that Holly was uninjured, I yanked open the driver's door. The airbag had deployed, protecting Devin from the wreck, but he wasn't safe from me. I reached into the car and yanked him out onto the ground, then planted one foot squarely in his back. He groaned and clutched his shoulder, which was clearly dislocated, maybe broken. I spotted Holly in the back seat, looking dazed but otherwise unharmed.

I heard a crash behind me and whirled around just in time to see the pastry cart smash into Gertie and send her sprawling again before the cart flipped over beside her. Gertie sat up and removed a croissant from her chest and took a bite.

"It's pretty good," she said.

I laughed as relief coursed through me.

Sirens approached, and I heard running behind me. Ida Belle moved her SUV and Detective Casey's car swung into the loading dock drive. Hospital staff hurried over now that my gun was back in place, and I waved at the back of the car.

"Holly's in the back seat. She's alive, but you'll want to check her out."

The head nurse nodded as she motioned for the others to help Holly out. "Thank you," she said to me.

"Looks like I'm too late for all the action again." Detective Casey walked up, grinning.

"You're in time for pastries," Gertie said.

"I didn't figure you'd make it here in time for the action," I said, "but you're just in time to arrest Devin Roberts for the murder of Lindsay Beech and kidnapping with intent of Holly Beech. Maybe it will improve the captain's opinion of me."

She laughed and clapped me on the back. "It just might."

CHAPTER TWENTY-SEVEN

By Wednesday noon, Ida Belle, Gertie, Ronald, and I were all in my hot tub, trying to recover from our adventures. Carter was down at the sheriff's department, putting together the documentation surrounding Holly's arrest and all the subsequent fallout. Merlin was in the living room, sitting in the middle of the floor, pouting because the rug was gone. Ronald had found a new dress for his party that he could wear with flats, and Sinful had returned to normal.

"Ally told me Celia went to NOLA yesterday to talk to an attorney about suing Skinny, Flint, the hounds, *and* the chickens," Ronald said.

Well, Sinful normal.

"Boy, Easter was rough this year," Gertie said as she tossed back a shot from a flask. "Anyone want some of this? It's Nora's latest painkiller."

"No!" We all answered at once.

"Suit yourself, but when you're still sore tomorrow and I'm skipping, you'll wish you'd tried it."

"I'll take my chances," I said, but I noticed Ronald's eyebrow had lifted at the word *skipping*.

"Don't even think about it," I said. "You've got to walk down stairs in a dress tonight."

"Another round of champagne then," he said and leaned out of the hot tub to start the refills.

He'd just gotten the champagne distributed when I heard laughing and looked up to see Detective Casey rounding the corner of my house.

"This is what you people do in the middle of the day on a Wednesday?" she asked.

"It is when you've had the week we have," Gertie said.

"Fair enough," she said and dropped into a patio chair. "I was at it until late last night, went home long enough to shower and change, and went right back at it this morning. But boy, have we unraveled a mess. I'm dead on my feet and probably should have called, but I wanted to tell you everything in person."

"We definitely appreciate it," I said. "And I owe you big for all your help. If your daughter hadn't come up with that employee and if she hadn't called, we would be having an entirely different conversation today."

"Don't remind me. She's been crowing around the house ever since I told her about it. That girl's ego doesn't need more stroking."

"You know you're proud of her," Gertie said.

Casey grinned. "Got that right. So I've got a doozy of a story to tell you, and it goes back almost fifteen years. I'm speculating on some of it because Devin isn't talking, but between questioning other people and information from the Spaldings and the FBI, I think I've got it all worked out."

"Holy crap, this sounds good," Gertie said.

"First off, Devin Roberts isn't Devin Roberts. His real name is Devin Porter. His father was the groundskeeper and handyman for the Robertses, and his mother was their maid.

His father died saving Mr. Roberts's life. They were installing a statue in the front yard of the Robertses' house when a drunk driver jumped the curb and ran into the yard. Devin's father pushed Mr. Roberts out of the way, and he was struck by the car and killed."

"That's horrible," Ida Belle said.

Casey nodded. "The driver had no insurance and no money, so there wasn't going to be a payout to make up for the financial loss. They lived on the estate, so housing wasn't a concern, but the Robertses felt horrible about it and wanted to do something more to help. Devin had been desperate to attend St. Marks, figuring if he graduated from there, he could get a scholarship to a good university, so Mr. Roberts agreed to cover the tuition if he was accepted."

Ronald whistled. "That's a good 50k a year."

"And that's when Devin Porter became Devin Roberts," I surmised.

"You got it," Casey said. "He knew Devin Porter didn't stand a chance of acceptance, but Devin Roberts would be guaranteed entry as a legacy. So he faked some documents and got his pricey education."

"Wasn't that risky?" Ida Belle asked. "Seems like it would have been easy to get busted."

"Not necessarily. The Robertses were already in the process of buying vineyards in Italy and they were only maintaining a residence in the US long enough to sell their other businesses, which was going to take about three years."

"Which just happened to correspond to Devin graduating from high school," I said.

"Exactly. The Robertses were always out of the country. St. Marks is a boarding school, and when Devin wasn't living on campus, he was living on the estate. So if friends came by to pick him up, he came out of the Robertses' house. If the school called, they got his mother, who pretended to be Mrs. Roberts."

"And he made friends with Brett Spalding," I said. "Another young man with part-time parents and who didn't live flashy. That way, Devin wouldn't be pushed to spend money he didn't have. Brilliant."

"I wondered about that part," Casey said, "but that makes sense. If Brett Spalding was a low-key spender, then latching onto him was the perfect play for Devin to maintain his cover. After graduation, the Robertses moved to Italy, Brett went off to Harvard, and Devin claimed he went to Oxford, but obviously we know that was a lie. A smaller university in the Midwest gave him a full ride and that's where he went. The interesting thing was he was actually accepted to two Ivy League schools but with only partial aid. LSU offered him a free ride as well, but he turned them all down."

"Why wouldn't he go to LSU instead of some lesser university?" Gertie asked.

"Because then he wouldn't risk running into anyone from St. Marks," I said. "Kelsey said Devin and Brett kept in touch all through college. Devin had already planned to return to NOLA and hit up his good friend for a job. But if anyone from NOLA saw him at school, he couldn't pitch the Oxford lie."

"Jesus," Ida Belle said. "Talk about running the long con."

Casey nodded. "He even had his name legally changed, which makes sense, of course, but he did it as soon as he turned eighteen, so I think Fortune called this one correctly."

"I wonder what his mother thought about that?" Gertie said.

"We'll never know," Casey said. "She passed several years back from cancer."

"And the aunt?" I asked.

"I talked to her and asked about it," Casey said. "She knew

about the high school thing, but when she noticed Devin's last name was still different on the Spalding website, he'd told her that he had to enter university with the same credentials he'd used in high school, which meant he needed to continue to be Devin Roberts so employers could verify his education. His aunt figured they owed him anyway and there was no real harm in it, so she just accepted it."

"Did she just accept him stealing her employee pass to gain entry to the locked-down wing where Holly was?"

"Definitely not. When we finally got around to explaining all the details of what had happened and all the things we believed Devin had done, she broke down. I felt sorry for her. She was sobbing and praying and thanking God for taking her sister before she'd seen what Devin had become."

"That's rough," Gertie said.

Casey nodded. "So this is where things start to get really interesting. I've been chatting with our friends at the FBI, who were exceptionally forthcoming now that we've figured out what was happening. Here's the deal—after college Devin started up at Spalding, got his first taste at making good money, and developed a gambling problem. He owed some bad people a chunk of change, got desperate, and figured out a way to skim money off client accounts."

"I thought he wasn't talking?" I asked.

"He's not, but the FBI's forensic accounting and IT people are incredible. They found the skimming right away, and it had been going on for years. They also found a keylogger that he'd installed on all the computers in the company. Did I mention Devin got a dual major—finance and IT?"

"So he was smart but dumb," Ronald said.

"Educated fool," Ida Belle agreed.

"Let me guess—you think Lindsay discovered he was skimming the money," I said. "He tried hitting on her, hoping she'd quit, and when that didn't work, he logged into her account and made a bad trade, hoping she'd be fired."

Casey grinned. "You're quick. But then Brett didn't fire her, and Devin was getting desperate. He had some of the skimmed money in offshore accounts but not enough to bounce and live well in another country. His spending habits had gotten the better of him. So he moved on to some bigger, older accounts, shooting for a larger payout. And that's what alerted the FBI."

She leaned forward and I could practically feel her excitement. "The Spaldings *had* been laundering money for bad people, but they were FBI informants."

"What?"

"You've got to be kidding me!"

"Holy crap!"

Ida Belle, Gertie, and Ronald all sounded off at once.

"They were in Aruba when they were approached by a drug cartel about laundering for them," Casey said. "They went straight to the FBI. Spalding had a friend who worked there that's since passed away. The FBI asked them if they'd be willing to handle the transactions so that the Bureau could figure out all the different branches of the organization. Once they were established with one cartel, they got the same request from another."

"Then one of the cartels killed the owner of another investment firm," Casey continued. "When the FBI told the Spaldings, they said they wanted out. They'd had a kid—something they hadn't planned on doing given what they were involved in—and now that Brett was getting older, they were worried about his safety."

"Well, that explains all the traveling," I said. "And the absentee parent thing. Did Brett ever know?"

"He had no idea. The Spaldings were out before Brett

graduated from Harvard. They didn't want him to have any part of it. The FBI filtered a story through the criminal community that they were sniffing around Spalding Financial so the rats mostly abandoned ship. The Spaldings told the shady clients that Mr. Spalding was dealing with health issues, and they were turning the business over to their very young and inexperienced son. The crux of it being that Spalding would no longer be handling certain types of accounts. All the cartels took their money out except for two who were heavily invested in businesses with really high returns. The Spaldings didn't like it, but the FBI told them to just let the accounts sit rather than raise eyebrows by insisting they remove the funds."

"If they've been working with the FBI all this time, then why were they arrested?" I asked.

"Because there was recent activity on one of those dormant accounts. And then the Spaldings showed back up in NOLA. The FBI detained them for their own protection until they could sort out exactly what was going on. And they had to detain Brett as well in order to shut down Spalding and figure everything out."

"So why did the Spaldings come back?" I asked.

"You're not going to believe this one. Because they met the Robertses at a party for one of their vineyards, got to talking, and realized they were speaking to Devin's parents. Except when they asked about their son—"

"The Robertses told them they didn't have one," I finished. "Over a decade of hiding his true identity, and his lies were exposed half a continent away. What are the odds? They met Devin at that hotel where they were arrested to confront him, didn't they?"

"Yes. They wanted to tell him that they knew the truth and give him a chance to explain. He said he'd lied in order to get educational advantages that he couldn't afford otherwise, but that he'd always been loyal to Brett and to Spalding."

"He must have been thrilled when the FBI detained them," Ida Belle said. "He figured even if the FBI found discrepancies, they'd never tie it back to him since he'd been using other people's log-ins to skim the money. In the meantime, he could play the poor fatherless victim to Brett to explain all the other lies. He'd get away with it all."

I nodded. "Except that Holly Beech started remembering."

"Nailed it," Casey said. "I really wish you weren't so dead set against being a cop. You'd make a great detective."

Ida Belle snorted. "You have these things called 'rules.'"

"So what about Lindsay's murder?" I asked. "Do you have enough to pin it on Devin? Holly might eventually remember, but I'm not sure her testimony would stand under questioning."

"I think we can make the case that Devin kidnapping Holly could have been for no other reason than to silence her. And Cantrell still has the knife in evidence. There's always the chance it will have Devin's DNA on it, but even if it doesn't, I think what we do have on him, even if some of it is circumstantial, is damning enough for a jury to convict."

"Even if they don't convict him for Lindsay's murder, he still kidnapped Holly and embezzled money from Spalding," Gertie said.

"Cartel money," Ida Belle pointed out. "Devin will be lucky if he makes it a day inside."

"Devin must have had a stroke when Ben turned out to be Ryan's son and Kelsey hired you to investigate Lyndsay's murder," Gertie said.

I nodded. "I'm certain that's why Devin was pushing Brett to shut up and write checks, and why he said he'd fund the surgery when Kelsey's accounts were seized. He hoped that if the surgery was successful, everyone would turn their attention away from Lindsay's murder."

Ronald snorted. "That was never going to happen. Once you take on a case, you don't stop until you have all the answers."

"Sometimes I don't have them all," I argued.

Ida Belle shook her head. "Sometimes you don't have all the *proof*. But I have no doubt you've answered all your questions."

Casey rose. "I've turned over everything we have to the ADA. Alexander has already asked for Ryan to be exonerated. I know the ADA will have to wade through it all and there will definitely be some questions, but it looks good. It looks really good. And now that you guys know as much as I do, I'm going to head home and hit the shower and the bed."

"Thanks again," I said. "I owe you and your daughter dinner."

Casey laughed. "You better pick. She's got expensive taste."

She gave us a wave and headed off.

"Poor Holly," Gertie said. "She *did* see her sister get murdered."

I nodded. "My guess is she went into the house after Lindsay was attacked to see if she was alive. She probably went into shock then and either pulled the knife out of Lindsay's body or picked it up off the floor. Then she went home, and Jared found her that way.

"And with her memory gone, she's probably spent all these years worried that she'd done it," Gertie said. "But one thing I don't understand—who sent that picture of Kelsey kissing Ryan to Brett?"

"If I had to guess, I'd say it was Devin," I said. "Once a gambler, always a gambler."

Ida Belle nodded. "You still think it was Raymond Beech who framed Ryan?"

"Yes. Remember when we asked Father Michael about staying in the hotel that night? And he said 'Proverbs 23:4' right before we decided he wasn't going to spout anything but nonsense?"

"How could I forget?"

"Well, I looked up that verse. It says, 'Labor not to be rich.' Then I checked to see who the church held their investments with. Back then, it was Raymond Beech's firm."

Ida Belle shook her head. "So Father Michael saw Raymond Beech that night and somewhere in the recesses of his mind it triggered a thought of money. Unbelievable. But I bet you're right."

Ronald lifted his glass. "To Fortune and her constant dedication to taking on nonviable cases to save the underdog."

"To Fortune."

———

A WEEK LATER, MERLIN WAS INSIDE, RUBBING HIMSELF ALL over the new rug, and I was sitting in my backyard reading a book. I received three phone calls.

The first one was from Kelsey, letting me know that the surgery was a success and that everyone was doing fine in recovery.

The second was from Alexander, letting me know the ADA had started the process to have Ryan exonerated.

The third was from Director Morrow, letting me know Colonel Kitts had been assassinated.

I dropped my phone onto the ground when Morrow disconnected and wondered what this meant for the DOD investigation.

And more importantly, what it meant for Carter.

WHAT WILL HAPPEN TO THE DOD INVESTIGATION NOW THAT Kitts is dead? Will Carter put it all behind him? And what mystery will surface next for Swamp Team 3?

DID YOU KNOW THAT JANA HAS A STORE? CHECK OUT THE books, audio, and Miss Fortune merchandise at janadeleonstore.com.

FOR NEW RELEASE INFO, SIGN UP FOR JANA'S NEWSLETTER AT janadeleon.com.

Made in the USA
Monee, IL
13 June 2024

59821843R00184